Sunshine Love

BAILEY HART

Sunshine Love
Heatstroke Hearts Book One

Cover: Echo Grayce of Wildheart Graphic Design

Editor: Victoria Curran

Proofreader: Claire Milto

For the women who just need someone to believe in them.
I believe in you.

One

JUNE

"THERE SHE IS." My boyfriend's mother sweeps toward me, her eyes sparkling like polished daggers. "The luckiest girl in the world."

I take a sip of my birthday champagne. I'm going to need it for this encounter. "Grace. It's nice to see you." Lies. All lies.

"As if I would miss my potential future daughter-in-law's party," she says, giving me a smile that doesn't go farther than the corners of her lips. The word "potential" is in unspoken air quotes.

Grace is the one who insisted on having a massive blowout for my thirty-third birthday. She didn't take no for an answer and CC'd me on a party organization email chain so long, it's a miracle my laptop didn't go up in a puff of smoke whenever I opened my inbox.

But that's what's expected of the girlfriend of the son of the wealthiest oil magnate in Texas.

Braydon Rowling II deserves the best, and I'm to play the part, even if I'd much rather spend the evening in my pj's mainlining M&M's and reading spicy books—living vicariously.

"Are you enjoying the party, dear?" Grace asks. A loaded question.

I scan the sweeping lawn, the sparkling infinity pool, Braydon's family's mansion with its gabled roofing, its countless cupolas, spires, and nooks. Floor-to-ceiling windows give a glimpse of the opulence inside: marble, Persian rugs, gold finishes, and chandeliers made of deer horn. Texas royalty chic.

Partygoers, wearing clothing that's probably worth more than my childhood home, move through the space. They're "friends of the family." My friends are back home in Heatstroke.

I clutch the champagne glass tighter. "You didn't have to go through all this trouble. I—"

"Nonsense," Grace says. "Only the best for a future Rowling. It's only a pity your mother couldn't be here to enjoy the party." Grace's lips thin. She's never gotten over the fact that her son chose me over one of the daughters of another equally rich, storied family.

"Mom's a busy woman. And this is a great party. I'm grateful, Grace." I smooth my hands over my yellow silk dress. It's my act of defiance—Grace hates the color yellow, and I've also gone with yellow ribbons woven into my French braid to complete the look.

"I did it for Braydon," Grace says. "He needs to let loose after the stress he's been under. Besides, I want him to know that things are taken care of at home, especially with his new endeavor on the horizon." The words are pointed. The dagger-eyes sharpen. "You understand how important this next year is going to be, don't you? The campaign trail? A Rowling woman, even a potential future Rowling woman, must know her place."

I'm not even his fiancée, but Grace has a set opinion of how I should behave. Cook the meals, perform in the bedroom—now that was a fun conversation—and speak when spoken to.

"Yes, we—"

"And a Rowling woman's place is supporting her husband. That's what has made this family what it is."

At times like these, I long for my mother. At least she's up-front with her insults.

When Braydon and I met—me serving him hash browns at an Achin' Bacon diner—I had dreams and no prospects, fresh out of high school and heartbreak. We'd started dating, and Braydon had provided for me. Asked me to move into his family home. Showered me with gifts.

And the years had passed. They'd passed so quickly I could barely fathom that I was already thirty-three. And still not a teacher. But when I told him I wanted to follow my dreams, he'd asked me to wait until the time was right. That he needed me to support his career first.

I open my mouth to tell Grace as much, but sudden silence saves me from the confrontation.

The speakers playing classical music a moment ago—I prefer country—have cut out, bringing frowns and murmurs from the gathered billionaires and high society.

"Now what?" Grace sighs, puffing her hair, her diamond tennis bracelet catching rainbows of light. "Darn Bluetooth, I told Braydon not to switch off his phone."

A sultry moan penetrates the backyard.

It takes me a second to put two and two together. The moans are coming from the speakers. What the—?

"That's it, babe. Just like that." Braydon's voice is a cold shock to my system.

"Braydon, I'm going to come."

"Fuck," he murmurs, in that whine that signals he's about to finish. "I wish you were here. I want you so bad, babe."

"Only two more nights and then you can come out and see me. No more phone sex. You can have all of this pussy."

Stunned faces turn toward me.

I choke on air, my cheeks flaming hot.

Grace chokes and sputters like she's swallowed a yellow jacket.

"You can have this ass too," the woman continues. "When are you going to leave her, honey bunny? You promised."

"Not now, babe, I'm about to squirt all over this—"

"Donald, cut the speakers!" Grace shrieks, waving her arms.

The sound stops, murmurs spread through the crowd, but I barely hear them. I barely see anything. The champagne glass isn't in my hand anymore, and my feet are moving. Rushing across the grass toward the back of the house.

Bodies shift out of my path, the crowd parting, faces I don't recognize.

Out. Out. Out.

I reach the house just as Braydon steps through the back door, straightening the tie I picked out for him this evening.

"Juney baby," he says, and I'm revolted by the pet name. "Happy birthday."

"Move out of my way, Braydon."

He ignores me, wearing a benevolent smile like he's gracing me with his presence at my bullshit birthday party. The one I should never have allowed to take place. But in a way, I'm grateful for it because now I know the truth.

Braydon lowers himself to one knee in front of the crowd of awkward onlookers. He removes a ring box from his top pocket. Words are leaving his mouth. I can't hear them because my ears are hot and ringing at my own stupidity, but I can tell because his treacherous lips are moving.

Sound rushes back. "Juney baby? Hello? Juney baby? Will you marry me?" He gives an awkward laugh. "Don't leave me hanging here. Kind of causing a scene."

I snatch the ring box out of his hand and bounce it off his head, drawing gasps from the crowd. "There's your scene, *honey bunny*." And then I dart past him, through the expansive mansion, past those cursed family portraits that glare down at me disapprovingly.

I grab my purse on the way through the foyer, then fling the grand doors open and run down the stone steps. Gravel crunches underfoot. My faded yellow VW Beetle is parked near the fountain. Ol' Rusty is the only part of me that I haven't allowed Braydon to sell or change.

I scramble for the keys in my purse.

"Juney baby, wait!"

I get inside and slam the door, jam the keys into the ignition.

"June!"

I look up and find him by my window, his blond hair slicked back. He's breathing hard and there's a red patch where the ring box hit his forehead. Braydon's always had that clean-cut frat-boy look, but now he's panicked. Ruffled.

It's hardly gratifying enough to ease the pain of his betrayal.

"June, stop acting like a fool and come inside. You're embarrassing yourself," he says. "You're embarrassing me."

"Goodbye, Braydon."

He slams his hand down on top of Ol' Rusty. "You drive away, and you'll regret it. You hear me? You can't leave me, June. Even if you wanted to. I own you and everything you are. I made you."

Tears sting the corners of my eyes, but I refuse to shed them in front of him. I put my foot down and speed off, out through the open gates, onto the road.

Two

CASH

"T MINUS 20 MINUTES!" I yell over my shoulder into the kitchen, while I repeatedly ram my finger into my phone screen. The fucking thing is refusing to cooperate, and today is not the day for bullshit.

It's Alex's last day of school before the summer break, and I want it to be perfect. I've packed her favorite lunch, including a treat—don't usually allow candy, but I'll make an exception on the last day of school—and I helped her pick out her wardrobe last night.

My 11-year-old daughter loves putting on fashion shows, and last night was the "most important night of her life" when it came to choosing between the purple dress or the black one covered in purple unicorns holding up "rock on" signs with their hooves. Don't ask me how the fuck that's possible.

"Work, you stupid shit." The phone is frozen on today's organizational calendar I've shared with the nanny, Mrs. Crouchbottom, and I'm about ready to throw it across the room.

"Swear jar, Dad." Alex's voice chirps behind me.

I jolt on the spot and turn toward her. "You didn't hear that," I said. "It was an auditory illusion."

She eyerolls me in her pre-teen way, and it makes my chest hurt.

Alex is growing up faster than I want her to. I don't want to be the lame dad who gets overly protective about his daughter switching her interest from books to boys, but guess who's got two thumbs and that exact problem?

I stare at her, tilting my head to the side.

"What?" she asks.

"Are you wearing makeup?"

"No."

"It looks like you're wearing makeup." I'm no expert. I can't tell if her eyelashes look a little longer than usual or if I'm imagining this, but I haven't bought her any makeup. Unless my sister decided to get her some? But Hannah would never do that without asking first.

I abandon my phone and fold my arms, still examining her. "You know you're not allowed to—"

"I'm not wearing makeup, Dad." She fluffs her short blonde hair. She looks nothing like me, but she's mine. My precious daughter who is most definitely wearing makeup.

"Wash it off," I say. "You've got—" I check my watch — "five minutes until the nanny gets here. And you know the dress code. I'm all for sticking it to the man, but the school has rules. And what do we do with rules?"

"Break them?"

I face-palm then point toward the stairs.

Alex has the good graces to blush and apologize before

darting off. She wants to express her independence, I get that, but I'm trying to establish routine.

My daughter prefers to go her own way. She reminds me of me when I was her age, except she's more into rock music whereas I was—

There's a knock at the front door, and I stride through the house only to find a deputy from the Sheriff's Department on the wraparound porch.

"Hands up, scumbag," he says, holding up his fingers in a mock gun. "You're under arrest for being a grumpy asshole."

"What are you doing here?"

Jesse gives me that shit-eating grin that has gotten him into more panties and trouble than his badge. "And hello to you too, brother." He punches me on the shoulder.

I grab his hand and twist his arm. He aims a kick at my shins.

The sound of Alex at the top of the stairs stops the scuffle right quick.

"Too responsible for your own good," Jesse says, lowering his voice. "What happened to country music star Cash who had to beat off the girls with a stick? How long has it been since you've left the house for a night?"

The implication Jesse's trying to make is how long has it been since I've gotten my dick wet. That's what my charmer of a brother calls it. "None of your damn business."

And it's been literal years.

Heatstroke is my hometown, it's quaint, with paved streets, broad sidewalks, and folk who've survived the summer temperatures and the bad tempers that come with it, but I didn't come back here to find a woman. In fact, the last thing I want is a commitment. I know where that leads.

"Uncle Jesse!" Alex cries from behind me. "It's the last day of school."

I step back to let him in.

"I know, you little devil," Jesse says, and fishes around in his pocket. "Cool outfit. Are those unicorns?"

Alex gives him the rock on sign. Jesse and Alex have always gotten on like two foxes in a hen coop.

"Here." Jesse hands her a candy bar that's probably half-melted, but Alex squeals with delight.

"I told Crouchbottom only one candy bar today," I say. I would have put it on the schedule too if my damn phone hadn't decided to freeze.

"Come on, dude," Jesse says. "Lighten up."

I give my brother a warning look before checking my watch. "T minus five minutes."

"Get a load of this guy," Jesse says, then covers his mouth. "Kssshk. Ground Control to Rocket Ship Alex. T minus five minutes until launch."

I consider punching him in the throat this time, just for fun, but I'm distracted by the fact that the nanny isn't here yet. Mrs. Crouchbottom has been Alex's nanny every summer since she was five, and I need her help this year more than any other.

"Honey, wait in the living room?"

"Can I watch BeysPlays?" she asks.

I nod before striding through to the kitchen to grab my phone. Jesse follows me like the natural-born pain in the ass he is. He's the oldest brother, but he's always acted younger than both Leo and me combined.

The first few chords of a too familiar song come on the radio. I shut it off, my heart pounding.

Jesse sighs behind me. "Still?"

I restart my phone and wait for it to switch on.

No notifications.

None.

Mrs. Crouchbottom hasn't let me know that she's going to be late. And if Alex doesn't get to school soon, she's going to be tardy, and her homeroom teacher is going to have two cows and a cat.

"Are you going to see him today?" Jesse asks.

I don't have to ask who he's talking about. I grunt by way of reply.

"Look, Cash, I just want you to know I appreciate what you're doing. He's not in his right mind at the moment, and this has been tough on all of us." His voice cracks a little. "We'll get through this, brother."

"It's my responsibility now. You've got your thing. This can be my thing."

"Whatever help you need, just let me know, all right?"

I appreciate the sentiment, but we'll be fine. My father and I are grown-ups. "Fuck," I say.

"Gesundheit."

"Crouchbottom is a no-show." I try calling her, but she doesn't pick up.

"She lives right across the street, doesn't she?" Jesse asks.

I nod, dialing again. No answer. "Fuck."

Jesse rubs a tan hand over his face, his dark eyebrows two slashes over blue eyes. "You want to check on her? I can take Alex to school."

"She usually walks her on the last day. It's their thing."

"I'll walk her," Jesse says. "It's no problem."

Jesse's an annoying fuck, but he is a law enforcement official. And I would and have trusted him with my life. "Thanks."

He grins and goes through to the living room to fetch my daughter. I hug her on the way out and promise that Crouchbottom, or another responsible adult, will be there to meet her at the bus stop when school ends. She's unconcerned.

I'm the opposite of that.

I have to get to my dad's bar as soon as possible, but I need to know that Mrs. Crouchbottom is all right. It's not like her to pull a no-show. She's in her seventies, and she loves spending time with Alex. Besides, if I don't have her as a nanny for the summer, I'm royally fucked.

I jog up the front path to Crouchbottom's two-story home, all shiplap, porch swings, and potted plants that she never forgets to water, and knock on the front door.

Loud music thrums from inside.

I'm no expert, but it sounds like a workout tape. Like one of those Jane Fonda specials from back in the day.

"Mrs. Crouchbottom?" I knock again. "Mrs. Crouch-bottom, are you in there?"

"Help." The cry is soft.

I take one giant step back, lift my leg, and kick the door in.

She's in the living room, lying on her side, clutching her hip while the workout video plays on her tiny TV. Her eyes are red, but she breaks out into a watery smile. "Oh, Cash, honey, I'm so sorry I didn't send you a message. I couldn't reach my phone. I-I think I've hurt myself. I don't want to be any trouble but would you—"

I'm already on the phone to an ambulance before her sentence is up. "Don't move, Elsa. Not a muscle."

I get her water and do my best to make her comfortable with a cushion underneath her head without moving her too much, and then I sit down on the sofa to wait.

I'll have to fix her door when I get home this evening. And I'll have to find another nanny for the summer. I've got the feeling Crouchbottom's going to be in hospital for a while. Fuck.

Three

JUNE

FIFTEEN YEARS HAVE PASSED, and Heatstroke is almost exactly the same as I remember it. The wrought iron lampposts, the benches on the sidewalks, the cobblestone streets, and the smell of fresh salty sea air.

My hometown is the type of place where people want to retire or go on vacation. It's tucked right along the coast, with a stretch of beach that attracts tourists during the summer, but with rolling fields and ranches that help keep the town running during the off-peak seasons.

Growing up, I never thought I would leave this place with its summer talent shows and hot pepper eating contest—biggest in the state, ask anyone in town and they'd wax lyrical about it.

All I wanted was to escape from this perfect town.

"Silly," I mutter.

What good is thinking about past heartbreak when I've got a real one going on right now?

I park outside the Heartstopper Diner, my pulse racing. *What are you doing, June?*

I'm back in Heatstroke because it's the only place I have family. My mother. Who I would rather not talk to about my problems, and who's going to lose her mind when she finds out that Braydon and I have broken up.

But when the going gets tough, us country girls have a tendency to pull on our boots and kick tough in the gonads, and that's exactly what I plan on doing.

That might be the exhaustion talking since I spent most of the night at a rest stop with my head on the wheel, drifting in and out of an uncomfortable sleep.

I check my reflection in the rearview mirror.

"Oof." Smudged mascara, dark circles under my eyes.

I adjust my blonde hair, the yellow ribbons I weaved through my French braid still there. I have got nothing but the clothes on my back, two hundred dollars in my bank account, and the old box of letters I keep in my trunk. I never moved it out of Ol' Rusty because a part of me didn't want Braydon to see it. At the time, I'd rationalized that it was because I had gotten over what happened.

I get out of the car and smooth the yellow silk dress that looks entirely ridiculous now that it's daylight. I take a deep breath and enter the Heartstopper Diner.

It's like being slapped with nostalgia. The early afternoon sunlight streams through the windows, highlighting the retro interior, with its cushy red barstools, linoleum flooring, and chrome-sided counter. The booths are half full. Familiar folks everywhere.

Marci Walsh looks up from behind the counter and her eyes go as round as donuts. Marci and I have kept in contact since I left, texting and FaceTiming whenever we get the chance. She was one of my friends in high school and the only girl who's stuck by me through thick and thin.

"Well, I'll be damned." That comes from Rod Coleman, who must be at least sixty years old now. He rises out of his seat across from his wife. "Is that—?"

"Sit down, Rod, before you break another hip craning your neck at pretty women…" His wife, Tilly, trails off. She rises too. "It can't be."

"June!" Marci cries. She circles the counter, her emerald-green eyes glistening, her long red hair, twisted into a messy bun on top of her head, bounces as she runs over. Marci squeezes me tight then holds me out at arm's length. "Well, you could've told me you were coming."

"Marci." I hug her back, relishing the physical contact. It feels like years have passed since I've experienced real affection.

"June Jackson," Rod says, grinning at me then smoothing a hand over his graying hair. "We didn't think we'd be seeing you again."

"Certainly didn't." Tilly, the head librarian at Heatstroke's public library, comes over and takes her turn giving me a hug. "Welcome home, honey pie. What brings you back? I heard you were living the highlife out in Dallas. Your mother's been talking the ear off anybody who stops long enough to listen. Telling everybody how you're a rich girl now."

"A rich girl who never visits. But guess that's all changed now, hasn't it?" Rod is eager for his hug, and I laugh and give him one. It's gut-wrenching to be home. I have amazing memories here mixed with terrible ones. I have to remind myself that I'm here for the summer, and that's it.

"I was about to get engaged."

That silences them. The quaint bell over the door tinkles as another customer enters. This time, it's Desiree from the antique store. "Well, I'll be damned," she says. "Is that—?"

Rod waves for her to shush up. "We're past that part already."

"We've moved on to the reason why," Tilly puts in.

"She was engaged," Rod says.

"About to be," Tilly corrects him.

The gathering crowd of well-meaning folks have picked up that something's gone wrong and Marci steps in. "This is a discussion we should have in private," she says.

"Marci Walsh," Tilly says, fisting her hips. "You're not seriously going to deprive us of the first good gossip we've had in years, are you?"

"Everybody who doesn't have their butt in a chair in the next five minutes isn't getting a refill on coffee," Marci says.

That gets them back to their booths real quick. Heat-strokers love nothing more than a good cup of coffee, and Marci happens to make the best—she's been working the counter since high school when her daddy owned the diner. Before she took over.

Marci guides me to a stool at the counter and fixes me a cup of said coffee. She pushes it along the countertop, her gaze laser-focused on me.

"You didn't text," she says softly. "What happened, June?"

I can feel the ears perking up around the diner.

I take a sip of coffee and am instantly transported to

heaven. Sweet, sweet relief. That rest stop coffee had no kick.

"It's a long story," I say, and then I tell her. Everything. At full volume. Partly because I know this will be all over Heatstroke before the hour is out anyway, and partly because it feels good to speak it out loud.

Marci's eyebrows lift on her freckled forehead the longer I talk.

When I'm done, she blinks. "Well, shit," she says. "Are you okay?"

"I mean," I gesture toward myself, "apart from the fact that I have no job, no future, and I'm going to have to sleep in my old room at my mom's place until I can get back on my feet? Sure." I don't have a choice to be not okay. I'm determined to view this as a fresh start.

And to avoid anything with a dick at all costs. Men are done. The past. Never happening again. It's finally time to focus on what I want.

Marci pulls a face. "You can stay with me upstairs! I've got a sofa ready and waiting."

I shake my head and grab her hand, squeezing it. "That's—I wouldn't want to inconvenience you."

"It's not an inconvenience to need help, June," Marci says. "That's what friends are for." Marci's a wild child, the type of woman who does what she wants, when she wants, whereas I've always been too afraid to do anything that would inconvenience someone else. I admire that about her.

I sip my coffee, and I'm already starting to feel better. "Yeah, but I'm going to stay with my mom. She'll be confused when she runs into me in town and I haven't stopped by." I pause. "It's surreal to be here."

"Back where it all started," Marci says with a grin. "I'm so happy you're here. The way you left was…"

I'm really glad she doesn't finish that sentence. Marci's the only person who knows what happened with Cash. And with Olivia, my best friend. Ex-best friend. Estranged best friend? It's in the past. It doesn't matter now, and Cash doesn't even live in Heatstroke anymore.

He moved away around about the same time I did, except where I fell into a relationship and failed to go after my dreams, Cash took his head-on. He's a country music star. One of the most famous. And the reason I avoid entertainment news like it spreads plague.

"Have you called your mother yet?" Marci asks.

I shake my head.

"Probably best you don't. You should just turn up and act like it's a big surprise." Marci knows what Mom is like. "Besides, she wouldn't turn you away." Even she doesn't sound that certain about it. "And hell, if things go south, you know where to find me."

Before I can say anything, the bell tinkles over the door again and a girl strolls into the diner.

She's the cutest button of a thing I've ever seen. Curly blonde hair, with a slightly upturned nose and blue, blue eyes. She's wearing a black dress covered in unicorns holding up "rock on" signs. My heart twists as she gives a big sniff and takes a seat at a booth by the window alone. A tear runs down her cheek.

"June," Marci says suddenly, "there's something you should—"

"Just a sec," I say. "That little girl looks upset." I abandon my coffee and go over to her.

Marci squeaks something out, but I don't hear what she says.

The girl doesn't look up. She's fiddling with her dress, trying to stop from crying.

"Hi," I say brightly.

She starts and meets my gaze. "H-hi."

"I'm June. Sorry, I didn't mean to scare you. Just, it looks like you're having as bad of a day as I am."

The girl doesn't respond immediately. I don't blame her. I'm the weird lady in a yellow silk dress.

"Do you need help?" I ask. "Do you need somebody to call your parents?"

She shakes her head quickly.

"May I sit down?" I offer her another smile, hoping to assure her that I am not, in fact, as crazy as I look.

The girl nods.

I slip into the booth opposite her. "So, I'm June, and I've had a pretty rough night," I say. "Sometimes life sucks."

"Yeah," the girl whispers. "Sometimes."

"Can I ask you a question?"

"I guess."

"What are you doing here alone?"

"School's out early and I, I just. My Ganny was meant to pick me up, and I…"

Ganny? There's only one woman I know in town who goes by the name "Ganny" and it's the matriarch of the Taylor family. Cash's grandmother. That means this little girl has to be the daughter of one of the Taylor siblings. There are five of them.

"Ganny didn't show up?" I had fond memories of Ganny Taylor. I'd spent countless hours at her house, playing in the old treehouse in her backyard with Cash as kids, swimming at the quarry while she kept a watchful eye.

The girl gnaws on her bottom lip. "I was meant to meet her," she whispers. "But I didn't get on the bus."

"May I ask why?"

The girl swallows. "I didn't want to go on the school bus. I don't like the bus." She presses her lips together in a line.

I take a deep breath. "I get that. Sometimes it's not easy to do things we don't like doing. But I'm pretty sure that Ganny's really worried about you right about now, and that she just wants to make sure you're okay. If we tell her you're here, she'll probably be relieved."

The girl plucks at her dress.

"Can I get Marci over there to call her?" I ask, pointing to my friend, who has gone pale and is gesturing to me frantically. I give her a quizzical look before turning back to the girl. "Are you allowed ice cream?"

She nods eagerly. I'm not sure if that's true or not, but I'm not above plying this child with ice cream if it will cheer her up. "A Spoonful of Sugar" is one of my favorite childhood songs. Besides, I remember Ganny Taylor doling out cherry-topped sundaes when I was about this girl's age.

"All right, so here's the deal. I'll call Ganny so she can pick you up, and I'll get you an ice cream to sweeten the deal. Sound good?"

The girl's lips part. "Alex."

"Alex? That's a cool name."

She breaks into a broad smile that looks oddly familiar. "June's cool too."

"Well, how about that? We have something in common." I look over at Marci. "Can you call Ganny Taylor and tell her Alex is here?"

Marci swallows like I've asked her to perform open-heart surgery. "I already have." Why does she look so unhappy about it?

Four

CASH

"SHE'S FINE, CASH," Ganny says, walking along beside me.

We're almost at the Heartstopper—an accurate description of how I'm feeling right about now. I tighten my grip on my grandmother's arm. Ganny is closing in on ninety and she absolutely can't be a permanent solution to my nanny issue, especially not now that Alex has pulled this stunt.

I don't know what's gotten into my kid, and that scares me.

Why would she not get on the school bus? It's not like her. She's my little rocker kid, my little rebel, but she's never done anything this disobedient before.

I'm a mixture of angry and sick. Angry because this situation is out of my control, sick because I feel like this is my fault. I can't be everywhere at once. I can't—

Ganny squeezes my arm and peers up into my face. She's got the blue eyes that are the hallmark of the Taylor family, and she pairs them with a stare that could cut glass.

At her age, she should be all soft around the edges, in need of extra care, but she's aged like leather and equally as tough. She reaches up and pats me on the cheek, gray-blue hair bobbling. "Take it easy, Cash, honey. She's a girl. She's finding herself."

"She could have wound up in danger."

Ganny doesn't point out that Heatstroke is safe, and that maybe I'm being unreasonable, and I appreciate that.

I open the door, the bell tinkling overhead only serving to piss me off.

Marci Walsh stares at me from behind the counter, round-eyed. "H-hi—"

"Where's—?" I start, but before I can say more than a word, two arms wrap around my middle.

"Dad, I'm sorry," Alex whispers. "I didn't mean to. I—"

My gaze fixes on my daughter, tuning out the rest of the diner. I tilt her chin upward. "I don't know why or what this was about but we're going to talk about this at home this evening."

Alex nods, tears spilling down her cheeks. Rage floods me so fast I have to take a breath to control the reaction. "Are you hurt? Did someone hurt you?"

"No, Dad," she says. "Nothing like that. I'm fine. A nice lady helped me."

Helped her? Helped her how? "Oh." I let out a breath. "Oh. Well, Ganny's here to take you home, all right?"

"Come on, darling," Ganny says, putting out a hand. "How about we make something nice to eat. Cookies? Would you like that?"

Alex blinks tears away and gives Ganny a watery smile. "Yeah."

"Great, come on, let's leave your dad to it. He's got to get back to work."

Alex gives me another hug, and I'm not sure I'm comfortable leaving to go back and help my father at the bar. "You want me to call the rest of the workday off?" I ask. "Want to go home instead?"

"No, Dad. No, I'm fine." Alex puts on a brave smile. "Sorry I made you worry. And Ganny too."

I give her one last hug. What a damn day this has been. First Mrs. Crouchbottom in the hospital and now this.

Alex heads for the exit with Ganny but pauses in the doorway. "Bye, June!" Alex grins. "Thanks for the ice cream!"

June?

There's only one June in my world.

I follow my daughter's gaze toward the booth near the front window. And the woman standing beside it.

June.

It's June.

It's like every dream, every fantasy I've ever had has materialized.

Seeing June Jackson for the first time in fifteen fucking years is like being struck by lightning. Every cell in my body is alive. I can breathe again.

June is more beautiful than she was when she left.

She's standing there, her hands tucked behind her back, her head dipped a little so that she peers up at me with those green eyes, her blonde hair threaded through with yellow ribbons. She looks sweet. And it threatens to turn me inside out. Her pink lips are parted in shock.

And her body.

Oh, my fucking God.

A yellow dress presses against her tan skin, modestly cut in the front, but with one fuck of a slit up the side that shows enough skin to torture me. She's slim, toned, her breasts perky, and I know if I stare for too long, I'm going to embarrass myself.

Is it really her? Fuck. How can it be?

She left.

She left and she stopped writing me six months after.

"Cash," she says, her voice like molten sunshine.

The spell breaks.

I close the space between us in three steps.

"June," I say, and then I draw her into my arms and hug her to my chest.

She feels impossibly good, treacherously so, but June was never for me. We were always just friends. It's difficult to remember it at this moment. If I felt like I was being struck by lightning before, now, I'm on fucking fire.

She smells like citrus and feels so good I have to let her go because my cock is already hardening from the brief contact.

Not happening. Doesn't matter if it's June. I don't do relationships anymore.

I come to my senses and step away. "You're back."

"It's good to see you again, Cash." She sounds uncertain.

I settle for a grunt and take another step back. June or not, I am not interested in having my life derailed by a woman again. Doesn't matter why she stopped writing me. Why she's here.

"I'm not here for long," she says suddenly. "Just for the summer, probably. I don't know. It's until I can get my life back together and then I'll be on my way."

Why is her life not together?

Last I heard, she had some asshole boyfriend in Dallas. Had he done something to her? "What happened?"

June opens her mouth to answer as my phone buzzes in the back pocket of my jeans.

Sounds rush back in. People talking. The clink of knives and forks on plates. The hiss of the grill in the kitchen.

Every single person is staring at us. Rod Coleman gives me a thumbs-up from the corner. Tilly whispers something to him, and I can't help scowling.

No one knows about the flame I held for June except for my buddy, Savage, and my brothers, but damn if they wouldn't talk about it if they did. And I've had enough stories circulating about me. The last thing I need is a renewed interest in my life now that I have Alex to look after.

And flames burn hot, but they also burn out.

"Your phone," June says.

I look back at her, and it's a struggle. I bring my phone out of my pocket. My father's number flashes on the screen. "I've got to take it. It's Dad."

"Sure," June says. "It was nice to see you, Cash." The words don't sound truthful. She rushes past me and out the diner door before I can reply.

My phone keeps ringing. The diners keep staring. Marci is pulling faces behind the counter and beckoning me over.

June Jackson is back.

$\mathcal{F}ive$

JUNE

CASH TAYLOR IS IN HEATSTROKE.

I sit in the car in front of my mother's house, the house I grew up in, the one that's right next door to Cash's childhood home, and try to take deep, even breaths.

This is the last thing I need.

I'm already dealing with the whole "Braydon is a cheating asshole" issue. Throw in my secret high school crush and this is too much to handle.

Olivia and Cash and I had been best friends, partly because my mother had been more of a parent to Olivia than her own. Olivia and I had practically shared my bedroom.

The three of us were inseparable until we weren't anymore.

My gaze wanders over to Cash's dad's place. It looks neat as a pin, well cared for, but Cash doesn't live there anymore. Is he just visiting? Alex is his kid. Does that mean he's married? Married to Olivia? What the hell is he even doing in Heatstroke? Is Olivia here?

Cash is a country music star. The last I heard, years ago, he was touring to sold-out shows across the country.

Forget it. It doesn't matter.

But the way his arms wrapped around me, the way it felt. The way he smelled. Like a man—leather, a hint of spice, and the scent of his skin.

He's even more gorgeous than he was years ago.

Tattoos down one muscular forearm, disappearing up the sleeve of his shirt. A shirt that strained against his muscles. Cash has always been tall, but he's filled out and he's grown a beard.

He's the total opposite of my ex. And it doesn't even matter because not only is he the past, but I'm leaving Heatstroke the first chance I get.

I grab my purse from the passenger seat and force myself out of Ol' Rusty and onto the sun-beaten sidewalk. The last time I talked to Mom was yesterday morning, and she told me to soak up all the attention I could get on my birthday, because one day I'd be old, my looks would be gone, and I'd have nothing left.

Patricia Jackson, ladies and gentlemen.

Nobody could accuse my mother of mincing her words.

You can do this. It's just Mom.

But the sooner I ask my mother if I can stay for a while, the sooner I can start looking for a job to fund my future. My dream. It seems like an impassable mountain, my goal right at the top, but nobody ever got to where they were going by not taking the first step.

My mother's house isn't as fancy as Cash's dad's. The front yard is smaller, the windows are dirty, and the cream shiplap needs a coat of paint. The picket gate creaks as I open it and make my way up the stone front steps and onto the porch.

At the sight of the front door with its misted glass panes and the old swing seat, I'm struck hard by nostalgia.

I press the doorbell.

Mom curses somewhere inside. Her figure appears in the misted glass and the latch clacks.

"Hi, Mom."

My mother has her graying hair scooped back into a bun that tugs at her roots. She's a little hunched over, fast approaching sixty and she stares at me, brow wrinkled. "June?"

"I should have called. But I, uh, I was wondering if I can stay in my old bedroom for a while?"

Mom looks past me, and it hits me that she's looking for Braydon. We've flown her out a couple of times, and she thinks Braydon is God's gift to our family. Because he's rich and sends her money whenever she asks.

"What are you doing here?"

Nice to see you too. I put up a sweet smile. "I, uh, I need help."

"Where's Braydon?"

"We broke up."

My mother's upper lip curls before I reach the end of that sentence. "What? Why? What did you do?"

"I didn't do anything," I say, "except for catching him cheating on me." I wasn't going to tell her why because it might hit too close to home for her after what happened with Dad, but it doesn't make sense not to say it.

"Cheating on you. Cheating how?"

There are a finite number of ways a person can cheat in

a relationship, and all of them are pretty bad. "He's having an affair," I say. "I—may I come in?"

My mother hedges. She steps back. "I was making cookies," she says. "You should have some."

My mother ranges between being lovely and sweet, baking cookies and sending cute texts with puppy dog memes, and telling me how I can't do better than Braydon and that she wishes she had a daughter to be proud of. That I'm the reason her life fell apart.

The dichotomy gives me whiplash.

It makes me feel guilty. Like, if I had my shit together then I wouldn't be asking for help.

My mother's flip-flops squidge through the house, and I follow her past the living room with its floral print sofas and childhood pictures, many of them of Cash, Olivia, and me playing together at the quarry, and I repress the shiver that comes at that memory.

In every picture, Olivia stands between us, her arms draped over our shoulders, wearing her bright smile.

It's weird to see her face now that we don't talk any more.

In the kitchen, Mom grabs her oven mitt and pulls a tray of fresh-baked chocolate chip cookies out of the oven. She places it on the counter. "Don't see how the two of you can give up on such a good long-term relationship so quickly."

I sit down at the kitchen table, placing my purse on top of it. I have to be careful in how I broach this topic. "That's the thing, Mom, it wasn't going great."

"What do you mean it wasn't going great? If it was going badly, why did you stick around for so long?"

"It was insipid," I say. "It was—"

"Don't use big words," Mom says.

"It seemed fine from the outside, but Braydon wanted me to stay home and didn't seem to care what I wanted. And every time I told him I wanted a career, he would have a reason that it couldn't happen. It wasn't just the cheating," I say, "but that part was bad enough."

"Cheating," my mother says irritably. "Cheating. That's not a big deal. You shouldn't let a good man go, just because he makes a mistake."

She isn't hearing me. Maybe because she doesn't want to hear me. "Can I please stay here for the summer? Or just a couple of weeks until I can get a job and afford to pay rent."

"You can stay for the summer," she says. "As long as you help me out financially. I've been struggling for months, as you well know." She puts cookies on a plate and places them in front of me.

"Thanks." I take a bite, and they are deliciously sweet, even if I'm confused about how to feel right now. Always the same when we talk.

"I'm sure you won't be here for that long anyway," Mom says. "Braydon will come down here and get you. That's the type of man he is, unlike your father."

"He's the type of man who cheats," I say, "and that's not the type of man I want for myself."

"Then what do you want? To live in a backward town like this until your days are done? Wind up alone, baking cookies with nothing to look forward to?"

An awkward silence.

"Things are going to get better," she adds. "You just wait until he comes for you. He'll sweep you off your feet again. Besides, anything worth having is worth fighting for."

I give her a small smile and put down the cookie. "I've got to get some stuff from the car." There's only one thing in the car, and that's the box of letters. It feels right to take them out now that I'm "home." It's totally not because Cash is in town.

"Sure." Mom moves out of the kitchen, leaving me with the cookies and a sense of unease.

I head out into the afternoon and grab the letters from my trunk before taking the old box up to my bedroom.

My bed is gone.

I blink rapidly.

There's a sofa, a TV, and a few of my old posters— Garth Brooks and the Chicks—and pictures on the wall, but everything else that's mine is gone. "Mom?"

"Yeah?" she shouts from downstairs.

"My bed?"

I can hear her footsteps on the stairs, and she peers past me as if she's not even sure what happened to it. "Oh, right. I figured you'd never come back so I sold it. Turned your room into an entertainment space. Sofa's comfy." And then she shuffles off again. "I'll get you a comforter and a couple of pillows."

I can rough it. That's fine. Not a problem. "Thanks," I call.

But a wedge of emotion has seated itself in my throat. I stow the box of letters on the top shelf in my closet then shut the door and walk to the window. It looks out on Cash's old house and gives me a view of his bedroom. The curtains are shut.

I sit down on the sofa and refuse to cry, pulling my phone out of my purse.

A notification from Marci puts a smile on my face.

> **MARCI**
> Girl. If you need anything, just let me know, all right? Like clothes, food, friggin' anything.

> I won't say no to the clothes. And I hate to ask, but do you know of anywhere I can find a job? Like, anything. I'll do whatever it takes.

> Clothes? Hell yeah. Stop by in like half an hour when I have my break? I've got some cute tops you will love. As for the job, I wish I could offer you one at the diner, but we're fully staffed. I'll put the word out for you. <3

> You are a super star and the best. Seriously.

> I'm just glad I finally have you nearby so I can unload all my emotional baggage on you. Hehehehehe.

> Be there soon. <3

If anyone's got emotional baggage, it's me. But I'm relieved to have Marci as a support system. Living in the same town as my mother is a punishment I don't want to take. I won't stop until I've figured life out and escaped Heatstroke for the last time.

Six

CASH

I'M in a foul fucking mood tonight.

Alex won't tell me why she didn't get on the bus this afternoon. Every time I ask, she clams up, and forcing the issue isn't going to make this any easier. Ganny's taking her tomorrow, on the first day of her summer break, and I've spent the last nine hours helping my father with the bar.

And June Jackson is back in Heatstroke.

That sends a spike of heat straight through my torso.

She's back in Heatstroke. She can be as perfect as she likes, as beautiful and warm and welcoming, smelling of citrus and fucking memories, but it doesn't matter.

June is a memory, and Alex has my whole heart. I haven't got room for complications.

Carter clicks his fingers under my nose. "You alive over there, bud?"

Carter, or Savage as we call him, rolled up on his Harley right after I got home and stayed for dinner. He's been on my ass about not taking it easy enough for weeks. I'd kick him out, but he's been my friend since middle school, and he's basically a brother to me and an uncle to Alex at this point.

I abandon the beans on my plate and sit back. I make a mean chicken-fried steak, but I'm useless when it comes to vegetables. The only reason I try to make them is because growing girls need their vitamins and fiber.

"I'm fine."

Savage gives me a knowing look but turns to Alex. "What's eating your old man's ass?"

I grunt. "Swear jar."

Alex giggles, pressing a hand over her mouth. It's a new habit she's picked up—covering her mouth when she smiles—and I've added it to the list of shit I worry about before I fall asleep. She's not confident enough. She's a rock star, but she won't let herself be one, and I keep thinking it's my fucking fault.

"Talkative, huh?" Savage says, nudging Alex. The man can barely fit at our kitchen table. Savage likes to spend time in the gym, and he keeps a beard and tattoos up the side of his neck that are meant to be a signpost not to fuck with him. Really, he's a teddy bear, especially when it comes to his goddaughter. "How was the last day of school, Alex? Somebody's got to keep me entertained while we eat these god-awful beans."

"Beans, beans, they're good for your heart," Alex chants and dutifully eats a forkful. "School was mid."

"Mid?" Savage frowns. "What is mid?"

"It means fine." Alex shrugs and looks down at her food, and my frustration doubles. "Yeah, fine. It was normal. I'm glad it's summer break, but Mrs. Crouch-bottom broke her hip so now I don't have a nanny anymore. I wanted to stay home and play computer games, but I have to go to Ganny's tomorrow."

"I thought you liked hanging out at Ganny's," I say.

"I do, Dad," Alex replies. "But there's other stuff I like too."

I scratch the back of my neck. "And you can't do them at Ganny's?"

Alex puffs out her lips and rolls her eyes. "I can do some of them, but it's not like I can play my games or anything."

"Back in my day," Savage says, sounding like he's sixty rather than in his thirties, "we played outside. Don't kids ever go to the quarry anymore? We used to fish and swim and get up to all kinds of shit."

"Swear jar," Alex and I say in unison.

My daughter shoots me an uncertain smile. I return it. I'm angry about earlier, but I'm more concerned about why. And why she won't tell me. I've never had to ground her before, and I don't want to start now, but we're entering dangerous territory.

"Kids don't go to the quarry any more. It's so 1999," Alex says. "I just, I like games."

Savage leans forward, the chair creaking under his weight. "But Alex, how are you going to meet cute boys if you don't go to the quarry?"

"I will throttle you," I say, pointing a finger at him.

Alex laughs. "Dad, I'm done. Can I go watch YouTube?"

"Yeah." We've already talked about how her behavior today was unacceptable and that there will be repercussions. I'm still figuring out what they are. There are parenting books, but theory and practical work are worlds apart.

Alex cleans off her plate, stacks it next to the dishwasher and hurries off to the living room to sit down.

"You're going to let her watch YouTube after the stunt she pulled?" Savage asks.

"Yeah," I say. "I'm figuring it out. This parenting stuff isn't for the weak."

Savage nods. "I bet. So, what are you going to do about the nanny situation? Crouchbottom's in the hospital? What did the doctor say?"

"That she won't be on her feet for months," I reply. "So, she's not going to be around to nanny. I'll figure something out." I have to. I can't leave dad hanging when he needs me, and I won't compromise on childcare for Alex.

I'm not panicked, but I'm certainly fucking concerned. If I could just—

"Just about every woman in this town would bend over backward to be a live-in nanny for you. I can hear them gossiping from here."

"Yeah, well, that's exactly the problem," I said. "I don't want a woman around who wants 'Cash Taylor' country music star." It's the reason Crouchbottom was perfect for the job, and totally uncomplicated.

"I heard June Jackson's in town."

My fist drops to the table so hard, the knives and forks clatter in our plates. "Oh."

"Oh?" Savage eyes me. "You haven't heard about that?"

"I saw her today."

Savage waits for more from me. I'm not giving it.

He gives a low chuckle. "Come on, Cash."

I get up and take his plate, not caring whether he's done or not. "Beer?"

"Sure," he says. "But I think you need one more than I do."

Savage is smiling so hard, I can hear it with my back turned to him.

"Cash, you've always had a hard-on for that woman, and now that she's back, you're not going to make a move?"

"You don't know what the fuck you're talking about. And keep your voice down." But I know Alex won't hear us. The sounds of her favorite gaming streamer's goofy laughter is penetrating the entirety of the bottom floor of the house.

"I do know what the fuck I'm talking about," Savage says. "You were the one who told me that she's the one who got away."

"Didn't say that."

"Yeah, you did. Every time we go out and grab a few drinks, which is never anymore, you talk about her. You talk about her more than you talk about your ex, and you didn't even fuck June," Savage says. "You can't tell me you're not tempted. What happened to the country music star who could have any woman he wanted?"

"He's long gone. He was gone the minute Olivia gave birth to Alex, and the minute I brought my baby back to this town. I don't want or need a woman."

"Fine," Savage says, "but I heard something interesting about her today."

"Fucking Chatty Cathy over here," I mutter, grabbing a can of beer from the fridge and handing it to him. I get one for myself as well, even though I don't usually drink during the week. I pop the tab because I need this tonight.

Savage downs some beer then lets out a burp and grins. "I heard through the Heatstroke grapevine that she's looking for work."

I don't react.

"June Jackson is as broke as the day she left Heatstroke. She's staying with her mother," Savage says, "right next door."

Not reacting is getting increasingly difficult.

"She needs help," Savage says. "And her mother does too."

I never liked June's mother. She's always been a taker, and June bent over backward to please her all through high school because of what Patricia put her through after her father left.

"Not my problem," I say, and the words feel so much like bullshit it must show on my face. Savage laughs again.

"Whatever you say, man." Savage downs the rest of the beer and crushes the can, leaving it on the table like the asshole he is. "See you tomorrow. Try not to drown in your grumpy-ass sorrows while I'm gone."

I flip him off as he leaves. The screen door slams. His motorcycle starts up a couple of minutes later and growls away.

June Jackson needs work.

You're insane if you do this. You've lost your mind.

I've spent the day trying not to think about her. But knowing she's next door is painful. Knowing she needs help is worse. She needs help, and so do I, and if I can't find a nanny within the next twenty-four hours, I'm fucked.

I push my chair back, leaving my beer on the table. Alex is sprawled on the sofa.

"I'm going next door," I say. "I'll be right back."

"Okay! But Dad, you've got to see this when you get back. BeysPlays found this secret tunnel in BingeCraft, and it's not even like a game mod or something." Her expression is deathly serious. "Can you watch with me?"

"Minute I get back," I say, even though I have no idea what the hell any of that meant.

And then I step out into the hot summer's night and turn toward June's house.

JUNE

MY MOTHER IS ALREADY UPSTAIRS in bed after a dinner of boxed mac 'n' cheese. She doesn't like to cook, and I'm pooped after the drive and the surround-sound Braydon phone sex-betrayal extravaganza.

Seeing Cash was weird too. Like a blast from the past I didn't want or ask for. God knows, the last thing I need is to get all twisted up about him again.

I sit on the sofa in the living room, trying to summon life from my mom's old laptop.

"The plan," I murmur, determined to stay positive. "Focus on the plan."

Design and print out a few flyers to put up around town. Find a job. Save money. Get the hell out of Heatstroke. Follow my dreams for the first time ever.

We'll call it the *yassification* of June. The extended uncut movie version.

As a corollary to my list: never let a man tell me what I can and can't do ever again, whether implied or directly.

A knock rattles the front door, and I frown, glancing

through to the entrance hall of my childhood home. The wooden floors with their creaks in specific spots, and the old family picture of my mom and me, Olivia hovering in the background.

I get up and open the door.

I regret it.

Because Cash is standing on the porch, and my cheeks are instantly hot.

So much for that never letting a man get in your head thing.

"Cash," I manage to say.

There we go. Not so difficult. He was just my high school crush. Just the person I'd pined after for years until he'd started dating my best friend instead.

Cash stares at me, his deep, ocean-blue eyes seeing straight into my soul. The Taylor brothers all have that stare, but none compare to Cash.

I take stock of his body in the silent heat of the Texas summer night, aware that the awkward quiet has continued for far too long.

Cash is taller than most men, well over six-four, broad-shouldered, muscular in the chest and arms and legs, and damn well everywhere else, but with the easy grace of an artist. His dark hair is short, the top longer than the sides, and styled like he's just rolled out of bed.

His nose is crooked from where Reggie Donald broke it with his dad's Louisville Slugger—accident when we were kids—and he's got those three freckles on his left cheekbone that I used to doodle in the backs of my textbooks.

"June," he says, his voice a rumble that penetrates me to the core.

Get over yourself.

"It's good to see you again," he says.

There's another quiet broken only by the chirping of crickets. "You, too."

He lets out a low breath, and I, like an absolute psycho, want to lean in and feel it against my skin.

"Sorry to interrupt your evening," he says.

"I was just trying to get my mom's old laptop to work, and let's just say I don't think there's an IT guy in the country who could bring it back to life. I'm surprised it didn't zap me when I tried to turn it on."

Cash's lips don't even twitch. The boy who used to laugh and kid around with me is gone and has been replaced by this surly man.

I swallow. This is so friggin' awkward.

"I heard you were looking for work," he says.

"News travels fast." I laugh. "Yeah, I'm kind of looking to get back on my feet. I was hoping Marci needed help at the Heartstopper, but she's fully staffed, so..." I trail off because I'm not sure why he's here. I glance sideways at his dad's house. "Are you visiting your dad?"

"Nope."

"So, you—"

"I need a nanny," he says, like he can't wait to get the words out. Almost like he's mad at me for having to say them. "You're a good person, June, and you're good with kids. You get that teaching degree you always wanted?"

Cash remembers. He remembers my dream.

Wait. Did he just ask me to be his nanny?

Cash shifts his weight from one foot to the other. "Look," Cash continues, running a broad tan hand over the back of his neck, "I'm in a tricky spot. I need a nanny for Alex for the summer. I need someone responsible who'll keep her from melting her eyeballs in front of the TV or computer." More tumbling words, half-angry. Or is he just in a bad mood?

"And you thought of me? Isn't there anyone else who could help you?" I ask. "I'm back so that I can work up the funds to start school, but I'm not sure nannying is what I want to do."

"I can help you with that," he says. "Money's not a problem."

I smile. "That's very modest of you, Cash."

"Didn't mean it like that. I just meant that I'll take care of you," he says.

My heart turns over.

"Financially. If you choose to be Alex's nanny."

"What happened to her previous nanny?" I'm too curious for my own good, and the questions I've been holding back are on their way out now. "I mean, you've always been the organized one, Cash. I can't imagine a world in which you don't have all your ducks in a cute little row."

"Mrs. Crouchbottom broke her hip."

My hand comes up to my throat. His gaze fixates on it. "I'm so sorry. That's terrible."

"Doing a Zumba workout tape."

"I'm not sure why that's relevant," I say, with a half smile, "but I hope she's okay?"

"She's going to be out for months."

"I—"

"If you're interested in helping me out, come by tomorrow."

I suck in a breath. Every part of me wants to jump at

the opportunity. I love kids. Alex is super sweet, and we got on well in the diner. I like Cash. A little too much.

I'm so attracted to him I can barely think straight.

"Where do you live?"

"Next door."

My stomach inverts. "Next door. So, you would just want a nanny for the day, right? I could stay here, and—"

"No."

"No?" I ask.

"I need a live-in nanny," Cash says. "Dad is not doing great."

I know Cash's mom passed away a couple of years back. I sent Ganny and his father flowers and my condolences.

"I'm so sorry, Cash."

"I might need to leave at night on short notice," he says. "So, I need you there at all times."

"What about Olivia?" The words are out before I can stop them because I've been desperate to ask. "Can't she come by and look after Alex?"

Cash's expression shutters. "She's not in the picture."

"But she's Alex's mom, right?"

Cash nods once.

Olivia and Cash dated for years, they'd lived the celebrity life together when Cash's band made it big. I have no idea what transpired between them, but I can't understand why a mother would leave her child.

Cash, unreadable, watches me. "Come by tomorrow morning if you want the job. I need the help if you're willing to offer it. I'll pay you well."

"Thanks, Cash, I—"

He takes a step toward me, so close I can smell his

spicy, leathery cologne. He smells the same, but better. More manly.

I look up at him. "Cash, I—?"

His blue-eyed gaze sweeps over my face, lingering on my lips and eyes. He's intense and always has been—that much hasn't changed. "Eight in the morning."

"Eight?"

"If you want the job," he says, and then, I'm sure it must be my imagination, but I swear he half lifts his hand, almost like he wants to touch me. Cash turns and walks off down the old front steps of my mother's house.

The emptiness that he leaves behind is as stark as it was when we were young.

I let myself back into the house and sag against the door.

I'm not really going to do this, am I?

Eight

CASH

I KEEP LYING to myself that I only asked her to be the nanny because I need the help. But it's a bullshit excuse and I know it. I need a nanny, but having June around is only going to make things hard for me. Just the thought of her, standing there, looking up at me with those pretty green eyes, her blonde hair messy, her lips parted just right, has me on edge.

I stand in the kitchen, staring out the window at Mrs. Crouchbottom's house opposite, hating that this morning happened. Not only because she got hurt, but because I'm going to have June under my roof.

Under my roof.

This was the one goddamn summer I needed a live-in nanny, and this had to happen. No matter what, I can't let myself get too close to her, no matter how much I wanted her in the past.

Upstairs, the toilet flushes, and it snaps me out of my reverie.

"Bedtime," I call up. "I'll be there in a second to tuck you in."

"Thanks, Dad!"

I love Alex so much, but it's difficult to deal with the guilt. If I'd chosen better at the start, maybe she would have a mother who wanted to be a part of her life. I clench my fists, shake my head, and let my anger and frustration drive away the last of my thoughts of June and her lithe, perfect body.

I head up to Alex's room, which is a mess by my standards and perfect by hers. She's got posters of the Red Hot Chili Peppers, Imagine Dragons, and the Raconteurs plastered against the violet walls, and her clothes are strewn over the back of the chair in front of her desk.

Alex is cuddled up underneath her fluffy black-and-purple comforter—her two favorite colors—and she gives me an impish grin. "Tomorrow is the first day of summer," she sings. "I can't wait. I'm going to play BingeCraft and visit with Ganny, and I'm going to—"

"Spend some time outside with friends." I sit on the edge of her bed, sweeping her hair back from her forehead.

"Dad," she whines, "I like being indoors."

"I get that, but life is about balance." I take a deep breath and study her closely. "You going to tell me what happened today? I don't want to ground you, Alex, but you can't pull that kind of stunt again."

She purses her lips and wriggles downward in bed. "I said sorry."

"And I believe you, but if there's something going on at school that's bothering you, I need to know about it."

Alex peers up at me with wide eyes but doesn't say anything.

"Because if anybody hurts you, Alex," I say, "I'll fuck 'em up."

"Swear jar!" She squeaks it out automatically.

I smile. "You have to tell me the serious stuff. It's our father-daughter promise, remember?"

"Yeah."

"So, is there anything you want to talk about?"

She thinks about it for a second then shakes her head. "Nothing bad."

I'm not going to push her for now, but I will be putting a call in to the school. I've got to respect her boundaries while making sure that she's safe. "All right," I say. "Goodnight, sugar plum."

"I love you, Dad."

I hug her and give her a kiss on the forehead. "I love you too." And then I get up, switch on her nightlight that casts constellations on her ceiling—she's been obsessed with stars ever since she found Dad's telescope when she was five—and head into the hall.

The minute I've shut the door, my thoughts turn to June again.

What is she doing back in Heatstroke? A wave of irritation moves through me hot and fast, and I force myself to dismiss it.

She's not mine. I don't get to look after her.

I enter my bedroom down the hall and switch on the lights. The window is open, letting in the warm night air, the smell of mesquite and fresh-cut grass, and the chirping of crickets. I grimace and tug my shirt over my head, dropping it onto the end of my bed.

My old guitar is gathering dust where I hung it on the wall.

I barely glance at it most days. It's just another decoration, one that I avoid looking at or thinking about.

June is back.

I walk over to the black Gibson.

The memories are echoes of sound at first. Chords. The cheering of the audience. And then smells—sweat, booze, leather, straw—a mix that reminds me of anticipation. There's a hint of perfume I don't want to remember, the flicker of lights.

I lift a hand and strum my thumb over the strings, the sound moving through the room like a living thing. The guitar is out of tune.

I stare at it for a minute longer, my fingers moving at my side, and then I make myself stop, shaking my hand out.

I rub my palm over my chest hair, trying to rid myself of the feeling of the strings, and then rub my fingertips together, feeling for the calluses that I've had since I was a boy.

I turn toward the window and find June staring right back at me.

What the fuck?

June is in her old high school bedroom across from mine. Her gaze is fixed on me, those pink lips parted, her hand pressed against that delicate throat like she's clutching her damn pearls.

I lift a hand in greeting.

June jolts on the spot, looks left and right, and then dives out of view.

I can't help but laugh. This grown-ass woman dove out

of sight because she saw me without a shirt? I'm not sure what it means, but I know that living next door to her is painful. So, what's it going to be like, living under the same roof?

With my father in the state he's in this year, I can't have it any other way. If Jesse calls in the middle of the night for help, or Dad wrecks Ganny's house, I have to be there to pick up the pieces. Day or night.

I turn off the light and sit on the edge of my bed, staring at her window.

It takes a minute for her to reappear, and when she does, she shuts her curtains and switches off the light without glancing my way.

Better that she does. If I could have June, I'd make her forget her own name. I'd make her scream and beg until her body was wrung out, until she was so exhausted from the pleasure I'd put her through that she couldn't think, couldn't move, couldn't want anything else than what I'd given her.

I shut the curtains, then lay back in bed, and my hand fists my throbbing cock before my head hits the pillow.

Nine

THE MINUTE CASH answers the door at eight o'clock sharp, the memory of him half naked, standing in front of his bedroom window, nearly paralyzes me with need.

Defined abs and pecs, a tattoo arcing across his chest and down one arm, just enough chest hair to show he's all man, and the edges of a perfect V just above the waistband of his jeans.

And that's exactly why you shouldn't be here. I'm not getting my heart broken again.

But what kind of person will I be if I don't help a neighbor in need? That's what living in Heatstroke has always been about. We help each other here, even if it's difficult.

I smile, hoping he won't notice how pink my cheeks are. "Good morning," I sing. "Did you have a good night's rest?"

Cash arches a dark eyebrow, and that brooding over-whelming presence nearly suffocates me again.

I have to get over that. He's hot. Yeah, he's a hot guy. I used to have a crush on him, but that's over now.

Professionalism. Just remain professional.

And this summer job might even look good on my college applications. That's the next thing on my list: an appointment with a college entrance advisor.

Cash takes a step back.

I move past him, the scent of his cologne invading the space between us, and I force myself not to react or stare at him. Cash's childhood home is almost the same as it used to be. Sure, there are a few new furnishings, the TV is completely new, but the same pictures hang on the walls. Pictures of the Taylor family. I stop in front of one of them, smiling.

It brings back good memories. Painful memories. It's a weird combination, but I force myself to act happy anyway.

"How are your brothers and sisters?" I ask.

"Fine," Cash replies.

He never used to be this closed off. Then again, we haven't seen each other in years. "Did Leo end up going to the Eagles?" He was a rugby fanatic when we were kids.

"Yeah." His expression is unreadable.

"What about Hannah? Lily? Jesse?"

Cash checks his watch. "They're good. Alex is upstairs. She'll be down in a second to say hi, and then I'll show you around."

All right, so he wasn't in a chatty mood. Roger that.

"Great," I say. "I—I haven't made a firm decision yet. I don't want to get your hopes up, but I wanted to come by and see if we're a good fit. Alex and I, I mean."

Cash nods. "Makes sense. I'll show you around, and if

you feel like you can help us by the end of the tour, you let me know. Alex will be with her Ganny today, but tomorrow's a problem for us. Need a nanny by then." He checks his watch again.

"Sorry, am I keeping you from something?" I ask. "You're checking your watch a lot."

"I'm late for work."

"Work." I figured that a rich country music star would be getting royalties. "Are you, uh, you're not playing with the band anymore?"

Cash gives me a blank stare. "No. I'm helping my dad at his bar."

"Oh. Oh, okay."

"We're doing construction," he says. "Place was about to fall apart."

Mr. Taylor's bar was popular with the locals when I was a kid. He bought it and ran it with Cash's mother. "That's great, Cash," I say.

He nods slowly, and that awkward silence between us builds.

I want to broach the topic of the letters and the fact that I stopped writing. I want to talk to him like we did when we were young and inseparable, but so much has changed. Olivia, Cash, and I were the three harbingers of the apocalypse in this town, and now we're nothing. No longer friends. And a part of that is my fault. If I'd been able to handle the fact that Cash and Olivia were dating, we would have stayed connected.

Footsteps clatter down the steps and Alex appears, grinning up at her dad. She's like a little ray of sunshine packaged in black and purple. She's wearing a black skirt and a purple shirt covered in flowers. "June!" she says. "What are you doing here?"

"June might be your nanny," Cash says. "What do you think of that, Alex?"

"That's cool," Alex says. "I mean, do you like kids or whatever?"

It's a funny and very practical question. "Yeah, I do. I want to go to college to be a teacher."

"Aren't you kind of old for that?"

Cash palms his face. "Alex."

"That's fine." I laugh. "Yeah, I am kind of old for that. I guess you can say I'm catching my second wind." I flap my arms in what I hope is a comical fashion, and Alex laughs.

She casts a sidelong glance at her dad. "I think it would be nice if you were my nanny," she says, "but I don't know if my dad's going to like it."

"Oh?"

"He's likes things done like, properly. Like, in a specific way," Alex says, patting the side of one hand into her other palm. "The dishes at a certain time, stacked exactly right, and the beds always made, and—"

"Alex." Cash shakes his head.

"Don't worry," I say to her. "I'm pretty good at following instructions."

"But one of the instructions is no ice cream." Alex sighs. "On weekdays."

"That's not a bad thing," I say. "Too much ice cream isn't good for the digestive system." I'm on the brink of telling Alex that it gives me the trots before I remember that Cash is literally right here.

And as much as I'd love to discuss bowel movements

with my old best friend slash crush, I'm thinking I've been through enough over the past couple of days.

"Maybe for old people stomachs." Alex wriggles her nose. "Kids are great with ice cream. Like, I bet I could eat a tub of ice cream right now and run all the way to Ganny's house and back. But Dad won't let me do that. He also has a schedule for when I get to play computer games. So lame."

"Alex," Cash says. "I can hear you, you realize that, right?"

I stifle a laugh. Alex is a card. She's a little trouble-maker, and I like her already. "Do you like to read?" I ask.

"Yeah, sometimes," she says. "It depends on the books."

"Have you tried any fantasy books? Because there are a couple I could share with you." I meet Cash's gaze. "They're for kids, don't worry."

He breaks eye contact. "Alex, have you made your bed and gotten ready for Ganny to pick you up?"

"Yeah," Alex says. "I'm ready."

"Great. You can play out back until she arrives."

Alex grins and waves at me before running through the house to the back door.

"No running in the house," Cash calls after her.

The screen door at the back slams shut a second later. "She's great," I say, turning toward him. "You've done an amazing job with her."

"I can't take all the credit," he says. "She's just like that."

"Well, she got it from somewhere."

Cash's expression closes off like it did last night when I

asked about Olivia, and I curse myself for putting my huge foot in my even bigger mouth.

I tuck my hands into the back pockets of my new blue jeans, and Cash studies me. "So," I say, "you have schedules and instructions for everything."

"It's in a document online. I have SOPs. To simplify the process."

"SOPs. For childcare. Got it."

"You say that like it's a weird thing."

"Not at all," I say. "I think that's great."

"If you take the job, I'll need your email so I can share the folder with you. It includes emergency contact numbers and all the information you'll need to get started." Cash moves toward the staircase and holds onto the edge of the balustrade. "I'll show you where you'll be staying."

"If I take the job."

Another awkward silence.

"Yeah." Cash nods up the stairs.

He waits for me to go ahead of him. We walk up the stairs together, Cash behind me.

Cash shows me Alex's room, which is as adorable as she is, with posters of rock stars on the walls and a computer in one corner with a display of anime characters above it. He moves toward another bedroom and stops. "This is my room."

My cheeks heat again. "Right. Your dad isn't around? I figured you'd be sleeping in the master bedroom."

"He lives with Ganny. Master bedroom is too big for me. Bought the place from him after we moved here."

"When did that happen?"

Cash's jaw clenches and releases. "After Alex was born. Twelve years ago."

"Twelve years! You've been here for twelve years?" My mother didn't mention it once.

Cash walks a door down and opens it. "This will be your room. Was the guest bedroom."

My heart is pounding.

If I take the job, I'll be in the room right next to Cash's. The house is a double story, with four bedrooms—I remember the sisters, Hannah and Lily, sharing a room, and Cash and Leo sharing another, with Jesse as the eldest on his own.

The queen-sized bed has white sheets. The headboard is pressed against the wall.

Cash's bed is on the other side.

It's a pretty room, with a view of the well-kept back-yard, the wooden slats of the border fence separating my mother's property from the Taylor's. There's a comfy armchair, a bookcase, an armoire, and a rug at the foot of the bed. Plenty of space. Warm and cozy.

And right next door to Cash's room.

I can't do this.

I turn away and bump into his broad chest.

Cash glances down at me, frying my insides with a look.

I back up a step. "Oh, sorry about that. I didn't see you there."

"You don't need to apologize, June."

"Huh?"

"You don't need to apologize." There's a heavier meaning behind his words, but I can barely concentrate because I'm staring into those piercing blue eyes.

Cash Taylor, why do you make me feel like a girl again? I don't need this after what happened with Braydon.

A door bangs downstairs.

Cash doesn't move toward me or away, just watches me. "The room okay?"

I nod slowly, as if my body is trapped in molasses. "Yeah. It's beautiful. Cozy. Nice." Too close to yours.

"The only other room in the house with a bed," Cash says regretfully, glancing at the bed.

I look at it too, the heat building in my throat. This is even worse than how I felt when we were teens with the hormonal pining.

"The master bedroom doesn't have—?"

"Cash!" Jesse, Cash's brother, saunters into the room then stops dead. He's shorter than Cash, but just as well-built. The Taylor brothers were the heartbreakers of Heat-stroke for a good reason. "Well, smack my ass and call me daddy. June Jackson."

"Smack your ass and call you what?" A pretty woman walks in behind him, her dark hair in glossy curls, her skin tanned like she just stepped off the beach. She's wearing a sweeping skirt and a crop top, and she looks like she could be a model. Hannah Taylor is an effortless beauty and always has been. She's five years younger than us, but she's always been more mature than her brothers. "June! Oh my God, are you kidding me?"

"Jayjay's back in action," Jesse says, grinning.

"Oh, my God, Jesse, you're so fucking cringe." Hannah pulls a face. "Ignore him, June. He's spent the better part of his boomer years trying to act like he fits in with the younger crowd at the bar. Sad."

"Hey. I'm a millennial," Jesse replies. "Get your facts straight."

"That's got to be the most boomer thing I've ever heard."

I laugh and sweep Hannah into a hug.

Hannah holds my hands for a second afterward. "Wow. Can you say glow up? You look amazing, June."

"No, you," I say.

She laughs. "This is perfect. You're back. You're back in Heatstroke to save me from a fate worse than death." Hannah presses the back of her hand to her head. "Boredom."

"My turn," Jesse announces.

He's wearing a uniform, and I spot a deputy badge on his shirt before he sweeps me into a bear hug. "Jayjay!"

"That's enough," Cash snaps.

Jesse releases me but loops an easy arm around my shoulder. "Lighten up, brother. We're just saying hello to an old friend."

"What are you doing back in town?" Hannah asks. "Not that I'm looking a gift horse in the mouth or anything, but I heard you were living the high society life in Dallas."

I haven't stopped smiling since the two of them entered the room. Until now .

"She's going to be Alex's nanny," Cash says, saving me from further questioning.

"For real?" Hannah asks. "That's awesome, June."

"Yeah," Jesse says, his tone deepening as he makes eye contact with his brother. "Awesome."

Cash glares back at him.

"I heard about Mrs. Crouchbottom," Hannah says,

brushing a stray lock of hair back from her face. She reminds me of a modern Cindy Crawford with darker hair. "The doctor says it's going to be months. We should take her some flowers sometime."

"Cash already has," Jesse says.

Another grimace from the grump, directed at his brother.

I hadn't made a decision until now, but the warmth in this house is such a juxtaposition to how I feel living at home, that it's almost instinctual to say yes. Especially when I have such history with the Taylor family. It won't be that difficult to resist Cash. He's just an old high school crush. I can put that behind me if it will help the Taylor family. They've lost so much, struggled so much. And then there's Alex. She's such a sweet girl, and I'm kind of worried about her after yesterday in the diner.

"So, you're going to be the nanny?" Jesse prompts. "Like, a live-in nanny?"

I hesitate. "Yeah," I say, turning to Cash.

He stares at me like he can see right through me, and brushes his hand over his jaw.

"What time do you need me here tonight?"

Ten

CASH

LAST NIGHT WAS the first night June slept under my roof, in the bedroom right fucking next to mine, and it took everything in me not to imagine her in bed. Imagine my body on top of hers, the way she'd react to my touch, the way she'd taste.

This morning, I'd rushed the fuck out of there before anyone was awake and headed to the bar. I didn't want to see June in her pj's.

I've had my fair share of heartbreak. I want Alex to grow up with a good foundation, and that means not taking the risk of another woman in her life. One who will leave.

I pack away the last of my tools in my toolbox. There are more important things to worry about.

I walk over to the neatly sanded counter in the bar and run a palm over it. The silence here is deafening. The lights are on, the interior is stripped bare.

When my father mentioned he was thinking of selling the place, I knew I had to step in. It's the pain talking. The pain of losing Mom. So, we're spending the summer fixing it up so he can run it again because this bar is all he has left of Mom that's tangible. Maybe if he has it to run, he'll come back to us again.

"I'm done for the day," I call out.

Dad's been in the back for the past half an hour. The office is his private space, the only area he won't let me change.

"Dad?" I walk around the bar and toward the door that leads into the tiny room, stacked with a filing cabinet, a desk, and two chairs so old that they squeak when you look at them.

Things have been downright fucked up since the funeral. Only time my father is happy is when he's peering into an empty bottle.

He looks up from behind the desk, his cheeks gaunt, and it's like looking into a mirror of my future. Old, alone, unhappy, broken. His blue eyes are dull. He runs a tan hand over his graying beard. "Cash," he says, "you're still here? Figured you would've gone home to Alex."

"I'm finishing up."

He nods, turning away from me to look at the laptop on his desk.

"What are you looking at?" I ask.

"Nothing important." He shuts the laptop and rises, groaning and knuckling the small of his back. "You hear about that new family in town? Living out in those fancy houses along the beach?"

I grunt. I have heard about them, and I don't like it.

"They're buying up property left and right," Dad says. "Tourism as it is in this town, they want a slice of it. I'm surprised they haven't come knocking yet."

"They won't," I say. "And if they do, we'll tell them where to shove it." The Deverauxs have been on a tear through Heatstroke, buying up property along the beachfront. Chuckles Bar, my dad's place—Mom chose the name —is practically an institution in town and it happens to be on the rise overlooking the beach. Prime real estate.

"Yeah, well." My father sounds noncommittal, and I don't like it. "Only a matter of time."

"Dad?"

He forces a smile. "Nothing, son. Nothing."

"You need a ride home?"

"Naw," he replies. "I've got the Jeep."

"You haven't had anything to drink." I state it rather than asking, and Dad gives me a look.

"Come on, now, son. You know me better than that."

Trouble is, I don't. I glance around the office, checking for any sign of alcohol, and my father grunts irritably. "Go on, get," he says. "Go home to my grandbaby. Give her a hug for me."

I remain for a second longer before leaving the room and heading out the front door. My father spends more time at Chuckles than he does at Ganny's house nowadays. I whip out my phone and shoot Jesse a quick text.

> Leaving now. You make sure he doesn't do anything wild?

> Come on, Cash, he's a grown man. He'll be fine.

> You remember what happened the last time, don't you?

> I'm the one who arrested him, so I'll say, yeah, that memory is pretty much firmly ingrained in my brain, dickwad.

Fuck you.

> I'll check in on him. Be there in five. Go home to Alex and your live-in fantasy.

Double fuck you.

I grit my teeth and slip my phone into the front pocket of my jeans. I get into my pick-up, start her up, and take the long drive home, my thoughts on the bar, my father, and Alex. I try to keep them that way, but they drift to June.

June in her yellow silk dress in the diner, smiling as she talks to Alex, wishing me good night at the top of the stairs last night.

June, the one that got away. Who left town before I could say goodbye properly. Who stopped writing.

I pull up to the house and park.

June's in the kitchen, visible through the windows that look out on the porch and the front yard. She's got a yellow ribbon twined in her hair, and she's wearing a tight camisole that presses against her perky breasts. She laughs at something.

I grind my teeth again.

She's so perfect.

Alex comes into view, gesturing wildly, and talking to June like they've been best buds for years. It figures that they'd get on. June's always been good with kids, and Alex needs a friend.

That thought cools my jets. I get out of the pickup and head up to the house, sore from a long day.

I open the front door.

"Dad!" Alex comes around the corner and throws her arms around my waist.

I squeeze her back. "I missed you," I say.

"Me more! But you've got to come sit down right now. June and I made fried pickles with ranch dressing as a side for dinner."

"You did *what*?"

June peeks around the corner, smiling at me in a way that makes my blood burn. "Hey! How was work, Cash? I hope you don't mind, but we made fried pickles."

"I hate fried pickles."

Alex looks like I've personally offended her. June's face is a mirror image of hers.

"Dad," Alex says. "Dad, no. No, you have to try them, they're the best."

I drop my keys and wallet on the entrance hall table and follow her into the kitchen, trying not to pay too much attention to June.

The nanny. Just think of her as the nanny. Think of her like Mrs. Crouchbottom.

They've whipped up chicken fried steak, mashed potatoes, greens, and the accursed fried fucking pickles with ranch sauce. It's an amazing spread.

I sit down at the head of the table and grunt.

"Try them," Alex says, blinking up at me. "Come on, please?"

June's attempt at stifling a smile isn't working. She sits down too, reaching out to the vase of bluebells she's put on the table as a centerpiece. She's wrapped yet another one of those yellow ribbons around the vase.

"Come on," Alex pleads.

I can tell my daughter is in high spirits. She's happier than I've seen her in a while. I despise pickles, but I spear one with my fork and insert it between my lips.

It's vile. Crispy pickle is somehow worse than regular pickle. I chew slowly and force myself to make an appreciative noise.

Alex claps her hands. "See? I knew you would like them."

But June is onto me. She gives me a knowing look, her lips tilting upward at the sides. Is she trying to fuck with me? June knows I don't like pickles.

It's time to change the topic before she victimizes me with another serving. I cut into my chicken fried steak. "Have a good day?"

"It was great! June and I did our nails, and tomorrow we're going shopping."

"Oh?" I glance over at June.

"Sorry," she says. "I was going to ask you first, but, uh, Alex needs some stuff."

"Stuff?"

Alex colors red.

"Feminine products," June says.

"Oh." I nod. "Sure, okay. Yeah. I'll leave my card here for you to use. You get whatever you need."

An awkward silence follows, and I fill it by eating. The food is amazing—barring the pickles. A part of me hoped it would be shit, just so June could be a little less perfect than she already is.

"How was your day?" June asks.

I stare at her, chewing. "Fine."

She breaks eye contact and smiles at Alex across the table.

I consider taking my food into the living room just to be away from her. I can't think. Distraction. I just need a distraction. "You hear back about that slumber party?" I ask my daughter.

"Not yet, Dad. Maybelle hasn't sent out invitations yet."

"Thought you said it was this weekend."

Alex shrugs and shoves a forkful of mashed potato into her mouth. She chews slowly.

Shit. Somehow, I've fucked up dinner. When I got home, they were laughing and smiling, and now the table is as quiet as a tomb.

June clears her throat. "Should we put on some music?" she asks, half rising out of her chair.

"No," I say, and place my hand on her arm. Touching her is a bad idea, and I release her again.

"Dad doesn't like to listen to the radio," Alex says. "In case they play his songs. He doesn't like country music anymore."

I stiffen but don't correct her.

June frowns, gnaws on her lush bottom lip, lowers herself back into her chair. "Oh."

The rest of the dinner is a little better. Alex explains what they did today—reorganizing her room, playing outdoors, visiting Marci at the Heartstopper, playing music together, deciding on which dishes we're going to take to Ganny's potluck dinner tomorrow night, and planning for the upcoming end of summer talent show.

"I've been telling Alex she should go for it," June says.

"I don't know yet," Alex says. "But I'll think about it."

I nod. "Sounds like fun." But the thought of Alex putting herself out there for judgment makes me a little queasy. I push my plate aside. "That was great. Thank you, June."

"That's what you pay me for," she says merrily.

I don't know what the fuck that's supposed to mean, but she rises from the table and turns her back on me before I can reply. Alex heads into the living room, happy as can be, to turn on the TV.

"She have a lot of screen time today?" I ask, rising from the table and grabbing my plate and Alex's.

"Nope. I stuck to your schedule," June replies, back still to me.

She's tall, but shorter than me, wisps of golden-blonde hair falling out of her high ponytail, against the base of her neck. She's wearing cutoff jeans that sit tight against her hips.

Fuck. I am in so much trouble.

"Thanks," I say.

"That's what you're paying me for."

"Stop saying that."

June turns to me, confusion flickering over that pretty face. Up close, I can appreciate her in too much detail. Freckles across her button nose, full lips, wide, blue eyes, high cheekbones. June is painfully beautiful and always has been.

"Saying what?"

"That I'm paying you. I'm not paying you to cook, and I don't want you to take that on as a duty."

"Oh. That's fine. I really enjoy cooking, so it's no trouble. Besides, Alex and I had a blast cooking, and I—"

"Fine. Cook if you want to. I'll raise your pay."

"What? No, that's not what I—"

"Excuse me." The words come out deeper than I intended, more harshly, and her eyelashes flutter.

I leave the dishes on the counter and start up the stairs.

I slam the door to my bedroom shut behind me, breathing hard. I enter my bathroom, open my shower door, and turn on the cold water. I step under the stream fully clothed, bowing my head and letting the water rush over me.

Eleven

JUNE

I'M SERIOUSLY SECOND-GUESSING my decision to be Cash's nanny. It's not that I don't enjoy spending time with Alex—that part is great—but being around him is a constant challenge. I'm not sure if I'm raw and tender over what happened with Braydon or what, but the more time I spend around Cash Taylor, the more those old feelings, the ones I buried years ago, resurface.

The best thing I can do is keep my distance. Remain professional because I'm never going to let a man take away my power again and I want out of this town. Besides, Cash doesn't want me and never has, so this silly crush needs to go back to high school and get a darn education.

"Ready to go?" I call up the stairs.

Alex and I are going shopping today, and I am so ready for some fun girly time at one of Heatstroke's many boutiques. Heatstroke has great stores thanks to the town's tourist appeal.

Alex clatters down the stairs, pretty in a pink striped shirt and a puffy black skirt.

"Are you ready for a shopping extravaganza?" I ask.

She gives me an uncertain smile. "Yeah."

"What's up?"

"Nothing."

"Come on, now," I say, "I wasn't born yesterday. I'd be bald if I was."

Alex giggles, but she gnaws on her lip. "I've never had a bra before." She says the word "bra" like it's a forbidden cuss word.

"Hey," I say, smiling. "I know this might feel a little weird, but it's going to be fine. Promise. Once you get one, you'll see it's not as big a deal as it feels right now. Besides, you can pick out something you like."

"What do you mean?" Alex asks.

I grab my purse off the table and sling it over one shoulder. It's the same sparkly one I chose for my failed birthday party. "I mean that they're not all the same, training bras."

"They're not?"

"No way. You get all different colors and sizes. It's just a soft bra that you can get in black if you want. Or purple. Maybe we can find one covered in unicorns."

Alex lights up at that.

I grin as we head out the front door.

"Do you want to walk?" I ask. "Or do you want to take Ol' Rusty?" I point to my car, still parked in my mom's driveway next door.

"That's your car?"

I laugh. "Yeah. He's like an old family friend. He's not

comfortable, he makes strange farting noises from time to time, but he's part of the family."

Alex gives me a dubious look.

"Walking it is," I say. "Good for the heart."

We set off together through the suburbs and toward the shops and restaurants facing the bay and the boardwalk. The sidewalks are already alive with tourists shopping the specials, kids with ice cream, people in beachwear.

Alex grabs my hand and squeezes it tight.

"Are you okay?" I ask.

She nods, staring at a point in the distance.

I frown. I'm not sure what's going on with this kid but seeing her this shy in public is alarming. Alex is going through something.

"In here," I say, and dip into a boutique targeting pre-teens and teen girls. The interior is loud, with splashes of pink and orange on the walls, and mannequins wearing denim skirts and colorful camisoles with matching bracelets.

"What do you think?" I ask. "Want to look around?"

Alex releases my hand. "Yeah. This place looks nice."

"There are some training bras over there. I'll find the assistant so we can figure out what size you are. Are you fine to look at them by yourself?"

"Yeah. I'm fine." She hurries off toward the underwear section.

I want her to have that moment of independence, even if I'm just a couple of feet away. Doing things by yourself is a confidence-building exercise in life. Even thinking that frustrates me. How did I ever let Braydon into my life? How did I let him take advantage of me like that?

The truth is, I was in a difficult spot, heartbroken,

young, and naïve. And I'd wanted so badly to believe in a happily ever after. But now I know that's a lie.

I circle through the store, searching for an assistant. She's busy with someone else, so I walk back to the underwear section.

"So sad." It's a girl's voice.

"Whatever, Leah," Alex says softly. "Just leave me alone."

"Aren't you alone, anyway?" The girl, she's got a nasal whine that's so annoying, stands in front of Alex, her fists on her hips. She's got dark hair, and she's wearing jeans and a frilly pink top covered in flowers.

The girl's stance is familiar to me.

It's that "too cool to even look in your direction" stance. Hip popped, examining her fingernails. I knew girls like this when I was in middle school.

They haven't noticed me yet.

"My nanny is—"

"Your nanny?" Leah giggles. "I can't believe you have a nanny. But, oh, I forgot. You don't have a mom, right?"

Alex's expression falls. She glances away, and I can tell she's trying to hide how much the comment upset her.

I grab a T-shirt off the rack. "Hey, Alex, check this out."

Alex hastily scrubs a hand underneath either eye and feigns interest in the T-shirt.

I turn toward Leah—upturned nose, a bored expression—and smile. "Hello," I say. "June Jackson. What's your name?"

"Leah," the girl replies, losing steam now that there's an adult present.

"Leah." I nod. "Are you one of Alex's friends?"

"Uh."

Before she can make something up, a woman appears in the aisle. She's got the same upturned nose and raven hair as Leah, and she's wearing a red ruched bustier with a pair of tight-fitting skinny jeans. "Leah, honey, did you pick something out? I want to—oh!" The mother stops. "Is that Alexandra Taylor?"

"Just Alex," Alex says.

"Alex, honey," the woman says, "how are you?"

"Fine. How are you, Ms. Pamini?"

The woman turns toward me. "And you must be…?"

"June Jackson. I'm Alex's nanny." I extend a hand.

The woman grips my fingertips and shakes them daintily. "Ooh, the nanny? Delicious. I'm Zara. This is Leah."

I open my mouth to respond, but Zara is on a roll.

"Working as the nanny for Cash Taylor?" Zara lets out a breath heavy with excitement. "That must be wild. I mean, you know he's a country music star, right? There are all kinds of rumors about that man."

"Mom, can we go?" Leah inserts.

Zara pats her daughter on the head. "Honey, go look at the blouses. Why don't you take Alex with you?"

The girls stare at each other.

"Alex and I were in the middle of shopping, actually," I say.

"Oh, well, gosh, I'll have to get your number," Zara says. "You know, Cash Taylor is the most eligible bachelor in Heatstroke. Every woman in town is after that piece of—"

I clear my throat. "It was nice meeting you, Zara."

"Sure, you too." Her smile doesn't carry any warmth. "You know, there's a talent show coming up at the end of summer. The town hosts one every year along with that ridiculous pepper-eating contest. We only moved here a couple of years ago, and I'll never get over it. Alex isn't thinking of competing, is she? In the talent show?" There's a sharpness to her tone now. "Because Leah and her girl group are going to do a little number, and they're a shoo-in to win."

Of course, Leah has a girl group. I glance down at Alex. "We'll see," I say. "We'll have to leave you with bated breath. Have a good day, Zara."

Zara herds her daughter away. Leah gives me a strange look before leaving.

"You okay?" I ask Alex.

"Yeah."

I don't buy it. "Is Leah the reason you were in the diner the other day?"

Alex presses her lips together.

"Does she say stuff like that a lot?"

Alex fiddles with the shirt I handed her.

"Leah's a bully," I say.

"But she's right."

"Right? No, she's not right. Your parents and your past don't make you who you are. That's a choice you make every day. By yourself. And Alex, you choose to be a rock star every morning. That's all that matters."

Alex's cheeks go pink, and she gives me a grin that shows off her dimples.

"When I was your age, I had a friend who saved me from a bully just like Leah." I don't mention that it was Olivia. "And she was the one who taught me that I could stand up for myself."

"That's nice of her."

"It was," I say.

"Are you still friends? Is it Marci?"

"Not Marci, no," I say. "And no, we're not friends. We kind of drifted apart." The truth is more painful. "So, the talent show?" I wave down the shop assistant. "You want to do it?"

"Kind of. But I don't know yet."

"It would be a shame if Heatstroke didn't get to see how talented you are," I say, and leave it at that.

If I was considering giving up this job before, because of how uncomfortable it is to live with Cash, there's no chance I'm doing it now.

Twelve

CASH

GANNY'S POTLUCK dinners are legendary in the Taylor family, heck, in Heatstroke too. Getting an invitation to one of our family dinners is akin to winning the social lottery in town, mostly because Ganny's so well-connected. She's the type of person who knows everyone's names and business, gives to charity, and loves meddling in people's affairs because it's for their own good.

But there's another element to it. Heatstroke was founded by two families. The Taylors and the Walshes, and our family has lasted the longest out here.

Being at Ganny's house has always made me feel at home in my own skin.

But tonight is different.

Tonight, June is wearing a white cotton dress that's modest, but might as well be threadbare. I trace the lines of her body through the fabric, trailing my gaze upward to her face.

She's in the middle of a conversation with my sister, Hannah, and her annoying best friend, Belle Simms, who's been the Thelma to Hannah's Louise since as far back as I can remember. They call themselves partners in crime, for fuck's sake.

June laughs, the sound tinkling through the air, and her green eyes find mine.

There's a moment of connection, but I break it quickly, scowling at myself.

She's the nanny. She was my best friend.

We've barely exchanged two words since she started working for me.

It's been a day, and Alex is happy. When I got home this evening, she couldn't wait to tell me about how they went shopping together, how she's thinking about entering the talent show, and how they made a potato bake for the potluck.

"You going to stand in the living room staring a hole through the wall all night?" Jesse asks. Just fucking great. The last thing I need is my brother on my ass. He wants "what's best for me" and it's annoying. He glances over at June, who's moving into the kitchen to help Ganny, her hips swaying. "How are things with the nanny?"

"Don't you mean Jayjay?"

He chuckles. "I knew you were sore about that. Man, you like her." Jesse points a finger at me around the Coke can in his grasp.

Alex shrieks and runs through the house, chased by Ganny's Chihuahua, Fireball. The pair take turns chasing each other, first her then him. Alex waves at me before running off, her cheeks pink with excitement.

It's good to see my daughter this happy.

"You must really like her if you brought her with you to the potluck," Jesse says.

"Ganny invited her."

"That your story and you're sticking with it?"

I sit down on the sofa and rest my hand on the back of it, tapping irritably. "How's Marci?"

"Ha." Jesse takes a sip of coke. "Fuck you."

"I hear she's having some trouble at the diner."

"Don't know, don't care."

I've got Jesse cornered here. He's got this weird hate-crush thing going on with Marci, and he'll never admit it. He's more stubborn than I am, and Marci's oblivious. She thinks he despises her because Jesse arrested her low-life brother.

I'm about to abandon the living room when the front door opens and Dad comes in, closely followed by Savage —my best friend has a standing invite to the potluck and takes advantage of it whenever he can.

I rise and greet my father, a quick hug and pat on the back. He smells like alcohol, and my jaw clenches.

Not again.

I'm all for having a beer after a long day of work, but Dad has a problem.

Savage grins at me and lifts a dish. "Cornbread."

"Dibs!" Jesse says.

Savage's cornbread is almost as legendary as Ganny's potlucks. He goes into the kitchen and I catch a glimpse of Hannah, all wide blue eyes, staring up at him like a trapped mouse.

Savage has that effect on women, but he wouldn't dare go near my sister.

Dad sits down, groaning and shifting his neck this way and that. "Ain't easy getting old, I'll tell you that."

"You're not old," Jesse says. "You're aged. Like a barrel of whisky."

"Speaking of," Dad replies, "how about one of you boys grab me a glass of something cold?"

I grimace at my brother.

He strokes a hand over his forehead and face, annoyed at himself. "Dad," he says, "nobody's drinking tonight. How about a Coke?"

"Looking for something a little stronger," he replies.

Things have not been right since Mom passed, and there's nothing that will fill the hole it's left behind. Except for the bar. That was their baby, but it fell into disrepair when she got sick. If I can fix it up, maybe I can bring my father back to the man he truly is. Make life worth living again, instead of burying his head in a vat of fucking alcohol.

Savage arrives bearing two cans of Coke, pops a tab and hands one to my father. I nod my thanks.

Savage scratches under his beard. "What are we talking about?"

Jesse opens his mouth and I shoot him a warning look. If he says one fucking thing about June, I'll make him sorry. He laughs under his breath at me.

I must seem like a fool to him. I feel like one.

But I can't help myself. I find myself looking for her. Turning my head, hoping to catch a glimpse of her golden hair, the scent of that citrus-sunshine perfume.

It's bullshit.

"Renovations are going well," I say. "We've replaced the entire bar. I want to sand those tables down and distress them. Might give the bar a more rustic vibe."

My father takes a sip of his Coke and pulls a face. "Chuckles was rustic before we started changing things."

"Dad, Chuckles was half-rotten before you started work on it," Jesse says, and it's in that moment, I appreciate my brother. It's a pity that Leo isn't here to help us deal with this, but he's got bigger aspirations, and I can't begrudge him a successful career doing what he loves.

Just because I chose to give up my dreams, doesn't mean my brother has to.

"I'm sure the place will turn out great," Savage says.

June and Alex come in from the dining area, and go into the kitchen. June gets down a glass and fills it with water.

Alex glugs the water down like she's never had a sip of the stuff in her life, while Fireball barks and yips, wagging his little butt in anticipation of their next game of tag.

June strokes my daughter's hair, blonde like June's, and if I ignore everything that's happened, I can imagine us together.

What if Jesse was right?

I didn't go for it when I had the chance, and I've spent over a decade regretting it, hiding the pain with music, with drugs at one point, with a woman who didn't care for me.

"—Deveraux family," Dad finishes.

The tail end of that sentence makes me flush hot. "What?"

"I've heard they're interested in the bar," Dad says. "You know what Heatstroke is like. People talk."

"They can keep talking," I say. "And the Deveraux can chew on a bag of sweetbread. They're not getting the bar."

My father takes a sip of his Coke but doesn't say anything. I get up, tugged toward the kitchen by June's presence. We make eye contact again, and she smiles. I don't react, opting to dip into the dining room instead to help Ganny set the table.

I don't want to want June Jackson, but every minute spent near her weakens my resolve. I'm starting to think my brother isn't as much of a jackass as he pretends to be.

What if you do take the shot?

Thirteen

CASH

"CASH," she says, her voice like liquid fucking gold, as I walk past, "can I talk to you for a second?"

June is in the living room, watching TV. Alex is already in bed, exhausted after a good dinner at Ganny's and a lot of running around with Fireball. My daughter is spoiled rotten whenever she visits her great-grandmother, and it reminds me of when I was a kid and things were simpler.

"Cash?" June rises from the sofa, wearing that white dress that sits flush against her tan skin. "It's about Alex."

"What about her?" I ask. "Something wrong?" Concern overwhelms my better instincts.

June has already muted the TV. "I think so." She frowns, and even that's cute. She glances upward, as if she's worried that my daughter will hear her.

"You want to talk on the back porch?" I ask.

"Yeah, that'll be great."

"Want a beer?"

She hesitates. "A beer?"

"Sure."

June presses her lips together and then releases them. "I mean, sure." She smiles. "Sure. That would be nice."

It feels like I've just asked her out, and it puts me in a state of heightened anxiety. I'm not an anxious person. I'm a face-my-problems-head-on kind of guy. So, this is new territory for me.

"I'll meet you on the back porch in a minute," I say.

"All right." She moves past me in the doorway, and I have this unconscious urge to stop her or follow her or both. I shut my eyes for a second after she's moved down the hall, then go to the kitchen.

I've never felt for a woman the way I felt for June in high school. I dismissed it as a crush or an obsession. Some bullshit hormonal boy shit. But I'm a man now, and nothing has changed. I still want to keep her, take her, protect her, free her, and everything wrapped into one when she's nearby.

Because June is and always has been better than me and this town. She makes friends wherever she turns. She helps people. She cares. And she's got this tough "fuck what people think" streak running right down the center of all of that. It makes her nearly irresistible.

I grab two beers out of the fridge, holding them by their necks.

Opening the screen door with my elbow, I step onto the back porch.

June smiles up at me from the porch swing. I screw off the bottle caps and hand her one of the beers. "Thanks," she says, and touches the side of the bottle against mine. "Cheers."

"Cheers." I sit next to her on the swing, clasping the bottle between my hands. "What's going on with Alex?"

June sets her bottle down on the wood planking with a clink. "That's the thing, I'm not sure, but I'm worried. We went to the boutique today to get some feminine stuff for her. A bra, mainly."

"All right."

"And we ran into another girl there. Leah."

"Leah. That's, uh, what's-her-face's daughter?" The mother who always sends me bedroom eyes and tries to get me involved in PTA baking events.

"Yeah," June says. "Except her name is Zara Pamini."

"Right, sure."

"I think Leah's been bullying Alex."

I stiffen. "What? Well, I'll have to give Ms. Pamini a fucking call, won't I?"

"I'm not sure that's necessary yet," June says. "I mean, it's a judgment call, but I think it would be a good idea for Alex to fight her own battles on this one. With help."

"Help."

"Yeah. There are a couple of great resources you can use to teach her how to handle bullies. And by that I don't mean punching them in the face."

I don't ask how she knows that's my go-to option. Not the healthiest path forward. "That would be great."

She nods. "I just think she needs to talk to Leah herself, and if that doesn't solve the problem and it gets worse, then maybe it's time to talk to the mom."

"That's why she didn't get on the bus." Why didn't Alex tell me this?

"I think so," June says. "But making a huge deal out of that, well, she might withdraw. I haven't been around that long, so you'll know the best way forward. I'm just telling you what I've observed."

"You've always had good intuition when it comes to this stuff."

"Probably because I've spent my life trying to appease my mother, but whatever," she jokes. There's a hint of pain there, and I hate it.

I sit back on the porch swing, laying one hand over the back of it. I'm close enough to touch her, but I don't.

"So," I say, "how are you liking the job?"

"I love it," June replies instantly, her cheeks pink. Her gaze darts toward me and then out to the backyard. "It's great. Alex is fun to be around, and you have a lovely home."

"Thank you. I tried to make it as warm as it was when my mother was alive."

"I'm so sorry about that, Cash," June says. "Why did your dad move out?"

I take a swig of beer. "Didn't want the memories, so he moved in with Ganny."

"I'm sorry."

"Don't be," I say, irritated about the apology. She spends too much time doing that. Almost like she's apologizing for taking up space that is rightfully hers.

Another quiet, which stretches longer than the first. Why is she here? What happened to her?

June breaks the silence. "What happened, Cash?"

"Huh?"

"I know we lost contact," she says, "but when we used to write, you and Olivia were touring. Everything seemed to be going great."

I freeze up for a second. "We broke up," I say slowly. "She, uh, she wasn't the person I thought she was, and things weren't good from the start. Maybe they looked that way from the outside, but they weren't. Olivia isn't part of Alex's life by choice. She signed away her rights to me. She's not even allowed near her because I took out a court order. Drugs." I don't want to talk more about it, but if she pushes me, well, fuck, it's not like I can refuse her.

It's June, for fuck's sake. I've looked her up countless times over the years, whenever I'm lonely or I think back on those old days. The hot summers we spent kidding around out at the quarry or at Ganny's or haunting Marci's dad's diner.

"Oh. I'm sorry, Cash. I had no idea that had happened," June says. "I hope she got the help she needed."

"I offered. She didn't want it." And then I take a sip of beer and look away. "Anyway."

"I noticed you don't play music anymore. I miss the sound of your voice, Cash. You're talented. But you know that. I'm sure all those flowers and panties women threw on stage were enough of an indicator." She grins, devilishly cute.

But it hurts like a son of a bitch.

"Yeah. I don't do that anymore. Don't have room for it in my life. Alex and my family are all that matters now."

Again, June looks like she wants to question me but shakes her head like she thinks better of it.

That irritates me too because she's worried about making me uncomfortable. So worried that she'd rather not get answers to her questions.

Fuck, I want her. I want her, and I can't have her, and it's been two fucking days and it's already impossible to bear. I don't do sex with random women, I don't want an emotional attachment, but June is difficult.

"What about you?" I ask. "What brings you back to Heatstroke?"

She opens her mouth.

I raise a finger. "And don't give me that shit about getting back on your feet."

"It's not shit," June says, tossing her hair back. June's always had a hot streak, and I've always liked it. "I am getting back on my feet. I'm going to apply to colleges and get a teaching degree, and then I'm going to find a nice place to settle down and start living the life I've always wanted to live. And this time, nobody, not a man or anyone, is going to stop me. Particularly not any assholes. I've recently discovered I have an aversion to assholes."

"Except your own?"

"I mean, I don't have a choice when it comes to that one."

"That's great, June. The teaching thing. Not the assholes."

"Thanks."

"It's also a bullshit answer."

"Oh, so you can just not tell me what happened with Olivia, but I have to tell you about my ex?"

I set the bottle down. "Your ex?"

She colors. "It's fresh."

Her phone rings on the arm of the porch swing, and she glances at the screen. The look on her face is as if she's been punched in the gut. She looks ready to cry, ready to chew through a wall.

"June?"

Fourteen

JUNE

I DON'T RECOGNIZE the number. It's not Braydon. He can't call me because I've blocked his number, and I have his mother's saved, so it can't be her. Never mind the fact that Grace Rowling would rather eat a plate full of sea cucumbers than call me first. She's like my mother, except the richer, less needy version.

I shake my head. "Sorry. Not sure who this is." It might be Marci or my mom, since she's changed her number several times. Panic scratches at me, at the thought of either of them in danger or need.

"Go ahead and answer it." Cash gets up. "Refill?"

"I'm good."

He smiles at me, his first genuine smile since I arrived in Heatstroke, and it's stunning.

The continued trilling of my phone brings me back to the moment, and I scoop it up and answer. "Hello?"

A scratchy noise on the other end of the line.

"Hello? Who's there?"

"June."

No.

It's Braydon.

His smooth, unctuous, sell-you-the-stars voice is painfully recognizable.

"What do you want?" I snap.

"June, come on, it's me. It's your Baby Bray."

I've never called him that in my life. "Are you drunk?"

"What does that matter?" he asks, his words slurring a little. "Look, I miss you, June. You are such an amazing woman, and I can't— Fuck off, Marty. Wait. Ha!"

I grit my teeth. I don't want to wait, and I don't want to talk to him. "I'm hanging up now. Don't ever call this number again."

"Sorry, Marty's here with me. He's telling me to tell you that you've got a sweet ass that won't quit."

"Goodbye." Braydon seldom let his mask slip in front of me, but when he's been drinking, he's insufferable.

"Don't be a bitch, June. You know what your problem is, you think you're better than everyone else just because you're nice. Well guess what, Juney baby, nice is boring."

The phone is removed from my hand forcibly.

Cash is standing behind me, his eyes filled with fury. He lifts the phone to his ear. "Who's this?" he asks.

I can't hear the reply on the other end.

"This is her new boyfriend," Cash says. "You ever call this number again, I will hunt you down like the rabid fucking dog you are, rip off your dick and feed it to you. Is that understood? You keep June's name out of your mouth and her number off your phone if you want to keep that shriveled piece of jerky you call a cock attached to your body." He stabs the screen then hands me back the phone, his expression neutral.

"What the—?" I swallow. "Cash?"

He sits down, holding a bag of unopened barbecue-flavored chips. "Want some?"

"Are you kidding me?"

"What?"

"You can't just do that. You can't just take my phone and…" Protect me. Care.

"Why didn't you hang up on him?" Cash asks.

"I was about to."

"You were about to." He's not buying it, and he tilts his head to one side, gritting his teeth.

"Yeah. I was saying goodbye when he started ranting."

"And you decided to stay on the line because you're a sucker for punishment?" Cash asks, setting the bag aside, unopened. "You need to stand up for yourself, June. Do what you want rather than what everybody else wants you to do."

"Excuse me, but I literally left him. I—"

"If you won't stand up for yourself then I will. I won't let anyone talk to you that way, least of all some limp-dick rich boy out in Dallas."

I get up from the porch swing to leave, and then it hits me. "Wait, what?"

"What?"

"You know about Braydon?"

"I didn't know his name, and I didn't care to fucking know it," Cash says.

"But you know that he's rich and where he lives? How?"

"I was curious," Cash says.

"So, what?"

Cash shrugs.

"You looked me up?"

He doesn't respond but gets up as well and stands in front of me, his hands tucked into the pockets of his jeans, that enigmatic look in his eyes.

"June." The word is a growl.

He steps closer, so that there's hardly any separation between us. I can't breathe at the intensity of his presence, but my skin tingles. I feel raw, exposed, like any movement he makes will shatter me.

In my wildest dreams, in those high school years, I dreamed of a moment like this. When Cash would stand close to me, press his lips to mine.

"You can't answer my phone," I say. "It's not right."

"Fine."

"Fine?"

"Anything else?" he asks, and his hand comes up. He caresses my cheek. His palm is warm, a little rough, calluses on his fingertips.

"Cash?"

His gaze lingers on my lips.

This must be a dream. He was never interested. Why now?

"June."

"Cash. W-what are you doing?"

"What I want," he says. "You should try it some time."

And then he closes the space between us and presses his lips to mine.

Heat and pressure. Arousal floods my body so fast, I moan against his mouth and weaken in his arms.

Cash collects me like I'm water spilling away. He holds me against his chest and deepens the kiss, one hand moving up to my hair. His fingers twine through the strands, tugging my head back. He parts my lips and his tongue brushes against mine, light at first and then insistent.

I moan again, losing my breath, and kiss him back with years of pent-up longing. My hands move up his body, resting first against his defined pecs and then moving up to loop around his neck, pulling him down. I want more, I want it all, and Cash is willing to give it.

He nips my bottom lip, kisses me harder, walks me backward and presses me to the wall beside the screen door, his hands caressing my throat, moving lower and—

A bang next door breaks the moment.

I stiffen.

Cash stops kissing me immediately and steps back, his lips still wet, his eyes blazing with lust.

My fingers move to my mouth, which is still hot from the kiss, aching from the intensity. Never in my entire life have I been kissed that way.

But this is Cash. Cash who chose Olivia.

Cash who is my boss. Cash who has a daughter with my ex-best friend.

"June," he says, "I'm sorry." And the regret in his voice is like a dagger.

It reminds me of that night, when we were young, when he told me that he was dating Olivia. That she was the one for him.

I shake my head. "I should go up to bed." And I turn and go back inside, leaving him there because I have no idea what else to do. Cash Taylor kissed me, and I'm not sure what it means or if it matters either way.

Fifteen

CASH

"FUCK."

I stare at the closed screen door, my cock throbbing against my jeans, my hands balled into fists. I'm an idiot.

I can't ruin things with her. We were friends. Are friends. Kind of. And if there's even a chance I've upset her, or that she didn't want the kiss, then I've got to make this right and apologize.

I'm pretty damn fucking good at reading when a woman wants me, and in that moment, the way June looked at me…

"Fuck," I repeat, and then I tear the screen door open and rush through the house, up the stairs, to her closed bedroom door, right next to mine.

I lean against the jamb, catch my breath, school my dick to behave.

Finally, I knock.

Movement inside.

A hesitation.

The door opens, and June stares out at me, beautiful, but her eyes are filled with tears.

"I'm sorry," I say.

June opens those perfect lips, still red from our kiss. "What?"

"I'm sorry. I shouldn't have done that."

June looks ready to say something but doesn't.

"I feel like an ass, not that it fucking matters how I feel, but I, uh, I shouldn't have taken advantage of you in that moment."

"Taken advantage of me." June sounds pissed.

Shit.

"Yeah. You were upset about your ex and—"

"You're telling me I was upset about my ex. You. You're telling me that." She laughs under her breath, shaking her head. "Cash. You know what? It's fine."

"Fine."

"Yeah."

She has every right to be mad. "June, if you don't want to work for me anymore, I'll understand," I say gruffly.

"I—what? No. I don't want to quit," she says. "Alex is great, this job pays well, and I've got everything I need to set myself up for the future." June gnaws on her bottom lip, peering up at me through long lashes.

Fuck. I want to kiss her all over again. I want to press her against the wall and make good on what we started. Strip that white summery dress from her frame, expose her naked flesh, suck her nipples into my mouth.

June squares her shoulders. "I've spent too long wanting my life to change and not actually changing it. I'm scared, Cash."

"Of?" If she says me, my cock will deflate like a punctured raft.

"Failing," she says. "I think. I don't know. And I want this job badly, but it's difficult."

"Why?"

"Because it is. It's difficult." She glances off to one side. There's something she's holding back, but she isn't upset about what happened.

Finally, June turns her gaze toward mine, and there's fire in her eyes.

"We're adults," she says. "Not kids anymore. Adults have needs, and that's totally normal. We had a moment of weakness."

I did read what she wanted correctly. Sex and nothing more.

I stare at her, holding back a deluge of images, flashes of her naked body, my fingers wrapped in her hair, her mouth around my cock. I grunt because talking is inadvisable.

"But," she says, at last, her lips mesmerizing, "we probably—"

"Shouldn't do it again," I say, finishing the sentence for her. "I've got to make it clear to you, June, I don't want a relationship. I don't have room for a woman in my life."

"And you're my boss."

"Exactly."

She hesitates. "We were friends."

"Were friends?" I ask, arching an eyebrow.

"We haven't talked in years, Cash."

"You stopped writing."

Her grip tightens on the door, but she doesn't say anything.

"Were friends," I repeat.

Quiet. The sounds of the summer night drifts through her bedroom window to break it. A chirping of crickets, and suburban noises.

"I should get some sleep," she says.

I step backward. "Goodnight, June."

"Goodnight, Cash." Her voice is soft, and the way her lips form my name is intoxicating.

I go into my room. Were friends. We were friends. Not friends any more. How long has it been since I had this feeling?

The pitiful truth is that this is the feeling that I associate with June. As a teen, I thought it was just a hormonal crush. Now, I know better.

But not friends?

Yeah. That's not happening.

June needs every friend she can get. She deserves friends who will protect her from the vultures that circle women like her. The ones who prey on goodwill and kindness and empathy. June can look out for herself, sure, but I can't let her do it on her own. I just can't.

Not when she's just been kicked in the ass by that fuck on the other end of the line. What kind of a name is Braydon, anyway?

I shut my bedroom door and walk to the wall that we share. I press my forehead against it, shut my eyes and inhale deeply, imagining for a second that I'm on the other side of it, my arms around her, gently kissing her neck, working my way up to her ear lobe. The warmth of her body against mine is a real thing now that I've felt it.

My frustration grows at a pace beside my need for her, and my cock is hard again. At this rate, I'm going to be raw from touching myself because of her. It's like I'm a horny teenager again, jacking off over the same woman.

It's like time has impacted with itself, and I'm here and there, trapped with myself and the emotions that I avoided.

Sixteen

JUNE

IT WAS JUST A KISS. Nothing but a kiss. Just a kiss.

I've repeated that mantra in my mind fifty times since I woke up this morning. I blame anxiety. But it's helping me keep thoughts of Cash's lips on mine at bay. I won't risk my future for a man, especially not one who dated my friend. Kisses, sex, feelings are too complicated for one summer.

"Ready to go?" I call out, as I take stock of everything I've packed in our massive striped tote for the day.

The plan is to go to the beach with Alex, catch some rays, read, play, build sandcastles, hopefully meet other kids who aren't as, frankly, crappy, as that Leah girl. There must be other like-minded eleven-year-olds in Heatstroke.

Then again, I know what it's like to not have friends. It was lucky that Cash, Olivia, and I found each other.

"Alex?"

"Coming!" Her voice is a little squeaky.

She enters the kitchen and stops in front of me, dipping

her head. She's got a one-piece on that's covered in purple sparkles, and she's chosen a pair of loud flip-flops.

"You look friggin' amazing," I say. "Wow! You've got to be, like, the coolest kid in school."

Alex's head snaps up. "You think?"

"I know."

"I'm not the coolest kid in school. Like, at all."

"Then you're going to be the coolest kid on the beach today," I say.

Alex rewards me with a grin.

"First things first," I root around in the tote, "sunscreen."

"Boo!"

"It's a necessity. It's in the Excel spreadsheet and linked Google Doc. And the manifesto." Cash has provided me with a Taylor family manifesto that is equal parts cute and alarming. Chief among the family goals? Keep Alex's skin safe from harmful UV rays.

"But I don't want to be pale," Alex whines. "You're all tan."

"Self-tanner," I say. "Not for kids, before you get any wise ideas."

Alex giggles, and I help her put sunscreen on.

I make a big show of putting on some myself. Just before we leave, I bring out my phone and dutifully shoot Cash a text, my insides betraying me at the sight of his name on the screen.

Alex and I are going to the beach today. We'll probably pop by Marci's diner for lunch.

Two ticks show the message has gone through. They turn blue. He doesn't reply.

I stow my phone, trying not to let the lack of response

get to me. I'm the nanny, and he's working with his dad. Just. A. Kiss.

"All right," I say, "let's show the sun and sand what we've got."

I lock the door behind us and we climb into Ol' Rusty. I spare a glance for my mother's house, but her curtains are shut.

I make sure Alex has got her seatbelt on, and then we putter off down the road together, the windows rolled down letting in the salty air. I switch on the radio, and Alex jams out to a rock song enthusiastically. I turn it up real loud so she can enjoy it to the max.

She drums on her knees, shaking from side to side. Just two girls on the loose, enjoying our freedom, no concerns for "the man" and what's expected of us.

We park along the winding road that looks down on the bay. Alex runs down to the sand, shrieking, and collides with the water like it's a long-lost friend.

I set up on the beach, grabbing the umbrella from the back of Ol' Rusty and pegging it into the sand. I keep an eye on Alex as she plays, splashing in and out of the waves. A couple of kids around her age are building a sandcastle, but she doesn't even look in their direction.

After twenty minutes, she joins me, out of breath and excited. I wrap a towel around her and sit her down in our spot under the umbrella. "There are some kids over there if you want to build a sandcastle."

Alex shrugs, accepting a bottle of water from me.

"You know," I say, "just because Leah's a bully, doesn't mean those kids will be. Do you know them from school?"

"No."

"Must be from out of town then." Still, some social

interaction with kids her age would be better than no social interaction. I'm not going to force it, though. Kids tend to balk at being told what to do at this age. At least, I did. "Have you put any thought into the talent show at the end of the summer?"

"I want to do it," Alex says, "but there's this other girl."

"Other girl?"

"Yeah. At school," she says. "Her name is Daisy, and she's new. But Leah is already friends with her."

"And you want to be friends with her?"

"She's nice," Alex replies, staring out at the waves. "She likes the same kind of music as me, and she plays in the band. The drums."

"Wow, she sounds awesome."

"Yeah."

And then the conversation fades into the soft sounds of the waves lapping the sand. One of the kids nearby shrieks and takes off down the beach, chased by the other one.

"Do you know where Daisy stays?"

"Yeah. I overheard her telling Leah that she lives in that old cottage on the beach."

"On Boiler?"

Alex nods.

"I have an idea," I say. "When I was your age, I started writing to my friends."

"Writing?" Alex says the word like it's foreign. Maybe it is for kids these days, given most of them have phones.

"So, your dad and I," I say, excluding Olivia from the conversation since I have no idea how much she knows about her mom or wants to talk about her, "we used to write each other letters. Pen pals. All the way through middle school, high school, and after I left town. Maybe you can write to Daisy asking her about the talent show."

"I don't know."

"I can even show you some of the letters your dad wrote me," I say on a whim. "I still have them."

"Really? You kept them that long?"

"Well, yeah. We were good friends. It might help you write one of your own." The letters Cash had written to me were innocent. Mine were the ones fraught with tension. My crush. "What do you say? It's worth a shot, right?"

Sometimes, things were easier to put on paper than they were to say out loud.

"Yeah." Alex sounds noncommittal but her eyes are alight. This poor girl wants friends and to be accepted.

"Thanks for bringing me to the beach," Alex says.

When I was a kid, I longed for my mom to spend quality time with me and take me places. I can imagine Alex wishes she had the same. Or maybe I'm reading too much into it, and she's just happy to be out in the sun.

She runs off again, and we spend most of the morning chatting about the pen pal idea, playing in the water, then relaxing and reading while we twiddle our toes in the sun. Alex informs me that her father has turned the master bedroom, the one that used to belong to her grandfather and grandmother, into a library, and I mentally curse Cash Taylor for being so darn perfect.

Lunchtime comes, and we enter Marci's diner, sun-kissed and hungry.

"June!" Marci rounds the counter and folds me into a hug. "You look gorgeous."

"So do you." Marci always looks like she's an actress

playing the part of a woman who works in a diner in a movie. She's using a polka dot silk scarf to hold back her red hair and is in a pair of cutoff jean shorts that I'm totally going to borrow later. "Hey, Alex."

"Hi." Alex waves.

"Chocolate milkshake and a Heartburn special?"

"Make that two," I say.

Alex and I take seats at the bar at the back of the retro diner, and I wave at Grant, the chef. He's been working at the Heartstopper since I was a kid, and he gives me his usual gap-toothed grin.

The Heartstopper is only just starting to fill up for lunch, and I spot a couple of the regulars from around town. There are unfamiliar faces too—tourists who've come for the sun and the beach. Timmy Schafer from the tiny video game store around the corner stops by to say hi, as do Rod and Tilly, and Moira from the cake shop. Every one of them is happy that I'm back in town, and even happier to see Alex, if the huge smiles they throw our way are any indication.

Alex sucks down her milkshake, spying on the TV overhead that's playing a rerun of a basketball game.

Marci finishes topping up someone's coffee and returns with our orders in little baskets with checked paper. "So," she says, casting a quick glance in Alex's direction, "how are things?"

She's talking about Cash. Because of course she's talking about Cash.

"Good," I say.

Marci's eyebrows spike upward. "Good?"

"Good."

"How good?"

"I'll text you."

"That good?" Marci asks.

Alex frowns, looking at her and then at me. "What are you talking about?"

"Nothing," we say in unison.

Marci clears her throat. "Do you have a night off any time soon?" she asks, and I'm so grateful she changed the subject. Alex is eleven, not five.

"Friday," I say.

"Awesome. There's a beach party over at Longhorn's. Belle, Hannah, and I were thinking about going. You've got to come."

"I don't know." I'd much rather curl up with a spicy book. But it's probably a good idea since Cash will be home and Alex is going to sleep over at Ganny's.

"It'll be fun. I'll text you the…" Marci's eyes widen as she looks at a point over my shoulder.

I turn.

Cash stands just inside the diner, holding two sunflowers. He locks gazes with me before walking across the diner, and every eye is on him except Alex's. Whispers start up, and I catch hints of phrases.

"Isn't that—?"

"The Cash Taylor?" says one of the tourists who recognizes the country music star Cash. The regulars watch because they love fresh gossip.

Cash stops in front of me. "Thought I'd join you ladies for lunch," he grumbles.

"Dad!" Alex has only just noticed him. She hugs him and he hands her a sunflower. "Thanks, Dad!" She tries to smell it and pokes her nose.

"Careful," he says, shifting the flower back.

"Weren't you busy renovating?" I ask.

"It's lunch," Cash replies simply with a shrug.

My heart pounds so hard, I'm sure everyone must hear it. Cash hasn't joined us for lunch in the few days I've been working for him.

Cash turns to me. "An apology," he says, and hands me the other sunflower.

Oh my God.

Did he remember that it's my favorite flower?

Cash gives me a brief, genuine smile that cracks me right down the center. Then he claps those large hands, the ones that were on my body last night, and rubs them together. "So, what are we eating?"

Seventeen

CASH

SPENDING time around June is dangerous. The way she carries herself, cares for Alex, talks, smiles, laughs, makes each second in the Heartstopper Diner stretch into a painful eternity.

"And we can come up with a song and maybe a dance together as well!" Alex says.

I nod, dragging my last fry through ketchup. "Sounds like a great idea."

June is tucked into the booth closest to the window and she's already finished her burger and fries. She peers out of the window, her chin resting in her palm, and I trace the shape of her profile with my eyes.

I release a breath. "Everybody done?"

"Yeah," Alex says. "Thanks, Dad."

"All right, I'll get the check. Meet you out front in a second."

"Thank you," June says, her fingers moving to the sunflower on the table beside her plate.

I grunt and rise. June is a constellation of temptations,

and I feel like a stargazer. I told myself that coming here was a bad idea, but I couldn't resist. It beats eating takeout and thinking about June.

The more I expose myself, however, the more difficult this becomes. I don't have anything to offer her here. She wants out of Heatstroke, I want to stay. I don't even know if I'm capable of love again after Olivia

I pay for the meal, ignoring the stares from the Heatstroke locals.

"Good lunch?" Marci smiles at me from behind the register. "Looked like y'all were having fun."

"Fun?"

"Sure. Chatting. It's kind of sweet, don't you think?"

"What is?"

"The way Alex and June are bonding," she says. "It's weird, but they even look alike."

I don't respond.

"Have a good day, Cash."

"You, too." I tuck my receipt into the back pocket of my jeans then walk out onto the sidewalk.

The door claps shut behind me.

A tall guy, tattoos down his neck, and the back of his hands, stands in front of June, smiling at her in a way that makes me want to punch him in the throat. He's wearing a suit that looks like it costs more than all the buildings in the street, and he's got a lean, wily look about him. Like he'd be slippery in a fight. Agile. The type who hides a knife up his sleeve.

I grind my teeth as he takes a step closer to her.

Alex sits on a bench on the street, her legs crossed, watching the exchange with interest, both sunflowers in her lap.

"I'll stop by here more often." The guy's voice is deep, and it makes the throat-punching idea even more alluring.

"Yeah, definitely," June says, her hand on the back of the bench, inches away from Alex. She glances down at my daughter. "It's a lovely town. Have you been here long?"

"Long? No."

"The Heartstopper is a great place."

The guy nods, flashing a white-toothed grin. "Yeah, it sure seems like it now."

June shifts her weight from one foot to the other. "Seriously, the food is great. And Marci, she's—"

"I'm going to level with you, June," the guy says, moving closer, "I'm not as interested in the diner as I am in you."

June's jaw drops. "Well," she says, "you're honest, I'll give you that. Unfortunately, I'm at work right now."

"Fine. Give me your number," he says, like he expects her to whip out her phone at his command. "I'll call you. We can set it up."

I join her, sizing the guy up. He's a little shorter than me. I can take him, easy.

"Cash," June says, her cheeks growing red, "there you are."

"Who's this?"

"Seth," the guy says, extending a hand. "Seth Deveraux."

This is the asshole who's interested in buying my father's bar.

"Cash Taylor," I say.

"I know who you are." Seth mimes a guitar. "You're that hot shot celebrity, right? The star. Can't walk two steps in this town without hearing your name. You're a regular town treasure."

"You need something, Deveraux?" I ask.

"Sure do," he says, running a thumb over his jaw. "Was asking June here for her number. Unless that's a problem with you, big man."

I sense June beside me, tense, concerned, and Alex watching with great interest.

"I'm good," June says suddenly. "Sorry, but I'm at work. And I'm, uh, not particularly interested in dating."

"That's a shame," Seth says. "If you change your—"

"She said no, fuck face."

"Whoa." Seth laughs. "Whoa, looks like I touched a nerve."

"Swear jar," Alex calls.

I take a breath, inhaling through my nose hard. I don't like this guy. I don't like him near June, near my daughter, near my father. I don't care that his family's money is good for the town. He looks and acts like trash, and I'm willing and able to take him out.

Seth tilts his head to one side like he's considering a fight, and even though I'm duty-bound to be a responsible father, a part of me wishes he would, so I could turn his face into ground beef.

"See you around," he says to June. And then he grins at me. "You too, Taylor." He strums that air guitar again as he leaves.

June turns toward me.

"I'll see you two at home tonight for dinner," I say quickly. "Be safe." And then I kiss Alex on the head. I don't look back at June.

I pull out my phone as I walk and shoot off a quick text.

> Sorry for acting like a dickhead back there.

The message is delivered, but she doesn't immediately respond so I tuck the phone away. I don't want June to feel like I'm encroaching on her privacy, but the thought of Seth anywhere near her makes my blood boil. She is mine.

The thought catches me off guard. June isn't mine and she never has been. She can't be because I have nothing to give her.

I arrive at Chuckles and let myself in. "Dad?" I call out. "You in there?"

The minute I step through the office door, I'm confronted by the smell of booze. The desk holds an empty tumbler and a half-full bottle of bourbon. My father's head rests on the desk, and he snorts in his sleep.

One hour and this is what happens. One fucking hour.

I can't step out for a minute without the entire family collapsing to shit. The Taylor family is split apart, shattered like glass, and I'm the asshole trying to glue the pieces back together without getting my fingers cut.

This is exactly why I can't get involved with anyone. If I fall apart, our family will have no one left.

I grab the bottle and tip the bourbon down the drain in the men's bathroom. I can't let Seth get to my father. I'm going to have to talk to Jesse and Hannah about this. Maybe even call Lily and Leo. Talk to Ganny.

This problem isn't going away, and I'm not sure even Chuckles Bar is going to save my father before it's too late.

Eighteen

JUNE

"DINNER'S ALMOST READY!"

The blaring rock music from Alex's room drowns me out, but I smile to myself. Alex is excited about the talent show, and about making a new friend, and I'm not going to tell her to shut her music off. Besides, I doubt Cash will mind. He was exactly the same at her age, except he was playing country and picking on his father's old guitar.

I gnaw on my bottom lip. I've put the two sunflowers in a vase on the kitchen table, and every time they catch my eye, I falter.

A flower for me. An apology.

It wasn't a damn declaration of love. I have to get it together. I swore at the start of this that I wouldn't trust a man again or let them take control of my destiny. Cash has to factor into that, but it's so difficult to bear that in mind because I know him. He wasn't the type of person who messed around. He was faithful to Olivia.

Or was he?

I have no idea what happened. I'm so curious, it's

eating me up inside, and I've lost count of how many times I've stopped and checked my phone, halfway toward looking him up. But if Cash was ready to tell me, he would. I'm not going to pry.

I'll stay in my lane and focus on college applications.

The front door of the house opens, and Cash storms into the kitchen.

His expression is dark, angry, until it lands on me. He frowns. "Loud music?"

"I know it's not in your spreadsheet," I say, "but she's pretty excited about the talent show."

"That's fine," he says, waving it off.

"And she wants to watch School of Rock after dinner," I say.

"Fine." He clears his throat, and I'm hyper focused on his Adam's apple, his muscular, tan neck, his shoulders.

I turn away from him and face the counter. "Dinner should be ready soon. I'm making fajitas."

"Thanks," he says, his breath brushing against my neck. Above us is the frantic thumping as Alex dances around in her bedroom.

He's so close, I know if I turn around, my breasts will brush against his chest. Is he toying with me? Because I can't take this. The way my body reacts to his presence is treacherous, and as much as I want to believe that I can sleep with Cash without strings attached, I know it's impossible for me.

I place my hands on the countertop, and I'm about to tell him exactly that, when a knock rattles the front door.

"I'll get it," I say, and walk past him without making eye contact.

I open the front door and my relief at being away from

Cash is short-lived. My mother stands on the front step, a half-smoked cigarette in one hand. She's wearing her work clothes from the grocery store, and she's got that mean look on her face. The one that precedes a slap or an insult.

"June Jackson," she says. "You should be ashamed of yourself."

I step out onto the porch and shut the door behind me. "Mom?"

"You're having an affair with Cash, aren't you?"

"An affair?" I frown. "I work for him. You know that."

"Well," my mother sighs, "I hope that's all that it is because I don't want a hussy for a daughter. Besides, what would Olivia say about this?"

I open my mouth to tell her that Olivia abandoned her only daughter, but my mother is already on a roll and talks right over me.

"I know you've got it in that head of yours to go to college and study, but this is not the way you do it. Taking advantage of friends," she says.

"I'm not."

"Listen, honey." Mom's voice softens, and she grabs hold of my arm and squeezes it. "Listen, I know you're hurting over Braydon, but things will get better. You don't have to sell yourself out to—"

"I'm the nanny," I say. "I told you that."

My mother purses her lips. "The nanny. That's not what I heard in town."

"It doesn't matter what you heard," I say, trying to be stern, "I'm working to earn money for the future." Heck, my mom was the one who asked for help with extra cash around the house.

"Good," she says, releasing my forearm. "As long as that's all it is."

I want to tell her to leave, but it's like I'm frozen when I think about it, paralyzed by guilt because she's lived here alone for years, and even though she's treated me like a passenger rather than a daughter, I feel like I owe her. Because that's what she's always claimed.

I owe her for ruining her relationship with my father.

I owe her for telling him, as a little girl, that I saw her with her boss at the restaurant.

I owe her because he left us.

"Listen, June, honey," she says, "this is all going to pass." She strokes my cheek, and it takes all of me not to flinch away. She takes a drag of her cigarette, stepping back and spilling ash on the porch. "And I'm glad to hear you're earning money for our family. It's been a real struggle for me lately, you know? I had to take out a loan to pay the bills. That Billy Walsh has been coming around asking for me to pay him back."

"Mom." I breathe it out like a curse.

Billy is trouble. Marci's brother has always skirted the law or gotten on the wrong side of it, and hearing that my mother has had dealings with him makes me sick.

"Mom, why would you ask Billy for money?"

She shrugs. "What was I supposed to do? Ask you? Graves won't give me an advance on my salary, so here we are. So, honey, I'm thinking that we should talk about how much money you owe for rent and board for—"

The front door opens and Cash steps out onto the porch.

My mother looks him up and down, then puts up a special simpering smile that she reserves for men or bosses. "Cash," she says, in a purr. "Honey, hi. It's been so long since I've seen you, neighbor."

Cash stares her down, expressionless. "There a reason you're on my porch, Patricia?"

"Goodness, I'm just paying my June a visit, isn't that right, June?"

Cash doesn't afford me the opportunity to respond. He removes his wallet from his back pocket and takes out a stack of bills. "How much?"

"What's that, Cash darlin'?"

"Don't act the fool, Patricia. How much?"

My mother wets her lips with the tip of her tongue. "Five hundred."

He leafs out the money and hands it to her. "You give that to Billy. Don't come back around here again. June's money is June's, not yours, you understand?"

Mom looks like she wants to argue.

"You should be ashamed of yourself, Patricia," he says, "trying to take advantage of your daughter like she's a fucking piggy bank."

"Cash darlin', I—"

"Get off my property."

My mother blinks, her eyes flashing with heat and anger, before she stamps her cigarette butt out on the sidewalk, then stalks off. Her front door slams moments later.

"What the hell are you doing?" I turn on Cash. "You can't—"

"Were you going to say anything?" he asks.

"Yeah, I was. I was going to tell her that I—"

"That you'd help her?"

I poke him in the chest, and my finger actually hurts from how hard it is. "Hey, stop interrupting me, would you? I don't need you to step in and protect me every time something happens. I was going to tell her to leave."

"I don't believe it."

"What?"

"June, you're too soft. You give and give and give to everyone else and never take anything for yourself," he says. "And she's part of the reason. She's the one who taught you how to do that, June. She's not a parent. She's a user. And she'll drain you dry if you let her. You want to go to college, you want to save up to follow your dreams, but she doesn't give a fuck about that or about you. She never has."

I glare up at him. "Why do you care?" I ask. "What does it matter who—?"

He closes the distance between us, and his hands move to my arms. He holds me in place, and I have to tilt my head back to make eye contact.

Cash's gaze pierces right through me, and I scan his face, the beard, his lips, parted, his deep blue eyes, the tan skin, the impression of wrinkles on his forehead.

"Cash?"

His touch electrifies me, but it's different to the night we kissed. Intentional and soft, reserved. He sweeps his palms down my arms and holds my hands for a second before stepping back. He balls his hands at his sides then releases them slowly and gives them a shake.

"You're my friend, June. Always have been. My best friend."

"I—"

"I will always care, always want to help," he says. "And I know you find it difficult to say no when it comes to her."

"Friend or not," I say, "I can fight my own battles." But it's hard to get the words out because Cash and Olivia were there for me after my father left. Just like we were there for Olivia when her parents abandoned her in Heatstroke.

It makes this entire situation worse.

"I know you can," Cash says after a beat. "I just find it difficult not to help."

The music cuts off upstairs. Dinner. Alex.

He opens the door for me, and I walk in, completely confused by old emotions that feel new again.

Nineteen

JUNE

"ARE you going to tell me what's going on, or am I going to have to squeeze it out of you like blood from a stone?" Marci asks, then takes a sip of her beer and gives me the stare. The "tell me everything before I implode" stare.

Belle and Hannah are at the bar, getting us a second round of drinks, both of them dressed in beachy casual wear that everyone has on tonight. Cutoff jeans, tight-fitting tops, bare feet. Longhorn's is the place most locals go for a bite and a drink after work. It helps that most of the tables are right on the sand, with a view of the distant waves, and that the moon is out tonight, glimmering on the ocean.

I tuck my hair behind my ear in the warm breeze, trying to avoid answering.

"You didn't text me," Marci says. "Come on, spill it before Belle and Han get back."

"Cash and I kissed," I say quietly, hoping the music from the speakers will drown out what I've just said.

But judging by Marci's dropped jaw, she heard.

"You're kidding me." It comes out as an excited hiss.

"Wait," I say, "don't get your hopes up. It wasn't like that."

"Like what? It wasn't hot?"

"No, it was incredibly hot. I just mean it wasn't anything serious. It was a one-off thing."

"Right, right," Marci says, grasping her nearly empty bottle of beer by the neck, one eyebrow raised. "Did this happen before or after he brought you a flower in my diner?"

"Before. The flower was an apology. He felt bad because I'm working for him. Look, you can't tell anyone about this. It's not going to happen again."

"Sure."

"Marci."

"Hey," she says, "I'm not going to tell a soul. Your secret is safe with me. But if you want my opinion—"

"I don't."

"Too bad. If you want my opinion," Marci says, with a sneaky grin, "this is only the start of it, June. There's no way you two can kiss and move on."

"We can. No, it's not even about that. I have to. I'm not going to open myself up to that again, Marce. Not after what happened with—"

"He who shall not be named." Marci crosses herself. "Just seems a shame."

"What does?"

"That you've waited so long for something to happen between you two, and now that it has, you're just ready to let it go?"

"Because I'm not a kid anymore," I say. "I'm not stuck in my fantasy world or whatever. I have to be realistic."

"Borrrinnnggg." Marci shakes her head. "You should fuck him."

"That's very testosterone-y of you, Marce."

"Oh, come on, wanting to get laid is not a guy thing. It's an everybody thing. Or most people thing. How long has it been since you've had a good session?" Marci's eyes glaze over. "Picture it. His hands running over your body, his mouth—"

"Is that the beer talking?" I have to stop her because the trouble is, I have been picturing it.

"No," she says, then tilts her head to one side, her crimson hair falling past her shoulder. "But it might be the dry spell."

"Huh."

"Look, I know that Cash likes you," Marci says. "I just know it. Men don't act the way he acts around you when they're not interested."

"You're forgetting something."

"What?"

"He has a daughter with my ex-best friend." I hesitate. "And he chose her, not me. This might be my ego talking, but I'm not going to be someone's second choice. Not even Cash Taylor's. Braydon made me a second choice for the entirety of our relationship."

There were women out there, thousands of them, who would kill for a date with the country music star, but I don't see him like that. He's just Cash.

"I don't buy it," Marci says.

"Buy what?"

"That he chose her over you," she replies. "I don't think you're second best. I don't know. I think if he knew what your feelings were back then, that he would have gone for it with you."

I sigh. "Let's be real about this."

"I am being real. He likes you and you like him. All the other stuff is bullshit." Marci has an affliction: getting things off her chest.

"I don't want to live in Heatstroke near my mother. I don't want any of this."

Marci looks ready to argue.

I'm saved from further prying by Belle and Hannah. They set down a tray of tequila shots on the table, and I cross two fingers in front of myself.

"Hell no," I say. "I have work tomorrow."

"We all have work tomorrow." Hannah, who has the Taylor family's good looks—blue eyes, dark hair, and pouty lips—sits down and nudges Belle. "Apart from this bitch. She's on vacation."

"Call it a sabbatical," Belle says. "I need a break. I think I'm going to die if I have to work with one more bratty sports star."

I frown.

Hannah hands out the tequila shots. "Belle works for one of those big PR firms out in Houston. Sexy sports guys are her bread and butter."

"Bread and butter?" Belle makes a gagging noise, and it's hilarious on a woman who is so well-put together. Even in casual wear, she has an air of grace. "They're my arch nemeses. Seriously, they're all brats. You think that those A-List celebrities with their teeny, tiny little poodles in purses and their retainers are bad? Try a six-foot-five football player."

"Why? What do they do?"

"It's not what they do," Belle says, and kicks back the shot. She smacks her lips then pulls a face. "It's what they don't do. They don't behave. They don't ask for anything politely. And they think they own the world and everyone in it."

"That last one is something they do do, isn't it?" Hannah asks.

Marci scoffs. "Ha! Do-do. Doo-doo."

"Really?" Hannah asks, her shot halfway to her mouth.

"What? Come on. Doo-doo." Marci takes a shot of tequila. "Like poop."

"I'm cutting her off," Belle announces, to the table and anyone who will listen.

We burst out laughing, and I feel lighter already. There's nothing like some good girl time, and I missed that so much when I was in Dallas. The only girl time I got was when I was forced into spaces with Grace Rowling's friends or family members or other willing victims. Marci was my saving grace in those times—I'd FaceTime her whenever possible.

"Hope you never meet Leo," Hannah says. "You would hate him."

"Why?" Belle asks.

"He's a rugby player," Hannah replies. "He's like a walking meat wall of ego. I mean, he's my brother and I love him, but the man's a pain in the ass."

Belle grimaces. "Hard pass."

I've had one cocktail tonight, and if I take this shot, I'm done for the evening. I down it and pull a face as the girls cheer. The guy behind the bar has turned up the music, and men and women make their way out onto the sand to dance. There's a dancefloor too, but the party spills out onto the beach, and it's a vibe.

"Ladies, we have to do this more often," Marci says. "The hanging out together part, not the tequila."

"Hear, hear," Hannah says. "Marc has got a point. You're going back to Houston soon, and June's only here for the summer, right?"

I nod. Only for the summer.

"Ooh! I know." Marci clicks her fingers. "We should go to the quarry."

A cold flush passes over me, and I clear my throat.

Marci's face falls. "Shit, I forgot about that, June. Sorry."

"Sorry?" Belle glances from Marci to me and back again. "About? What happened?"

"It's nothing actually," I say, waving a hand. "Just a silly thing that happened when we were kids and I couldn't swim." I chuckle. "It's like a gut reaction every time someone mentions the quarry. Silly."

"Olivia pushed June into the quarry from Diver's Point when we were kids," Marci says, since Hannah and Belle are a couple of years younger than us. "She nearly drowned."

"I couldn't swim great," I say, "and I got the wind knocked out of me. It's not as bad as it sounds. Just a memory."

"It sounds shitty to me," Belle replies. "I mean, what kind of kid pushes another kid into the water like that? From high up?"

I wave a hand. "She thought it was a funny prank. Anyway, uh, yeah. I think that would be fun. We could hike Old Man's Trail."

"Exactly." Marci slaps the table. "Then it's decided. Next weekend?" Marci's the type of person to run into things headfirst without hesitation. She'd also beat someone up for me if they looked at me wrong now. Back in high school, Marci kept her distance a lot of the time, mostly because of Billy getting in the way.

"Sounds great," I say, because I want more of this time. Time to think and breathe and pull myself together without being in Cash's sexy orbit. With these girls, I can relax.

It's silly, but the end of summer seems too close. I'm already anticipating what it will be like to leave Heatstroke. Cash. Alex.

That has to be the tequila.

"Oooh, don't look now, Han, but guess who just walked in the front door?" Belle nudges Cash's sister.

"Savage," Marci says, grinning from ear to ear. "Savage is here."

"Whatever." Hannah's cheeks are pink. "I don't care. He's just Savage. Doesn't even read. That's sacrilege to a librarian." But it's clear she cares a lot because her gaze is fixed on the bar.

I follow her line of sight, and my stomach jolts. Savage isn't alone. Cash is with him, and every woman in Longhorn's is staring right at him and whispering.

I look away quickly, taking a breath to calm myself. My head swims from the thought of another woman touching him. Good thing I didn't have another tequila.

Before I can do anything stupid, like, say, go over there and act like I'm more than just the nanny or a friend, a guy steps up to the side of the table. He's good-looking, but I don't recognize him from around town. Blond hair shaved on the sides, the top swept back. He's come over from the table of guys next to ours, and they all watch in anticipation.

"Hi," he says, sweeping a hand over his chin. "Name's Charlie."

"June."

The other girls watch the exchange with interest, except for Hannah, who's still staring at Savage.

"Wanna dance?"

"Charlie," I begin, as I look over at the bar where Cash has already collected an entourage of women, talking, touching, laughing. "Sure. Why not?"

Twenty

CASH

"HEAR you might be singing in that big talent show at the end of summer," the woman says, leaning on the bar beside me. She's making a show of pressing her breasts together under a strappy silk top and trying her best to direct my gaze toward her cleavage. She tosses her hair and lays her fingers on my forearm, stroking my skin.

I shift away from her. "Nope."

"You aren't?" she asks. "Aw, why not? You're the Cash Taylor. I bet if you played, folks from all over Texas would come."

Savage chuckles under his breath beside me, leaning around me to grin at the woman. "Cash doesn't sing anymore."

"Why not?" a second woman chimes in.

I'm pissed that I let Savage convince me to come to Longhorn's. Bars are not my scene anymore, and I despise the attention I get while I'm out. It's a constant reminder of the past.

"He gave it up," Savage says.

"Gave up music?" The first woman tries to lean in. She's too close, and I scrape my barstool back and get up.

Savage eyes me over the edge of his beer can but doesn't say anything.

"Restroom," I grunt, because I'm an asshole but not a rude asshole. I turn to leave Savage with the wolves and freeze.

June is here, in another man's arms.

The blond who's holding her wears a grin like he's won the lottery. I don't blame him for that. He has.

The guy sways June onto the dance floor. She laughs as he turns her in a circle. He wraps his arm around her, pulling her close, and a monstrous thing happens to me. An unfolding, snapping in my chest.

Before I know it, I'm across the bar, standing behind him. June catches sight of me over his shoulder and sucks in a breath, her eyes widening. "Cash?"

"No, honey, it's Charlie," the goof says.

I tap him on the shoulder, and he turns. "Huh?"

"Mind if I cut in?"

The guy sizes me up, weighing his options.

My fists clench, and my nostrils flare like I'm a caveman with a club. Everyone in Longhorn's stares at me, but I don't care.

The nanny.

"Sure, I guess," the guy says, and moves back a step.

I take June's hand and spin her into my arms. She lets out a whoop at the change in pace.

I move June across the dance floor, my arms around her waist, my hands pressed against her strappy top. It's covered in yellow flowers and rosebuds, and I want to rip it off her body and suck her flesh into my mouth. Her body feels perfect against mine, supple, like she was made to press against me like this.

I've had a sip of beer, for God's sake.

Her fingers are interlaced around my neck, her gaze flickers from my face, down my chest, away, and back again.

I study her, open my mouth to say something, but the DJ changes the song. The first notes of "Tougher Than the Rest" by Springsteen pound through the speakers, and June bites her bottom lip.

This song. It's like the asshole DJ has chosen this song specifically to fuck with me.

It's the song my mother and father danced to when I was a kid. It was one of the songs June and I jammed out to in our teens. We would sing it together, me playing guitar, and her keeping time on her thighs.

June swallows.

I want to run my hands all over her body, through her hair, make her look into my eyes and see what I'm feeling.

Instead, I hum along to the song.

Her head snaps up. "Cash," she murmurs.

"Hmm?"

"You're singing."

"Humming."

A hesitation, another biting down on her bottom lip. "Why don't you do it anymore? Sing?"

If it was anyone else asking, I wouldn't answer.

"Cash?"

"Because of what happened," I say. "The band broke up."

I sway her back and forth, staring at how beautiful she is. That light she's always had shines from within her.

"We broke up because Olivia fucked the drummer." The words come out bland and emotionless because I don't feel anything for them anymore. Either of them.

June's eyes widen and it takes her a moment to respond. "I had no idea. I'm sorry, Cash."

"Yeah." Because we stopped being friends. "Found out about it just before Olivia discovered she was pregnant. We got a paternity test, and when I realized Alex was mine? No going back. I didn't want to. But that isn't the reason I stopped singing."

"It's not."

"No. I just lost the love for it. Lost the reason I started singing in the first place."

"Do you think you'll ever get it back?"

I stare at her hard, and a warm thrumming starts up in my chest. "I think so."

She smiles.

The pressure between us returns, and the words of the song, the pounding of the drums, and the memories, are undeniable. June's body is tight against mine, soft curves pressed against my hard lines, and I have to take a breath to stop myself from kissing her again.

The dance floor disappears around us. It's just June. June's delicious citrus scent mingling with salty ocean air. A moment we've never had before and one I want to keep going forever.

But the song ends.

June steps out of my grasp, and I can feel the lack of her in my arms. She gives me a polite smile and starts to walk off.

I take hold of her forearm, and she stops.

"Cash?"

I'm aware of the bar again, the people staring. My sister is wide-eyed over on the sand, sitting with Belle and Marci.

"Come home with me," I murmur.

"What?" June can't hear me over the music. She steps closer.

I brush her hair back over her right ear, lean in. "Come. Home. With. Me. Now." I watch gooseflesh spread down the side of her neck, over her collar bone, beneath her top.

She hesitates then looks up at me, her eyes flicking left and right. "My purse."

I walk over to the table where the girls are seated and grab her purse. "Evening," I say.

None of them respond.

I return the purse to June, and then I place a hand at the small of her back and walk her out of Longhorn's toward my pickup.

Twenty~One

JUNE

I CLUTCH my purse in my lap as we take the long drive home. I'm tense, ready for his touch, hoping he'll reach out for me every time he moves his hand to the stick shift, and I'm starting to despise myself for it.

Cash doesn't say anything as he drives. He doesn't turn on the radio either but the words of the song we danced to are stuck in my head. His side profile is strong, the beard, the aquiline nose a little crooked, his blue eyes focused, lips parted. Lips that have touched me.

Lips I'll let touch me again.

Cash parks the car outside his house. My mother's place is dark next door.

Cash unclips his seatbelt and turns toward me. "How much have you had to drink, June?"

"Huh? A cocktail and a shot of tequila. What about you?"

He grunts and leans back against the door.

I take offense to the insinuation that I'm not in control of my faculties. I'm not the type of girl who gets sloppy and falls around drunk in bars. Those days are long gone, lost back in the years of working as a server and having too much fun.

"I don't want," he starts. "I'm not going to touch you unless you want to be touched."

I want him to touch me so bad it hurts, but I keep up my defenses. Because what does it matter if he's a good man, a gentleman, a person who won't take advantage of me? He wanted someone else while I pined after him like a fool.

"June."

I put up a hand. Maybe it is the alcohol talking, but I need him to hear this. "I don't want to ruin anything," I say, "and neither do you."

"Right."

"But you make it difficult for me when you look at me the way you do, when you talk to me the way you do. Hell, Cash, when you do anything, you make it real difficult."

"I make it difficult." He laughs like it's the funniest thing he's ever heard. "What about you?"

"What about me?" I have shreds of dignity left after Braydon, and I try to collect them. I'm not going to ask him if he likes me like we're in high school. I'm not going to ask him why he chose her instead of me. I'm not going to—

"Every second I spend with you makes it difficult for me to breathe."

Damn him to hell. It's like he's writing lyrics to a song, and it makes the girl in me swoon and whimper.

"I don't know what that means."

Cash runs a hand over the back of his neck. "Come on,

June. You know what it means. It means I want you. When I saw that guy with his arms around you," He grinds his teeth. "I wanted to break his face. I wanted to make him regret it."

His arm rests on the back of the seat, and his fingers are inches from my skin. "There are plenty of reasons not to do this," he says. "But we're adults, right? We can keep it as just physical. No need for emotional attachments."

His phone trills, and he cusses under his breath.

"It could be Alex," I say.

Cash grimaces and worms the phone out of his pocket. "Fuck." He answers it. "Jesse?"

I let out a breath of relief. If it's not Ganny, then Alex is fine and there's nothing to worry about. I reach for the door handle.

"Fuck," Cash grunts. "Yeah. Yeah. I'm on my way." And then he hangs up and turns to me. "My dad—"

"Is he all right?"

"I don't know, but I've got to get over there."

"Of course," I say. "Thanks for the ride home."

"June." He places a hand on the back of my neck, and I shiver at his touch. It's too much! I can't handle this level of need for him. It's not fair. It's like the universe is playing a cheap prank on me after everything that's happened.

I force a smile. "Seriously, Cash, look after your dad. Family comes first." And his father needs help. I know it. The rest of the town has been talking about it—whispers about the fall of the Taylor family—and it makes me angry every time I hear it. "I'm fine. We're fine."

"I want to be more than fine."

My heart flutters. "You always have been."

Cash opens his door and steps onto the sidewalk, but I let myself out before he can get my door for me. I wave and hurry up to the house, fumbling keys out of my purse. I slam the door shut once I'm in, leaning against it for a minute.

There's a beat before the pickup engine starts. I wait until he's gone, and then I pull my phone out of my purse as I run upstairs.

I lock my bedroom door behind me and open a tab on my phone. Five minutes later, I've found them. Lone Star College Counselors. Their website is encouraging, and they specialize in helping "later-in-life" students who want to change their career or study something fresh.

There's a button at the bottom of the web page.

Book a consultation with us today!

They're located in Austin, which is a three-hour drive from Heatstroke, and they're my shot to get out of here. My finger hovers over the button.

Twenty~Two

CASH

I PULL up outside my grandmother's house to find Jesse's squad parked out front, the lights still flashing. I grit my teeth and stare at the scene in front of me. Jesse's holding my father up and walking him toward the picket gate, my father's head hanging, feet dragging.

I take one night off, shift my focus from Dad and my family and the fucking bar to June for what feels like a second, and this happens.

My hands ball up into fists and I release them, along with a low breath.

I get out of my pickup and slam the door.

Jesse pauses, glancing over at me. "Found him on the sidewalk out front."

This is bad.

Jesse's on duty. He should be taking our father into custody for drunk and disorderly conduct. Every time my father acts this way, he endangers Jesse's job, he endangers our entire family, and it's selfish. He didn't have this problem until Mom died.

And that's exactly why I can't afford to get involved with June.

"Sucks that you had to cut your evening short," Jesse says. "I could have handled it. Thought you'd want to know."

I lift my father's other arm. "You're not going to detain him?"

"No," Jesse says, a hint of guilt in his voice. "He's right outside his house. Nobody called me over here either, so he wasn't causing a disturbance. I just happened to be driving by."

I nod.

"...go of it," Dad mumbles.

"All right, old man," Jesse says. "Let's get you upstairs and into bed."

"Fuck, Jesse," I say. "This is—"

"You can't do it!" Dad grabs hold of my shirt, fisting it and tugging me with the strength that only drunks have. "Listen to me, you can't do it."

"Calm down, Dad," I say, grinding it out.

It hurts like a son of a bitch to see him like this, but suggesting rehab has only made him double-down. Nothing we do seems to help. Nothing we say.

Nothing I do. I'm failing to be the son he needs, and it's eating me the fuck up inside.

Jesse and I guide him up the front steps of Ganny's house and to the door.

"You can't give up," Dad mumbles. "Taylors don't quit." And his gaze sweeps up, blue-eyed and surprisingly lucid. "Taylors don't quit, son." And then his look goes hazy again, and his head bobs.

"Get the door open," I say, taking my father's weight

from Jesse.

We all have keys to Ganny's house and have since we were kids. Jesse unlocks the door, and we carry my dad inside and up the stairs to his room. We get him onto the bed, and Jesse takes off his shoes. I turn him onto his side and make sure he's comfortable. Jesse gets a bucket, just in case.

"Goodnight, Dad," I say, as we leave.

On the sidewalk, I pause and stare up at the moon. "Fuck," I mutter, then shout, "Fuck!"

"You want me to arrest you for being disorderly instead of Dad?" Jesse asks, switching off the lights on his car. The side is printed with the Sheriff's Department logo.

I don't reply.

"We've got to do something about this," Jesse says.

"What?" It bursts out of me. "What are we supposed to do?"

"I don't know," Jesse replies, a whole lot calmer than me. "But we can't spend the rest of our lives picking up the pieces of a broken man."

"He won't listen."

"Yeah. He won't. But something's got to change. Look, I'll figure it out, okay?"

"It's not your job to figure it out," I say.

"Yeah? It ain't your job either."

I shake my head. Because it is my job. The minute I left this town and started getting famous, my entire family went to shit. Everything changed. Mom got sick. She suffered for years while Dad watched her waste away, beat the disease, fall into remission again.

Jesse leans in and inhales.

"The fuck?"

"You wearing cologne?" Jesse asks.

"Fuck off."

Jesse gives me a knowing look.

"Oh, come on," I say. "Savage and I went to Longhorn's."

But the knowing look stays. "How's June?"

"Fine."

"She doing a good job as a nanny?"

"Sure."

Jesse won't quit it, and it's annoying me. We have bigger problems.

"You know," Jesse says, "you wouldn't have all this repressed rage if you'd just do what you wanted to do."

"Who says I don't?"

"So, you've told June how you feel then?" Jesse asks.

The urge to scuffle with my brother is strong, but I'm exhausted. Watching your father fade away isn't easy. I don't have the energy to argue with him tonight.

"You should tell her," Jesse says.

"What are you, a relationship guru? I don't feel anything. I can't feel anything. Feelings lead to this kind of fucked up shit." I gesture toward the house.

"I'm your brother. You're not the only one who gives a shit about this family," Jesse says. "I don't get you, Cash. You've never been afraid of taking a shot. Fuck sakes, you were signed by a music label. You're the bravest man I know."

I was afraid of caring too much and collapsing when I ultimately wound up alone again. Whether it was because of a betrayal or because of something worse. Love ended in pain, and I couldn't afford to be weak when I had a family to care for.

"She wants you," Jesse says. "A blind man can tell. She's wanted you since high school. I'm serious. You can't live your life in limbo, brother. You can't keep trying to force everything to be perfect and not allowing yourself to live until it's how you want it. Besides, if you don't ask her out soon, someone else will. Sometimes, you gotta roll with the punches." He punches my arm.

I punch him back reflexively, and Jesse grins. He points at me. "You're lucky I'm on duty or I'd whoop your ass."

"In your imagination, you would. We both know who's tapping out first."

He laughs before returning to his squad car.

I get into the pickup and drive home. I hate to admit it, but my brother might have a point. Not about the ass whooping, I'll always take him in a fight.

The house is dark when I pull up. June must be asleep.

On the way to bed, I stop in front of her door, listening hard, hoping she's still awake. It's quiet. I go to bed, consumed with thoughts of her, about what could have been tonight. Of what should be.

"HE LIKES TORTILLA CHIPS," Alex says with a stern frown. "And remember the fried pickles? He loved those."

I pull a face. "I don't know about fried pickles," I say. "Those take a lot of effort to make."

She gives me a suspicious look. "He liked them."

"Alex, honey, I hate to break it to you, but your father only ate the fried pickles because you made them. He wouldn't touch them otherwise."

"Huh." She fists her hips, looking cute as a button in a black skirt and Metallica T-shirt. This morning, she asked for my help weaving a bright purple ribbon into her hair.

"Do you have your letter?"

"Yeah." Alex produces the pen pal letter she's written for Daisy. I had her go through my letters from her father —except the one that I never sent—so that she could write one of her own. She's ready to put it into Daisy's mailbox, and she's insisting we visit Cash at Chuckles Bar for a surprise picnic afterward.

For all her rocker chaos, Alex is pretty organized. She's

a joy this morning, and packs drinks into our picnic bag while I check the spreadsheet for anything I might've missed.

"Sunscreen?" I ask.

"Check."

"Multivitamin."

"Check."

"Did you water the plants?"

"I'll do it now!" And then she rushes out of the room. I laugh under my breath at her excitement. I wish I shared it.

I'm waiting to hear back about the consultation from the college advisors. I've filled in the booking form, and I'm ready. Apart from having the money for college tuition, of course, but I'm hoping they can help advise me on that too.

This has to work out.

"Ready!" Alex reappears, grinning from ear to ear, letter in hand.

Every time I look at her, I wonder how Olivia could have abandoned her. Olivia's not the friend I used to know, who stuck up for me when times were tough or spent hours gossiping late at night in my bedroom. We lost touch after I left town, but how did she change this much? Was it the celebrity lifestyle? She pushed me into quarry when we were kids as a "prank", but looking back on it now, it was just part of a pattern of behavior I accepted. Just like with Mom. Except with her, I didn't have a choice.

"Saddle up, sailor," I say, and grab the picnic basket.

"Saddle up?" Alex asks.

"I don't know. It made more sense in my head than it does out loud."

We lock the house and descend into the heat, fanning ourselves. Unfortunately, Ol' Rusty's air conditioning is nonexistent, so we ride through town with the windows rolled down, Alex holding her hand out of the window and catching the air.

I park the car outside Daisy's house—a cottage close to the beach—and Alex runs up to the mailbox and drops the letter in, her cheeks flushed with excitement.

"Go, go, go!" she cries, and I laugh. You'd swear this was a special ops mission.

Five minutes later, we park outside Chuckles Bar, and my joy fades into anxiety. The bar has shiplap walls, window shutters that are currently closed, and a heavy wooden door that's wedged open. The steps that lead up to it are worn from years of use, and the old live oak is still beside it, a testament to the history of the place. I remember playing under that tree when we were kids.

I gnaw on my lip.

Alex gets out of Ol' Rusty and starts up the steps without me.

You can do this.

Time to put my big girl panties on.

I grab the picnic basket out of the back seat and I'm two steps into the building when I find Cash, standing near the bar, power tools discarded, grinning down at his daughter.

He's shirtless.

Cash Taylor is shirtless. His body is unreal. Planes of muscle, tattoos arcing down the right side of his chest and onto his arm. He's covered in a thin sheen of sweat that makes him even sexier, and he runs his hand through his hair as he laughs and talks to Alex.

Our eyes meet and he does a double take, his throat working.

I lose my breath.

Cash stares.

"…picnic! We brought everything," Alex says. "And fried pickles. Because I know how much you love them."

Cash looks away from me. "Fried pickles?" His expression falters and he tries to smile. "Uh, that's great!"

Alex and I burst out laughing.

"What?" He frowns. "What?"

"Come on, Dad," Alex says. "I wasn't born yesterday. I know you don't like the fried pickles we made, even though they were amazing."

Cash gives her a sheepish grin, and I go a little weak at the knees. He's got such a tough exterior that seeing him soften for his daughter is special.

"What did you actually bring for this picnic?" Cash asks.

"Oh, everything. We've got candy, cupcakes, chips, and soda."

"Anything healthy in there?" Cash asks pointedly.

"Don't worry," I say, "I made her pack fruits, veggies, hummus, and other fun healthy snacks. There isn't that much bad stuff."

"Boo!" Alex flops down in the chair.

The sound of tires crunching on the gravel outside sends Alex out of her chair. Boots stomp on the stairs, and Jesse enters the bar, handsome in his uniform.

Alex shrieks and darts toward him, and he catches her in a hug. "There she is, the little devil."

"Uncle Jesse!"

He ruffles her hair and gives her a hug. "What are you

doing here? Come to bug your old man?" Jesse meets my gaze. "Jayjay."

"Hey, Jesse."

"Glad I joined the party. Is that a picnic basket?" Jesse takes it from me.

Cash is at my side in a heartbeat. He wrests the basket out of his brother's grasp, the muscles across his chest rippling. "I'll take that."

"Uncle Jesse, did you hear?"

"Hear what?"

"I'm going to be in the summer talent show," Alex says.

Jesse claps her on the shoulder, and Alex breaks down what she wants to perform and how she's hoping Daisy will join her. It's a sweet moment.

Yet I'm aware of how close Cash is, how half-naked he is. There's a smattering of hair across his chest that makes him all man, and I have to take a step away. Swooning in front of Cash's brother and Alex would be incredibly embarrassing.

I focus on the picnic basket in his tan, strong hands instead of his blue-blue eyes or his body. "We brought enough for everyone. I wasn't sure how many people would be here. I figured your dad might be—"

"He's at Ganny's," Cash says.

"Oh."

Cash nods.

"How is he, Cash? After everything that happened? After your mom?"

Cash lets out a rough breath. "Not good. Not good at all." He sets the picnic basket down on a table. Jesse and

Alex have started playing a game of tag in the interim, and we watch them idly as we talk.

"If there's anything I can do to help—"

"You do enough already," Cash says. "You're a full-time nanny, and the stuff you've been doing with Alex. I want you to know I appreciate it."

"I'm just doing my job."

"You're going above and beyond, June," he replies. "As for Dad, we'll get there."

I chew on my bottom lip. "If anyone can fix this place up, it's you," I say. "I'll never forget when you made that rocking chair for Ganny."

"Don't remind me." He laughs, and the sound is so natural. It's good to hear him happy. "She nearly fell out of it."

"It was a great first attempt," I say. "Gosh, you were, like, how old when you made that?"

"About Alex's age."

I laugh, and he brushes his fingers over the back of his neck, giving me a sexy, shy look from underneath his brows.

"Hey," he says, "I improved. I made you that book-shelf, remember?"

"I remember. My mom didn't want it in the house at first, but we smuggled it in when she wasn't looking."

"She always hated me," Cash says.

"She hated everyone," I reply, "except for Olivia. She always had a soft spot for her." Olivia was basically my sister growing up. She spent more nights at my house than at her own. And when her parents left Heatstroke, she stayed with us. I glance over at Alex, checking she didn't overhear me. "Sorry."

Cash shakes his head. "Alex knows who her mother is, and she knows that Olivia leaving isn't a reflection on her, but on Olivia herself. It's okay to mention her. I don't keep secrets from my daughter."

Oh, my God. Take me now. "Right," I say. "Well, that's good."

The easiness of our conversation has lulled me, and I realize that I've stepped closer to Cash, or he has to me. We're so close, I can feel the heat off his body.

He's captured me with his eyes again, and I can't break the stare. I can't shake the memory of his hands on my body, us dancing at Longhorn's, how little he cared about the attention on him. How I was his only focus. Cash, the celebrity. No. Just Cash, my friend.

Alex shrieks and darts past us, closely followed by Jesse, who roars like a lion. "You better run."

"Hey," Cash barks, "be careful. There are power tools right there." He points at the bar.

Jesse rolls his eyes. "Oh, lighten up, man. We're just messing around."

I let out a breath. "Picnic time!"

That puts an end to the game of tag, and we settle down at one of the old tables in Chuckles Bar to eat.

But I don't have much of an appetite.

The longer I'm near Cash, the more difficult it is to resist him.

Twenty~Four

CASH

I GET out of the pickup into the fading sunlight. I'm tired from a long day at the bar and spent thinking about June. She's going to leave after the summer. She acts like a friend, but she wants me. I can see it in the way she moves when she's near me, the way she gravitates toward me.

I stand with my hands tucked into the front pockets of my jeans, staring up at the house that I grew up in. The one that was filled with noise and joy but was silent when I moved home. Except, now June's back and it's full of life again.

She's not yours to keep.

I want her to be mine. I want to be selfish and claim her. Protect her. But that would mean having her in my life, and that's a recipe for disaster. I'm not going to become a shell of a man when she eventually leaves.

The sounds of singing stop me on the threshold.

I don't usually play music around the house. The only music I allow is what Alex listens to—old school rock rather than country. I like to limit the chance that I'll hear something of mine on the radio.

But this isn't music from the radio.

Upstairs, the door to the main bedroom, the one I converted into a library, is ajar, and the singing drifts out of it.

Alex and June are inside, among the bookshelves, sitting on the floor rather than the comfy armchairs.

June's singing a song for Alex, one I don't recognize, but she sounds like a fucking angel.

June pauses. "So, do you get what I'm saying?"

Alex nods and then starts to sing. My throat tightens as I witness my daughter practicing. I don't want her to go through the pain I went through, but I do want her to have a love for music.

This is not part of June's job description. And this is really something I should teach my child, but I'm awestruck by how beautiful they both sound, and how gentle June is as she teaches Alex.

It reminds me of our jam sessions when we were teens. Olivia never joined in. She always claimed it was "our" thing.

I squeeze my eyes shut for a second and back away from the door. I go to my bedroom and lift my guitar off the wall. I tuned it recently, after June moved in, but I haven't played it in years.

June and Alex look up as I enter the room, and June's eyes widen at the sight of the guitar in my hand.

I settled on the floor between them and strum a few chords.

"Are you going to play while we sing, Dad?" Alex is super excited. "My dad hasn't played guitar in a long time. I think the last time was when I was like five at my birthday party."

June gives me a look that's filled with emotion. "That long, huh?"

I don't respond but play a song that's been stuck in my head for years. One that I've never written down. It's always like this when I pick up my guitar. There are chords waiting for me, a tune, and as I strum them out, words come to me.

I sing them in my mind, lifting my gaze to June's face.

Alex claps and laughs.

I keep playing, my eyes drifting closed. Music is home for me, one I gave up, and I lose myself in it, accompanied by the scent of June's perfume, by the sounds of my daughter tapping her knees in time to the song. A song that isn't a song yet.

June hums, and at this point, it's taking everything I have not to kiss this woman, consequences be damned. Fuck the end of summer. Fuck the past. She spends time with Alex, and my daughter has blossomed in the short weeks she's been here. It's like June has injected life back into our family.

I strum out the last chord of the song and rest my hands against the strings. It's been so long since I played, the fingers on my chording hand sting. It's a good feeling.

"That was awesome!" Alex says. "I want to play like that. Can you teach me to play?"

I open my eyes. "You want that?"

"Yeah!"

"Sure, I can teach you to play. But another time. You go get ready for dinner, all right? Let's go out tonight. We can hit Beach Buoys."

Alex whoops and darts out of the library, her footsteps pounding down the hall toward her room.

June sits across from me, her lips parted as if she wants to speak.

I pick the strings, watching her as she takes me in. She breaks eye contact, taking a breath and glancing off to her left.

"I got it!" Alex yells.

I get up and then hold out a hand to June. She takes it, and I help her to her feet. The touch lingers, and I finally release her hand as Alex bursts into the room, holding an envelope in one hand and a piece of paper in the other.

"June, it worked! It worked!"

"What worked?" I ask.

"The letter. The pen pal letter I put in Daisy's mailbox." Alex holds out a letter. "She replied. She said she wants to meet up and learn a song with me. She wants to sing in the talent show with me."

I sweep her up into a hug. She's going to make a friend. Life is different to what it was when we were kids, but it bugs me that she struggles to make friends, and that she spends a lot of her time at home during the summer.

I set her down, and Alex hugs June around the waist.

She hugs her back, smiling down at the top of my daughter's head. "That's amazing, Alex," June says. "I'm so excited for you guys. Did she say when she wants to meet up?"

"No, but she put her mom's number in the letter." Alex shows it to June. "Do you think you can call her, and we can meet up?"

June looks up at me. "If that's okay with your father."

"Of course," I say. "Of course." I'm not going to stop

my daughter from making friends or enjoying music, just because I've given up on both of those things.

"This is amazing!" Alex does a little jig on the spot. "We're going to be rock stars! We're going to kick butt!"

"All right," I say, "sounds like you need some food to fuel that creativity."

"Beach Buoys!" Alex cries, folding the letter carefully and tucking it back into the envelope. She hugs June again, and it's a sight sweet enough to make your teeth hurt.

I go back to my bedroom and hang my guitar up on the wall, staring at it for a second. The feeling of the strings against my fingers remains.

Twenty~Five

CASH

I PACE back and forth in my room that night. I've showered. I've tried sleeping this off. It's like I've contracted something, and this is worse than a cold.

I'm fucking wasting away because I can't have June, and I'm losing my fucking patience with it and myself.

I run my hands through my damp hair, staring at the wall that June and I share. She's just on the other side of it, doing God knows what. I heard her moving around in there a few minutes ago, and it's torturing me.

I leave my bedroom and move down the hall to Alex's room.

She's fast asleep, an angel with her eyes shut and her hand flung above her head on the pillows. Her night light is on, casting stars across the ceiling and the walls. I lift the covers to her chin, then bend and kiss her on the forehead. She gives a deep satisfied sigh, and I smile.

There. That's better.

I can think clearly again. Alex is everything to me.

I shut my eyes for a second, leveling my thoughts, and then walk past a pile of laundry Alex should have put in the basket. I step on a piece of paper and frown, glancing down at it.

Cash Taylor.

My full name is scrawled across the front of an envelope, and the letters are in that looping scrawl I recognize intimately.

June's handwriting.

But what is one of June's old letters doing here? I've kept them in my closet on the highest shelf, where Alex can't reach them.

I glance back at Alex, but she's fast asleep, and my daughter knows better than to go through my things. There's a box of old letters nearby, and I open it, peer inside. They're all addressed to June. Ah, of course, they were writing a pen pal letter to that kid, Daisy, and using the letters I sent June as an example.

But this one is addressed to me.

I bend and pick up the envelope. It's still sealed.

But it's addressed to me, right?

I tear the top of the envelope open and extract the letter. I unfold it.

> Dear Cash,
> I don't know if I'll ever send this letter. It's probably the dumbest thing I've ever done, just writing it, but I have to get the words out on paper.
> Tonight, you told me that you're dating

Olivia. I wanted to be happy for you, but I can't be. I can't be happy for either of you, and maybe that makes me a bad friend, but I can't be. I just can't be.

I've been in love with you for as long as I can remember. For as long as I knew what love might be. And now you're with her, and I can't even stand the thought of spending time with either of you. I know that's really selfish, and I'll never try to do anything.

You chose her. I have to come to terms with that. It's going to take me some time. I think it might take me forever.

I love you, Cash Taylor.

If only you could have loved me back.

June

My heart has stopped beating.

I stare at the words on the page, reading them again.

I love you, Cash Taylor.

June loved me. June loved me and she left because of it. She loved me and never told me. She loved me and never sent this letter.

And I was the idiot kid who thought she didn't care, didn't want me, never would.

How many times had I wanted to ask her out, but been too chicken shit to try? Too afraid that she'd reject me because we were friends, and I didn't want to fuck up our friendship?

The letter shakes in my hand from the pressure of my grip. I walk out of Alex's room and shut her door quietly. And then I'm down the hall and in front of June's bedroom.

Twenty-Six

JUNE

THERE'S a knock at my door. Cash.

I set my book aside, marking my place with my bookmark, check my reflection in the mirror and then go open the door.

Cash is there, holding a sheet of paper, fire burning in his eyes. "What is this?" he asks, thrusting the page toward me.

I take it from him and scan it.

My stomach drops at the words I wrote years ago. The words I didn't have the guts to say.

"What is this?" Cash repeats. "You love me?"

"Cash."

"You love me?"

"Cash."

"You loved me."

"Why are you so angry?" I drop the letter. "It doesn't matter how I felt or—"

Cash grabs the side of my face, his thumb on my chin. His grip is gentle but firm. "Answer me."

Shivers travel down my spine. "What?"

"You loved me?"

His grip tightens, his thumb pulling on my skin, tugging my bottom lip down. "The truth, June."

"Yes," I murmur. "I loved you. I wanted you. I—"

Cash grasps me by the waist and pulls me toward him. His lips meet mine, and I melt against them.

The kiss is hot and greedy. He parts my lips and takes what he wants from me, his hands running up my body to cup my breasts.

I moan against his mouth, and he breaks the kiss, pressing a finger to my lips. "Not too much noise," he says, tapping the door shut with his foot. "I haven't even started yet."

I bite down on my bottom lip. His words are too much. It's like he's caressing me with them. The letter lies forgotten on the floor.

Cash drags that finger down my lips, parting them. "Such a pretty fucking mouth."

I try my best not to whimper.

"Let's put it to good use." He tangles his fingers through my hair, pulling my head back, and then he takes my mouth again. Cash's tongue massages mine, tasting sweet.

"I've waited so long for this. I can't stay away from you anymore, June."

I look at him wide-eyed because I can't form words. How am I meant to? This is the culmination of every fantasy, the long nights spent staring at the ceiling, many of them having occurred underneath this roof.

Cash walks me backward until my back hits the wall next to the window. He nips the soft skin along my jaw, then sucks and kisses his way down my throat, pulling the flesh between his lips, his hand fisting my hair and pulling my head back to allow him access.

His other palm cups my breast through the fabric of my cotton pj top. He pinches my nipple and makes an appreciative noise against my throat.

I tremble against him.

Cash takes hold of the waistband of my shorts and pulls them down. He grunts at the feeling of the lace underwear underneath and tears them down too. His fingers slip between the folds of my pussy, and my head bangs back against the wall, a gasp escaping me. "C-Cash," I moan.

He presses his other hand over my mouth, a smile tipping the corners of his mouth upward, his gaze hazy with desire.

Cash's callused fingers sweep against my wetness, and he sucks in a breath. "So wet for me," he whispers, and then he dips a finger inside me.

I tense, a noise wrenching free of my throat, barely blocked by his palm.

"More?" he asks.

I nod frantically.

"How much more?" He presses a second finger inside. "That much?"

I whine and nod again.

"How about this?" Cash places his thumb against my clit, and I'm lost. He massages gently, in circles, keeping a perfect rhythm that sends me straight toward an orgasm. It's like he knows me without ever having touched me before.

He pumps his finger inside me then returns to that

rhythm against my clit. Cash stares into my eyes, pressing his forehead against mine, and the weight of his body, the scent of his cologne, and the feel of him inside me is the perfect cocktail.

I crash over the edge and clench around him. The noises escaping me are unearthly, but he blocks them with his palm.

It takes at least thirty seconds before I'm back to earth.

Cash releases his palm from my mouth and kisses me, capturing my mouth. I kiss him back, relishing the way he feels. I'm not sure we'll get this opportunity again.

Cash removes his finger from inside me and lifts it to his lips. He sucks my juices off his finger, and says, "I should have been your first, but that's all right, June, because I'm going to make your body forget every touch except mine."

"I—"

Cash runs a finger over my swollen pussy, and I let out another noise then clamp my mouth shut.

"I'm going to eat your pussy now, June," he says. "I'm going to punish you for bringing me to the edge like this. I shouldn't touch you, but I'm going to anyway."

I clench at the thought. It's so deliciously naughty.

"Do you want that?" he asks, grabbing hold of my chin.

He kisses me, and I move my hands over his body, tugging on the shirt that should not be on.

"I want this off," I murmur.

Cash reaches back and drags it off, exposing toned abs, the smattering of hair across his broad chest, the tattoo arcing down one muscular arm. "Like that?"

"Yeah."

"What else?" he asks.

"You."

Cash cups my breasts through my shirt then works his hands down my body. He drops to his knees in front of me, hooks one of my legs over his shoulder, and kisses the inside of my thigh.

"Such a pretty pussy," he says, and then he tugs on my lower half, angling me so he can reach all of me. "I've been dying to eat this pussy since I saw you in the diner, June."

He blows gently on my clit then places his mouth over it and sucks it. The warmth and pressure when I'm already sensitive are too much.

Cash feasts on me. He parts my pussy and pumps his tongue in and out of me then moves it back to my clit, swirling it around and moving two fingers inside me at the same time. The sounds of his mouth on me, the soft wet sucking, is so naughty I can barely keep it together.

My knees weaken, and Cash holds me upright, keeping a steady and relentless pace.

I tilt my head back, clenching around his fingers again, my back arching, my foot slipping out from underneath me.

Cash catches me with ease. He shifts me around until he's holding me in his arms then rises, his lips still wet. He carries me to the bed and throws me onto it.

The outline of his dick presses against his jeans, and he grabs it stroking up and down.

"Take off your shirt," he says.

I remove it and toss it aside.

Cash grunts, a guttural sound. "You couldn't be more perfect, June."

"I want you," I murmur.

"Where?"

What's the right answer? Everywhere. I want him everywhere.

He unzips his jeans and takes hold of his cock.

I gasp. I'm not sure it's going to fit. It's thick and long, the tip wet with pre-cum.

"Where do you want it?" Cash repeats. "Show me."

I trail my hand down my body, between my breasts, to my pussy. "Here."

THE PROBLEM PRESENTS itself as I stroke my cock, watching June touch herself.

"I don't have a condom."

June's eyes widen. "I'm on the pill. And I've never had sex without a condom before."

"Never?"

"Not once."

My head drops back and I groan. Then I would be her first. The first time she's been with a man without a barrier.

June gnaws on the corner of her lip in the sexiest way imaginable, and I want to put my dick between her lips and watch her stretch to accommodate me. Watch her gag and beg for more.

"How long has it been since you—?" June starts.

"I'm clean." I got tested after Olivia, twelve years ago, and I haven't done anything since. That's how serious I've been about not getting involved with anyone again.

June's fingers work that sore spot between her legs, the

one that has to be aching after I made her come twice. "Cash," she murmurs, "I want you."

It's all I need.

I grab her by the hips and drag her to the edge of the bed, my fingers digging into her tan flesh. June's body is amazing, soft around the hips, lithe and long, her breasts full so that they bounce when I move her.

I place my dick at her entrance, and she rises onto her elbows to watch.

"Please," she whispers.

I press the tip inside, and she whines.

"You can only have it if you keep the noise down."

"It's too good." She's panting.

"It's only the tip, June." And I press into her, parting her pussy.

She claps a hand over her mouth and falls back against the bed, her breasts bouncing, pink nipples puckered, goosebumps traveling over her skin. Her legs move either side of me.

"Come on, you can take it all. Just a little. Bit. More." I sheath myself inside her, the velvety warmth sending shots of pleasure through me. She's so fucking swollen from her orgasms, so soft and ready.

But I want to savor this moment. I want to take her and own her completely before I let her have my cum.

My cock pulses inside her, and she whines again.

"You're going to be the death of me," I say, and then I pull out of her slowly, the length of my cock glistening. It feels obscenely good when I press back inside her. She accepts all of me, and I stroke her stomach with my fingers. "Good girl."

"Cash," she whispers it past her fingers. "Oh, my God, Cash."

I brace one arm above her head, shifting my weight over her. She loops her arms around my neck and runs them through my hair, pulling lightly.

"Legs around my waist," I say. "You'd better hang on." Because I've waited a over a decade to have her, and I'm going to make this worth every cold shower, every hot night touching myself with images of her in my mind.

June wraps her legs around me and tightens her grip.

I thrust into her, and she cries out. It feels so fucking good, it's a miracle I haven't exploded yet. I press my lips to hers to silence her, kissing her and owning her completely. I set a relentless pace, pounding into her and suck her tongue gently.

June's body arches underneath mine, streaked with sweat, her pussy making delicious noises, and I'm fucking breaking myself trying not to come. But I want June to have it all, every inch of what I wished I could have given her from the start.

I pin her leg back, folding her and angling her so I can hit her G-spot. I grab the pillow above her head and give it to her.

She bites down on it, and I relish the look on her face. She's close. Her cunt is swollen and hot, tightening around my cock.

Mine.

The thought sends me into fucking spasm. I grunt and moan, breaking my own rule.

June's ass tries to lift as she meets me in an orgasm of her own, but I hold her in place, claiming her, even as her eyes roll back in her head, her jaw goes slack.

She's beautiful, powerful, even when she's lost in her climax.

My cock pulses, filling her, and I ride it out.

I hold myself inside her after I'm done, remove the pillow from her grasp and stare down at her. She's gorgeous, red patches on her skin from my beard, her body marked by our sex. I am in so much fucking trouble now that we've done this, but I can't bring myself to regret it.

She shuts her eyes, placing a palm over them instead of her mouth.

"June, look at me. Let me see your eyes."

She peeks out at me from between her fingers, and I chuckle.

"Tonight," I say, "is about what you want. Forget everything else." And then I lower myself down on top of her and kiss her again, my lips moving over her mouth to the apples of her cheeks, to her closed eyes. I pin her hands above her head again. "Tonight, you're mine."

"Yours," she repeats, and I like the way it sounds on her tongue. I like it so much that I can't wait to take her again.

I pull out of her slowly, and she gasps and then sighs. Her eyelids are heavy, and I wrap my arms around her and pull her close, leaving tomorrow's worries for future Cash.

Right now, all I want is to be with June.

Twenty~Eight

JUNE

IF I WASN'T SO sore from last night, I would've dismissed it as a wild fantasy. But I can still feel Cash between my legs, and it makes me shaky. I stand in the kitchen, my hands on the counter, staring out at the street.

We had sex two more times in the middle of the night, and I am exhausted, beyond satisfied, and completely confused. When I woke this morning, he wasn't in my bed, but my sheets smelled of him, of us, and there was a hand-written note on my bedside table.

See you tonight, gorgeous.

I can't help worrying about the future. How is any of this going to pan out when we're heading in different directions? Cash's heart is here, and I'm set on leaving. Cash doesn't want more than sex, and I'm struggling to stay disconnected already.

"Almost ready!" Alex calls down the stairs.

Daisy wants to meet up and figure out what she and Alex are going to do for their performance.

My phone buzzes in the pocket of my cut-off jeans, and I curse myself for my nervous reaction.

Two notifications pop up on my screen.

One is a text message from Cash. The other is an email from Lone Star College Counselors.

I open the text message first.

> **CASH**
> Thinking about you. Can't wait to get home and make you mine again.

> We should talk about what happened.

> After.

My pussy thrums. Such a traitor, she is. But I'm helpless when it comes to him. The memories of him inside me are so strong, they overwhelm the guilty conscience that says I'm selling myself short. Cash made it clear he doesn't want a commitment.

I open the email from the college counselors.

Hi, June.

Thank you for your email. This is Sasha, from Lone Star College Counselors, and I'm happy to say that you don't need to come all the way out to Austin for your consultation.

I'm more than happy to do an online call with you if you're available for that.

Let me know which times suit you, and we can talk.

Kind regards,

Sasha Turnbull

I can talk to them from here—that's going to save me a lot of money and open up my options. I'm hoping there's a college nearby that has rolling admissions, but afford-ability is still an issue.

"June?"

Alex is adorable in a bright purple dress with more ribbons in her hair. "Ready to go?"

"You look happy," Alex says.

I hesitate. "I just found out I can meet with a college counselor online, without having to leave."

"A college counselor?" Alex scrunches up her nose. "Aren't you…?"

"Old? I know, but lots of older people study. I want to become a teacher so—"

"No, I meant, aren't you going to stay in Heatstroke?"

I hesitate. "My plan was to stay for the summer. I love it here, especially spending time with you, but I have to start doing something with my life."

"But being my nanny is doing something." Alex folds her arms.

"I know. It's the best," I say, "but you won't need me after the summer is over."

"It's not the same." Alex takes a step forward. "I want you to stay."

"Honey." I wrap my arms around her and hug her tight, an ache starting up in my throat. "I'm not going anywhere for the next few months. And I promise when I do, I'll come back and visit." Is that really a promise I can keep?

"You swear?" Alex asks.

I gnaw on my bottom lip.

"Swear on fried pickles?"

I laugh. "Sure, I swear on fried pickles with ranch."

Alex seems satisfied by the answer. I wipe tears off her

cheeks, and she gives me a watery grin. "Congratulations, June."

"Oh, thank you. You're too sweet. But nothing exciting has happened yet. It's just a consultation call."

"It's good news, though, right?"

"Right." I'm grateful for this little sweetheart. I can't believe I'm lucky enough to know her, and it makes me even angrier that her mother chose not to be a part of her life. "Let's get to Daisy's."

We're on the way to Ol' Rusty when my mother opens her front door.

"June!" Mom's voice is a rasp.

Keys in hand, I stop on the sidewalk.

Mom stands behind her picket fence, her arms folded, her robe stained and worn. I place myself between her and Alex. "Hey, Mom, what do you need?"

"Where are you going?"

"I'm running errands," I say. "Is there something—?"

"I need you to come over right now," my mother says, in that tone I associate with punishment. Punishment if I don't do what she wants. "Dishwasher has stopped working and I need you to clean out the sludge." The unspoken words are there. "You owe me."

"Ew," Alex whispers.

"Speak when spoken to," my mother snaps at her.

"Don't talk to Alex like that," I say, shrugging the purse farther up my shoulder. "And if you need help with your dishwasher, you should probably call a technician."

My mother's jaw drops at the audacity.

And right now, after last night, I'm feeling like an audacious bitch. I walk Alex to Ol' Rusty and unlock the doors, then get inside and start the engine.

Alex turns to me, frowning. "That's your mom?"

"Yeah."

"She's kind of mean."

"A bully," I say, finally voicing it. "Remember what we talked about when it comes to them?"

"That you have to stand up to them," Alex replies.

"Yeah." And I can't afford to show Alex anything different. What kind of person will I be if I tell her one thing and do another? I don't glance in my rearview mirror as we drive off because I don't care whether my mother is angry anymore.

There are more important things than what she thinks. I put on the radio and smile as Alex bobs along to a song.

Twenty~Nine

CASH

FOR THE FIRST time since my mother got sick, I've had a good day.

I worked hard, Jesse dropped by to shoot the shit, and Dad was sober and worked alongside me. Every fucking thing fell into place today, and I'm sure it's because of June. One night with June and my world is righting itself.

I want her for longer than the summer. I want her to stay, but I have to be careful because if I screw this up, I'll hurt more than just myself, more than June.

I swore off commitment, but it's hard when it comes to her.

I park my pickup outside the house and stare up at it. Memories flood back, my hands on June's body, the way she clawed at the sheets and bit down on the pillow to stop from screaming.

I would give anything to hear her scream my name. One of these nights, Alex will be away at Ganny's and we can have the space to ourselves.

The early summer evening is quiet, broken by Joe's

dog, Ballbuster, barking down the street. Stepping inside, I'm treated to the sounds of laughter and the scent of fresh-baked cookies.

"Dad!" Alex rushes into the hall and throws her arms around my middle. She's covered in flour, and I guess I am too now.

"Hey, honey." I sweep her hair back from her forehead. She's got those purple ribbons in her hair again. "How was your day?"

"Awesome! June took me to practice our song with Daisy. We met Daisy's mom, and she invited me for a sleepover, but June says you have to meet her first because you're the dad." Alex rattles that off at high speed. "But I really want to go, Dad. Please can I go? Please?"

It's the first time she's been invited to a slumber party in a long time. Things have been difficult since she started middle school. "Did you meet her dad too?"

"No, she doesn't have one. She has two moms," Alex says. "And they're both really nice. Please, Dad."

It's like my daughter has come alive again, her blue eyes sparkling. "I don't see why it would be a problem. But yeah, let me talk to the moms first."

"Yes." Alex pumps her fist in the air like she's already won the battle, even though there wasn't one.

I go into the kitchen and find June in front of the oven, bending to peer through the window at the baking cookies. Her hair is tied back in a messy bun, and she wears cutoff jeans, a strappy top, and my oversized apron.

I want to walk up behind her and hug her, bury my face in her neck, kiss her and hold her like she's my woman.

But she's not. Yet.

"June and I are making chocolate chip cookies," Alex says.

"Is that so." I can't keep the hungry bite from my tone as I take in the nanny, standing in my kitchen, looking like a snack herself.

June starts at the sound of my voice and turns, her gaze fixing on my face. Those plush lips part, and I'm already picturing them on my cock.

I clear my throat. "Seems like we're eating a lot of sugar lately."

"We're baking them for the bake sale to raise money for the homeless shelter," June says.

I want to take her upstairs right now. "So, none for us?"

"You're not really going to deprive the bake sale of these cookies, are you, Cash?" June asks. "That's borderline evil."

"Evil? Then I guess the Cookie Monster is evil too, huh?" I arch an eyebrow.

"You said it," June replies, and grabs the mitts from the side of the oven. "But we'll save one batch for us, assuming you're okay with the sugar content."

"You make me sound like I'm the food police."

"You were the one who put the sugar rule in the spreadsheet, weren't you?" June asks, her tone teasing.

Alex looks between us. "You guys are happy," she says.

June goes stiff.

"Why wouldn't we be?" I ask my daughter. "It's summer, the house smells like cookies."

The phone rings.

"I'll get it!" Alex runs into the living room.

June brings the baking sheet out of the oven and turns

toward me. There's fear written all over her face, and it's mixed with determination.

Before she can say anything, Alex comes into the kitchen holding the cordless. "It's Daisy! She wants to talk. Can I talk upstairs?"

"Of course," I say.

She rushes off, already jabbering away, her footsteps heavy on the stairs.

June puts the next sheet of cookies in the oven and turns on the radio. She moves through the kitchen, and I'm itching to reach out.

I rise from the table and move over to her. "June."

She freezes. "Cash."

The first chord of one of my songs starts up, and I reach over and shut off the radio before it can play.

"You know, you can't just switch off the past, right? It happened, Cash. We have to live with the fact that it happened. That Olivia—"

"We need to talk," I say.

She nods, her expression sobering. "Yeah. I know. What happened last night can never happen again."

"No."

"No?"

"No." I take her hand and bring it up to my lips. I brush a kiss over the back of her knuckles. "No. It has to happen again."

June's pupils dilate, and she shivers. "Cash?"

"I want it to happen again, do you understand? June, I need it to happen again. Like you said, we're adults. We can do this without getting emotionally involved."

Footsteps rattle on the stairs, and June steps away from me, clutching her hand to her chest, wide-eyed. Alex darts into the kitchen a second later. "She asked about the slumber party, Dad. She asked if I can go this weekend."

"I'll drop by and talk to her moms tomorrow."

Alex claps while June turns away, facing an empty cookie sheet. She starts doling out dough, and Alex joins her.

"Do you want to help, Dad?" Alex asks.

"Let me wash up, and then I'll be right down."

Because right now, I can't think of a better way to spend my early evening other than with Alex and June.

Thirty

JUNE

I STAND at the window in my bedroom, phone in hand, staring out at the backyard and the side of my mother's house, the moon high overhead.

I promised myself I would leave this town in my dust, but one night with him and it's like I'm ready to throw it all away. I've got that consultation coming up with the counselors, and now I'm torn between excitement and regret.

When I leave, I'll be leaving Alex and Cash. If I don't finally get my teaching certificate, I'll despise myself for it.

Getting way ahead of yourself.

"Ugh."

I abandon the window and flop down on the bed, but that's not any better. It smells like Cash, and I'm instantly hot all over.

A text blips through on my phone, and I peer at the screen.

> **MARCI**
> Can't wait for the hike this Saturday! Get keen, girls!

> **HANNAH**
> I was born ready for this.

> **BELLE**
> I didn't bring sneakers. Do I have to buy a pair?

> **MARCI**
> Unless you want to go hiking in your Louboutins, city girl.

I love the group chat we've got going on. The girls added me to it after the night at Longhorn's and, to their credit, they haven't asked me about Cash too much. I think mostly because Hannah's in the group and it would be super awkward.

I'm about to shoot off a text when another message comes through, but it's not from the girls.

An unknown number.

> **UNKNOWN**
> Hey, June! How are you? I've been thinking about you a lot lately, and I thought we should catch up. I know it's been forever but it's about time, right?

> Who is this?

Three dots appear on the screen and then disappear, but the soft swish of a letter being pushed underneath my door distracts me and I go pick it up.

My name is scrawled across the front in Cash's handwriting, and my heart palpitates as I open it.

June,
I can't stop thinking about you. I don't want things to go back to the way they were.
I don't think they can.
Cash
P.S. I left something in the hall for you.

I open the door and lose my breath.

Cash is shirtless in the hall, one muscular tan arm up, resting against the door jamb. His hair is wet and curly, and that blue-eyed stare consumes me.

"Cash."

"I write you a love letter and all you can say is my name?" he asks, his lips parting into a heartbreaking smile. "Again."

"Huh?" I can barely function.

"Say it again."

"Cash," I say.

"May I come in?" he asks gruffly.

I step back to admit him, and he stalks into the room, taking up all the space and air.

I shut the door, even though I know that's looking for trouble. Being alone with him is difficult. "You said you don't want to stop."

"That's right." He leans against my desk, arms folded, and considers me. "I don't want to stop."

"Why?"

"Because I want you, June," he says.

I've waited so long to hear those words. "I want you too, but I'm not going to get my heart trampled again, and you're not interested in anything serious. And Olivia—"

"What has she got to do with anything?"

I let out a breath. "Oh, come on. Come on, Cash."

He tilts his head, spearing me with those deep blue eyes.

"You were engaged. You have a child together. You chose Olivia. Look," I say, "look, this is already complicated, but the fact that you're Olivia's ex is just another level of fucked up."

"She's not in Alex's life. She's not in yours or mine. Don't see why it's a problem."

"Because."

"Say it. Say what you want to say, June. Don't hold back because of someone else's feelings."

I swallow. "Because it's just weird. You and Olivia shared something deep, and you're not prepared to do that again. I'm not prepared to stick around in this town, not when my mother is living right next door, and even saying that is getting ahead of myself. I'm not sure I can be with you and not get emotional."

Cash pushes off the desk and crosses the distance between us. He takes me by the arms, stroking his thumbs over my skin, and making sure I look him in the eyes. "I wanted you first."

I shake my head. "Cash, you were the one who told me you were dating her, remember? That night? On the bleachers after the game? I'll never forget it because it felt like someone had driven a red-hot poker through my chest."

Cash presses a palm to my cheek, and I lean into his touch, hating myself for it. "Olivia told me that you were in love with someone else."

"What? Wait, what?"

"Told me that you were in love with Jason, that asshole who graduated a year ahead of us, and not interested in me. That was a month before we started dating. I was a stupid high school kid. I should've grown a pair of balls and come after you regardless of who you might have had a crush on. But I wanted you to be happy, and Olivia said you were happy. You seemed happy."

"Olivia told you I was in love with Jason?"

"Yeah."

"Olivia knew how much I liked you, Cash," I say. "She knew. And she came to me before you two started dating and told me that you wanted her. She asked me if I was okay with it, and I told her yes, because I wanted you two to be happy. Because you were my friends."

His expression darkens.

"I wasn't dating anyone," I say. "You knew that. We were inseparable, the three of us. Did you ever see me with Jason? The whole reason I left Heatstroke was because I couldn't handle seeing you two together. My mother certainly didn't help matters. So I left and started my own life."

And that was when I had started working at the Achin' Bacon, where I met Braydon.

Following the trail backward in time made me sick to my stomach.

I would never have believed Olivia was capable of this back in the day, maybe because I thought the best of everyone, naively, but now that she had abandoned her daughter. Cheated on Cash.

"But none of that actually matters. You want me." I pull out of his grip in what is the most difficult movement I've ever made. I like Cash's hands on my body. "You want me, and I want you, but for you, it's just a sexual, passionate thing that's happening. For me, it's always been more, and I cannot risk falling in love with you again." It's already too late. It's happening, and I need to get away.

"It's not just sexual," he says, running a hand over the back of his head. "June, it is not just sexual."

"How can that be possible? How am I supposed to believe that after you blatantly told me you don't want a commitment."

"You were right earlier. We can't ignore it. Can't switch it off or make it go away. But goddamn if I won't spend every waking moment trying to make it right."

He takes me by the back of my neck and gently pulls me toward him, wrapping an arm around my waist. "I don't know what this is, but I know I don't want it to stop. I know it's not just a physical thing. I'm willing to find out what's going on if you are."

I want to present a strong front, pretend to be in my right mind, but it's so damn hard with him this close.

Cash Taylor has me in the palm of his calloused hand.

He presses his lips to mine and parts them, his kiss hungry. I meet him with the same desperation, my hands tugging on his shirt. In this moment, all I want is to believe what he's said, even though there's a small insistent voice in my head screaming to be careful, that this is too good to be true, that the last time I trusted a man, I wound up destitute and a fool.

Cash lifts me, and I wrap my arms around his waist. He walks me backward and sits me on top of the desk, his mouth hot against mine. "What do you want, June?"

Thirty~One

CASH

I'M GOING to prove how I feel, how much I have always wanted her, with every kiss, touch, and taste. By the end of tonight, June is going to be a quivering mess. I'll erase the doubts from her mind, and if it doesn't work, there's always tomorrow and the next day, and every day until the end of summer.

I tear her shirt down, and her full tan breasts are free. My cock throbs, and I picture running it between her tits and fucking them.

I press her breasts together and suck both her nipples into my mouth, grazing them with my teeth, then sucking hungrily.

June plasters a hand over her mouth and cries out.

I release her, focusing my attention on one nipple, biting gently then tickling her with my breath, my tongue, my other hand sliding down to the button on her cutoff shorts.

"I've been thinking of pulling these down and fucking

you over the kitchen counter all evening," I say, around a mouthful of her breast.

June gasps as I undo the top button and unzip the shorts. I move my hand over her neatly shaven pussy and slip my finger between her lips.

"So wet for me already," I murmur.

June's hand is still covering her mouth, and it's probably a good thing, because I'm about to make her scream.

I nip her breast then plunge one finger inside her. She kicks, arches her back, her eyes roll in her head.

"That's it," I say, "show me how much you want it."

June reaches between us and grabs the front of my jeans, her hand finding the outline of my cock.

I throb and tense. "Keep doing that and I'm going to bend you over this desk anyway."

"I want it," she whispers. "I want it."

I'll always give June what she wants. I pull her off the table and stand her up then strip her jeans down to her ankles. Her panties are next. They're already a sodden mess.

I turn June and force her down on the desk, putting that peachy ass on display. I have the perfect view, her parted ass cheeks, her wet, pink pussy, and her cute little asshole. I want all of it, and I bend behind her, sucking her lips, working my finger over her clit, and pushing my tongue inside her, lapping up every drop.

June clings to the desk, moaning as softly as she can.

I slap her ass gently. "Quiet."

She shifts to cover her mouth, her legs trembling so much I have to place both palms on her ass and hold her still.

I feast on her, setting a rhythm that brings the best response from her body.

June shatters underneath me, her pussy clenching my tongue, and her cries are muffled by her hands.

"Good," I whisper. "That's good. You keep coming for me like that. It's all I want. Now, hold still."

"I want it," she murmurs again, a hint of impatience in her voice. "Cash. I want you."

"Which part of me?" I ask, holding the tip of my dick at her entrance. It's torture for me to hold back as much as it is for her, but I want to hear it from her. I want to hear how much she wants it.

"You."

"Say it, June. Say you want my cock."

"I want your cock," she murmurs.

I press my head inside her, taking her inch by inch and thoroughly enjoying her reaction to my girth. Her pussy is just as velvety soft as last night. Fuck, it feels even better.

June presses backward, hungry for me, and I chuckle and smack her ass again. I spit on that cute little asshole and rest my thumb there, massaging her gently as I pound her sweet cunt.

"Do you want it?" I ask, applying a little pressure with my thumb.

"Yes," she hisses. "Yes."

Gently, I press my thumb inside her, and she cries out.

I halt. "Good?"

"So good. So good."

"You're not hurting?"

"No," she whines. "Please, Cash, please."

"Keep it down," I say with a grunt, and then I set a pace that silences her. I bring my other hand around her hips and find her clit, massaging the already sensitive button again. I'm driven to give this woman as much pleasure as possible. I want June to forget everything but us. No more worries. No more heartbreak. Just my dick inside her, my hands on her body, banishing all negative thoughts.

Her pussy tightens around my length, and I keep my thrusts even, changing nothing about the way we move together, until she bites down on her palm to keep from screaming.

"Easy," I say, "don't hurt yourself."

She's left a little red mark on her hand, and my cock grows harder at the implication.

"It's too good," she whispers. "Cash, it's too good."

"You can take it." I thrust into her, driving myself home and watching as her skin reddens, her eyes go wide, and she turns her head to watch me over her shoulder. It's the most beautiful thing I've ever seen.

I claim her again, coming so hard, I'm the one who moans, and she rises to meet me, bending so that she can take it all. I hold myself inside her for a minute, then pull out, moaning at the sensation. "You're unbelievable."

June is spent, draped across the desk, dripping. I lift her carefully, then walk her into the en suite bathroom so we can clean up. She rests her head against my shoulder, and it's the perfect moment.

Thirty-Two

JUNE

I WAKE up in the darkness, moonlight illuminating the room, my body aching from Cash's touch. I shift against him. He's behind me, one arm underneath my neck, the other looped over my waist. I don't want to move in case it wakes him.

I don't want to think about what's going to happen when I leave, or how this will affect Alex, or what my plans for the future are.

I have to be realistic.

But Cash is offering me more than just sex, but I'm not sure he even wants that, not deep down. There's so much he's holding back because of what happened with Olivia, with his mother passing, that I don't know if he's equipped to handle more than sex.

"I've been waiting for you to wake up," Cash murmurs in my ear, his breath soft against my neck. He trails his fingers up my naked body and cups my breast. "You're too tense, June. Let me help you relax."

I melt at the sound of his voice, pressing myself backward into him.

With Braydon, we never really had the ripped sheets portion of our relationship. My ex was more concerned about what he could get out of sex, rather than how we felt afterward, and even though it was wrong, I wanted to be the best girlfriend.

Braydon wanted to dress me up like a doll and wheel me out. I think a sick part of him liked that he'd "saved me" from my country-girl lifestyle.

But Cash is different. His hand massages my breast then works its way up my chest to my throat. He moves up to my chin, turns my head.

"I can't stand to see you upset," he says.

Cash kisses the corner of my mouth, and I reach back and grasp a handful of hair at the base of his neck. He makes a deeply satisfied noise. "I love it when you touch me."

I want to thank him for how he's made me feel the past few days. For how protective and kind he's been. I turn over and kiss him full on the mouth, hoping to show him how happy he makes me. Cash kisses me back, soft and hot.

Slowly, I work my hands down his bare chest, to his cock, already hard for me. I grasp his shaft in my hand, and he throbs. "You can't touch me like this. I'm going to lose control again."

I bite down on my lip, staring up into his eyes. I don't want to talk. I'm afraid of what I'll say, so I kiss his neck, then the crest of his chest, right over those delicious tattoos, and work my way down his torso.

He catches my forearms. "June," he says, "you don't have to do that."

"I want to." Because I'm that bitch. I want to give him pleasure. I want to know that I'm the one who makes him lose his mind. I want to give him what he's given me.

Cash releases me, and I move down his body. He's so thick, I'm not sure how I'm going to fit him in my mouth.

His gaze is fixed on me, trusting, longing.

I encircle his head with my lips, and he grunts.

I suck on him, working my mouth over his head, and then taking as much of him as I can until I gag.

"Yesss. Fuck, that's so good," he says, fisting a handful of my hair.

I work his shaft with my mouth and hand, striking a pace that has him moaning softly. "That's it, June. I can't —" He cuts off, breathless. "I can't." He places both hands on my head and helps me set the pace, bringing his dick to the back of my throat. It's forceful and so sexy I'm already wet for him.

He fucks my mouth, and I reach between my legs to play with myself, unable to take it any longer.

Immediately, Cash stops. He drags me up his body, spins me around, and sucks my clit into his mouth.

I cry out softly.

"Put my cock in your mouth," Cash says. "Suck it to stop from screaming."

I do as he says, and it muffles the moans. Because I can't not make a noise when he's lavishing my pussy with such focused attention. It's like Cash is on a mission to make me come. Like he takes pride in it, and that thought makes me lose it.

I try my best to focus on giving him what he wants as he does the same to me.

Cash fucks me with his tongue, pulling me backward so he can reach my clit. He slaps my ass lazily, the pain sending a corresponding shock of pleasure through my core, and I jerk in his arms.

He brings me under control, holding me tight, pumping two fingers inside me in a measured rhythm, his tongue pressuring and circling my clit.

I suck and whine, rocking back and forth against him, my peak approaching fast.

"Cash," I moan, my lips pressing against his tip.

"Suck, June. You're so good at it."

I suck him into my mouth as an orgasm washes over me, and my body tenses against him.

"Yes, that's it. That's it."

Cash doesn't stop until I'm done. And then, he blows on my pussy gently.

I keep sucking, eager to give him what he's given me, but he doesn't give me a break. He sets to work on me again, licking then taking me in his mouth.

The pace becomes frantic. He presses three fingers into me, finding my G-spot and working that at the same time as he works my clit.

"Yes, June. Fuck," he says. "Fuck, I'm going to come."

My orgasm arrives, and at the last second before he comes, Cash turns me around and seats me on his length. He holds me down, his fingers biting into my thighs, thrusting through our shared climax. I cover my mouth at the sensation, the pulsing, the way I can feel every ridge, every vein, and ride through it with him.

Afterward, Cash lets out a breath. "I'm addicted to you, June. I've got to come inside you every time now." He brings me to his chest and holds me there.

I drift off, thoroughly satisfied, with Cash still inside me.

"YOU'RE sure you don't mind dropping her off?" I ask from the kitchen doorway.

Cash leans against the counter, studying me with a gaze that makes me hot all over. For the past three nights, he's been in my room. We're both a little sore from it, but I'm already tingly from a single look. It's so bad, and so good, and utterly messed up.

"June," Cash says, in that low sexy voice that takes me back to last night, "it's your day off. And I'm not working at the bar today. Stop worrying."

Alex is going to spend the night at Daisy's house. She's super excited, upstairs getting ready, and I'm so happy for her. Daisy is a great kid, and Alex needs a good friend. Quality over quantity, right?

"All right," I say, at last, "I just don't want to—"

Cash crosses the kitchen, takes me in his arms, and kisses me.

I stiffen then melt against him before pushing back.

"Hey," I whisper, pressing my fingers to my mouth, "we can't do that. She could see."

He scrapes his hand over the back of his neck. "You're looking so cute in your hiking gear I couldn't resist."

"Well, you'd better try," I say, and wink. I turn around, wiggle my ass at him for good measure.

"Watch it!" he shouts. "You'll take someone's eye out with that thing."

I guffaw in what has to be the least sexiest way ever, and Cash laughs from the kitchen.

I'm meeting Marci at the quarry for our hike. "Bye, Alex," I call up the stairs. "Have fun today!"

Before I can leave, Alex comes darting down the stairs. "Bye, June," she says. "I miss you already."

"I can't wait to hear all about it when you get back," I say. "I'm so excited."

She smiles. "Me too."

"Are you okay? You look a little pale."

"I'm fine," she says. "I'm just excited. And I've got a headache."

"Headache?" Cash appears, the picture of a concerned dad, which only serves to make him even sexier. Damn man.

Alex goes over to her father, and I leave them alone, waving a quick goodbye as I leave.

The drive to the quarry is filled with a mishmash of thoughts. I'm yo-yoing between wanting Cash and wanting to run away before I wind up with a broken heart again.

Cash gives me mixed messages. First tells me he doesn't want a relationship, then I'm his.

Marci meets me at the base of the hill that winds up to

Diver's Point, wearing a sensible pair of hiking boots, shorts, and a bikini top, her red hair tied up in a high ponytail. "You," She narrows her eyes. "Have had sex."

"Marce!"

"It's like a sixth sense I have," she says, circling a finger toward her face. "I can always tell when someone's been getting the good-good. And you, ma'am, have been receiving the best of the best."

"Would you keep your voice down?" I grab her arm, guiding her up the path a few steps. "Someone might hear."

"Relax," Marci says with a mischievous grin. "Belle and Hannah aren't here yet. Besides, the trail's pretty quiet today. So?"

"So?"

"Tell me all about it."

"I have no idea what you're talking about," I say, lifting my nose in the air.

"Oh, don't you give me that, June Jackson. You're all colors of satisfied, and I deserve to know the juicy details," Marci says. "Believe it or not, I'm invested in your relationship with Cash. You have no idea how frustrating it's been to watch you two from afar, both of you as blind as the other when it comes to love."

"Gee, thanks. And it's not love."

"Don't change the subject."

"I didn't."

"Well?"

I check the coast is clear and then lean in. "We might have done some things."

Marci lets out an excited squeal and claps her hands.

"Yes! I knew it. I so knew it. You two are meant to be. I told you so. Didn't I tell you so?"

"Hmm."

"I can't believe it," Marci says. "Actually, I can. You know, they say a stopped clock is right twice a day? Well, this clock is ticking baby, and I am right all the damn time."

"And so humble too."

Marci pops a hip and waggles her eyebrows at me, shifting her sunglasses down her button nose. "Who needs humble when you can be fabulously correct all the time?"

A car rolls up and parks, cutting our conversation short and sparing me from sharing the details. I'm not sure I can talk about it without blushing, and I'm not ready for Marci to ask me for sizes, positions, and satisfaction levels—as is her way.

Belle and Hannah emerge from Hannah's cute Chevy, Belle wearing a pair of sneakers she claims are the best she could do on short notice, and Hannah practical with full hiking gear, and a backpack she's loaded with enough water and snacks for a three-day trip.

"Is that a sleeping bag?" Marci asks, poking the roll at the top of Hannah's pack.

"You never know," Hannah replies sagely.

"Never know what?" Marci frowns. "Whether we'll be stranded a couple feet from the cars? Diver's Point isn't that far."

"Rather have it and not need it than need it and not have it," Hannah says.

"Like a condom," Belle adds.

I choke on my sip of water, ejecting a little down my front.

"The wet T-shirt contest is starting early this year, woo-hoo!" Marci does a little shake of her shoulders. That bikini top is hanging on by a thread, but she makes it work.

"You're insufferable," Hannah says.

"All right, you fabulous bitches," Marci says. "Let's get this shit show on the road. To Diver's Point!"

"Huzzah!" Belle cries.

I laugh and fall in beside them. We chat as we head up the hill, the trees casting dappled light over the path, and the summer heat building beneath the canopy as it grows dense. Our chatter fades as the path inclines, and Belle and Hannah fall behind—mostly because Belle is struggling.

Marci and I walk a little ahead.

"So?" Marci whispers.

I glance back at the girls. Belle is red-cheeked and seated on a rock beside the path, complaining to Hannah, who's lending a sympathetic, albeit sweaty ear.

"I don't know if there's anything to talk about."

"June, this was meant to be. The two of you should have happened years ago. Olivia just kind of got in the way," Marci says.

I'm confident the other two can't hear us, but I hesitate anyway.

"Why are you holding back?"

"Because I've spent the last, what, fifteen years with a man who put his needs first?" I suggest. "Even if Cash and I are "meant to be" which I don't even know if that's true, but even if we are, what am I supposed to do now, Marce? Give up on all my plans? I have a meeting with the counselor tomorrow, and then I'm going to start applying to colleges. And there's Alex to consider. If we decide to be together, how is she going to take it?"

"She loves you."

"She loves me as her nanny," I say. "That doesn't mean she'll love me as her dad's girlfriend. He's never dated before. She has no frame of reference. It wouldn't be right to put her through something and then leave. And I've said from the start that Heatstroke is a stop. I'm not going to spend the year here. I want to study."

"Yeah, but you want to study teaching."

"Correct."

"And then what?"

"I want to settle down," I say, "and teach in a small, cozy town."

"Like Heatstroke."

I brush my hand over my head. "There's more to it than that. Olivia. My mother. Alex. Cash blatantly told me he's not going to get into a long-term relationship again."

"Yeah, but that's just the pain talking. You saw how his dad collapsed after his mom died. The man is hurting. He's confused. Ugh, you're so responsible," Marci says, ruefully. "You've got to let that kitty out of the cage."

"I think it's fair to say that letting the kitty out of the cage is exactly what landed me in this predicament."

Marci gives me a devilish grin. "Touché." She pauses, wriggling her nose. "I guess it's fine not to know right now. Maybe the summer will change your mind."

The girls start walking again, and Marc and I take the lead up the hill.

"What about you and Jesse?" I ask.

"Huh?" Marci looks at me, wide-eyed. "Me and who?"

"Oh, come on."

"You cannot be referring to Jesse Taylor," Marci says. "Because Jesse Taylor, is the most insufferable human being to ever have walked this earth."

"Hmm. I don't buy it."

Marci rolls her eyes.

"You two have chemistry."

"Yeah, and you know what else happens in chemistry? Explosions. Big ones," Marci says.

"Marciiii."

She shrugs.

We trek to the top of the hill.

Finally, we reach Diver's Point overlooking the quarry. It's not too high up, but it's high enough to be scary for me after all these years. I dismiss the memory and move toward the lookout point. The wood on the decking is creaky, and there's a guardrail that's seen better days. The quarry is as beautiful as ever, the water a deep blue, the reflection of the clouds overhead scudding across the surface.

"We made it!" Marci sings.

Belle glares at her, sweat-streaked. "Made it? Made it. Made it to where? We still have to walk all the way back down that thing!"

"If you need a nap." Hannah removes her backpack and pats the sleeping roll on top. "You know where to find me."

"I'm going to throw you and that backpack off this cliff."

"Picture time!" Marci cries.

The girls gather round, and we squish in and hold up peace signs and make pouty faces for Marci's cellphone camera. Or, Hannah, Marci, and I do. City girl Belle glares, but she still looks cute.

"One more, one more."

I lean back against the wooden guardrail, grinning.

Marci tells us, "Say—"

There's a cracking noise that sends panic shooting through my veins. One second I'm upright, staring at our reflection in her cellphone, and the next I'm looking up at that beautiful blue sky, and then I tumble and I'm looking at the water. Wind rushes past me, and my stomach whoops as I plummet.

I scream, but the air is knocked out of me as I hit the surface. Water rushes up my nose and down my throat, and I choke. I try to kick, but my limbs refuse to work properly.

No!

The memories come flooding back. The sound of Olivia laughing. The ice-cold water. And I'm struggling to kick my way to the surface.

Warm arms wrap around my waist, and I'm dragged upward. I break the surface, spluttering, coughing up water.

"It's okay. You're okay." Cash's voice, warm and deep. His strong arms encircle me, protecting me from the water. He turns me around and his blue eyes banish the sky and the fear. "Can you breathe?"

I nod, and try to say something, but it only makes me cough more. My lungs and throat are burning.

And Cash is here. Cash saved me.

Thirty~Four

CASH

I HOLD June close to my chest, swiping her soaked hair back from her face and checking her. When I saw her fall from Diver's Point, I didn't hesitate. June's not great with water, and the way she screamed sent adrenaline through me.

"It's okay," I say, "you're good. Are you good?"

Finally, her coughing stops, and she meets my gaze with those beautiful green eyes. "Yeah," she says at last. "I —where did you come from?"

I'm treading water, holding her upright. The only thing I did before diving in was kick off my shoes.

"Jesse wanted to come out here for a swim. I didn't realize you were hiking here."

"Well, I wasn't hiking here exactly." She points at the water, giving me a small smile.

I laugh. "Glad to see the fall didn't knock your sense of humor."

"I don't think it knocked anything," she replies. "I just got a shock."

"Still going to make you go to the hospital."

"Seriously, I'm fine." She glances up at Diver's Point. The girls are up there, as well as a few other townsfolk and tourists, all staring down at us. June acts as if she wants to swim back to shore, but she makes it about two strokes before she starts sinking again.

I grab hold of her and bring her to the surface.

June coughs and blinks. "Guess swimming isn't my strong suit."

"Good thing you didn't come to the quarry to swim, right?"

I want to kiss her right here, right now, and I'm considering it seriously. I tuck her against my chest, my hands moving under the water to her ass. I squeeze gently, and June gasps. "Cash."

"No one can see."

I trail my fingers under the crease between her thighs and ass cheeks, so tempted by her, I can barely think straight.

A shrill whistle interrupts my progress toward her pussy.

I glance toward the shore and spot my brother standing there. He waves, holding up my phone.

What now?

June pulls a face. "I don't know if I can swim."

"On my back. Arms around my neck."

"I—what?"

I turn around and fix her arms on me. "Hold tight," I murmur.

June's breasts are pressed against my back. I want her as mine. I want everyone to know that June belongs with me, but I'm not sure I can take the pain of losing her when it happens. Because it's always going to happen. Love is pain. I swim back to the shore, and she lets go when her feet touch the silt underneath us.

I help her out of the water, and she looks good enough to eat, her shirt wet, her nipples plucking at the fabric. I stand in front of her to shield her from Jesse's eyes and take the phone from him with a questioning look.

"It's Daisy's mom, Sara."

"Sara?" I answer quickly.

"Cash." Sara sounds stressed. "Cash, I'm sorry to call you like this. I know you just dropped Alex off, but she's crying and asking after you. I don't know what happened, I—"

"I'll be there in ten minutes," I say, and hang up. I turn to June. "Alex is upset. I'm going to pick her up."

"Do you need me to come with you?" June asks, placing a hand on my forearm.

I want to say yes, but this is my daughter, and it's June's day off. "I've got it."

"Are you sure?"

I nod.

"Do you know what the problem is? Is Alex okay?" Jesse asks.

"Going to find out." Adrenaline is already pumping through my veins. If someone hurt my daughter, I'll tear them limb from limb.

June walks with me until we reach the start of the trail to Diver's Point. Marci rushes over, wide-eyed.

I grab June by the arm and turn her toward me. "Stay safe, June."

"She'll be fine," Marci starts, "she's a grown—"

I fix my stare on her and she gives a little squeak, her cheeks pinking. "She better be fine," I say.

"Cash," June says. "Relax."

I want to kiss her, but I resist, settling for a quick touch of my palm to her cheek. "See you at home." And then I charge off toward my pickup. I make it to Daisy's house in under five minutes, and I'm sure Jesse would've cited my ass for it, but I don't care.

Sara opens the door the minute I pull up, and Alex comes out, her cheeks streaked with tears.

I run up to her and hold her close. "What's wrong, honey?"

Alex shakes her head, biting her lip.

"You want to talk in the truck?"

She nods.

I thank Sara, and she asks that I update her. I'm sure Daisy's bummed that Alex can't stay over, but I don't see the girl. I walk my sweetheart to the truck and sit her inside, then get in and start the engine. We drive off a little and park down the street, so she doesn't feel like her friend's watching out the front windows of her house.

"What happened, Alex?" I ask. "Did Daisy do something? Was she mean to you?"

"I want June."

That's a gut punch. Not because I'm jealous that Alex wants June, but because June is going to leave at the end of summer, and what happens when Alex wants her then? "I know, honey," I say, "but June's got the day off, so you'll have to settle for me."

"It's not like that, Dad. It's just a girl thing."

"A girl thing?" I'm praying that Daisy wasn't mean to Alex. She's finally got a friend and— "A girl thing." The lightbulb clicks on in my brain. "Honey, is it the kind of girl thing that needs sanitary pads?" She can't already be that old, can she?

Alex's bottom lip wobbles, and she nods.

I let out a breath. "All right. We can deal with that. You know what, I'm going to get you what you need from the store, and you can just wait in the truck. Sound good?"

My daughter nods.

"Are you in pain?"

Another nod.

"I'll get you some Advil and a heating pad." I remember what Olivia was like during her time of the month, and she had it pretty bad. She needed attention, care, warmth, painkillers, and cookies.

I start the car and we drive down the street.

"Don't worry, honey." I'm not sure what else to say or what she needs to hear, but she seems satisfied by what I've done so far.

I park the pickup outside the General Store, leave it running and the AC on, then jump out to get her what she needs. I grab a cart and load it up with supplies—cookies, chocolate, tampons, sanitary pads of every kind—I have no idea what's the difference between the thick ones and thin ones, but getting extra can't hurt. By the time I arrive at the front desk, my cart is nearly overflowing.

Lucille, who's worked the checkout line at Roger's for a decade, gives me a sage look. "It's that time already?"

"Seems like it."

"They grow up too fast, don't they?"

My throat tightens. I pay for everything, bag it myself, and rush out. Alex is in the car, grimacing and bending over a little.

"We'll be home in a minute."

I drive as slow as I can so as not to hurt her. I get her into bed, then give her all the stuff. Alex looks a little lost.

"There are instructions on the packages," I say.

Tears well up.

"I'll call June."

Thirty-Five

JUNE

I WAKE up to soft kisses on my shoulder and neck. Sunlight streams through the gap between my curtains, and my pulse ticks up a notch at the sensation of Cash's beard grazing my skin.

Yesterday feels like a fever dream. Him diving into the water to save me, his call for help with Alex, the afternoon spent helping her with the new phase of her life and providing support, and then bedtime. Bedtime with Cash.

My skin tingles at the memory.

I keep my eyes closed, enjoying the attention. His palm glides down the side of my body. "The things I would do for you," he murmurs softly.

He kisses me on the cheek then carefully gets off the bed, quiet because he doesn't want to wake me.

I spy on him through the cracks in my eyelids, admiring his body, tan and muscular, the tattoos down one arm. His gaze flickers toward me, and a smile twists the corners of his lips. "You'll get a better view if you open your eyes all the way."

I blush furiously then glare at him. "You're not supposed to know I'm awake."

"You're a terrible actress," he says, and comes over, buttoning up his jeans he'd worn the night before. "But everything else? Zero complaints."

Butterflies tumble in my belly. He braces one arm on the bed and bends to kiss my forehead, the scent of him filling the space between us.

I have my consultation today. Cash has work at the bar. Alex will need a nanny and extra care today.

"See you tonight." Cash's voice is a deep, comforting grumble. He lingers as if he wishes he could stay, and then he finally leaves the room, the door clicking shut gently behind him.

I am so screwed.

The longer I spend with him, with Alex, the more I feel for both of them. I'm falling in love with this precious little family, with Cash, and I don't know what to do about it or how to feel about it.

And with the upcoming consultation, my nerves are through the roof. I've spent most of my life doing what other people want, and now I have the opportunity to be selfish.

"Enough," I mutter, and get out of bed.

I spend the next hour getting the kitchen clean, and the breakfast made, then check on Alex. She's in the throes of the dreaded second day of her period, but she smiles from ear to ear when I bring her pancakes with a side of bacon in bed.

Cooking is my comfort zone, mostly because I was the one who did most of it growing up, and watching Alex devour the pancakes brings me so much joy.

"June," Alex says between chews.

"Yeah?"

She finishes her bite and crinkles her nose. "Do you think Daisy's going to be mad at me for yesterday?"

"No way. If she's a true friend, she'll understand that you were going through something. Heck, she's probably going to go through it soon too."

"You think?"

"Yeah. She's going to hit puberty too. It's a rite of passage," I say. "A really sucky one."

Alex nods. "I didn't think it would hurt like that."

"I know," I say, "but there are ways to deal with it. And if it's ever too sore, you can talk to a doctor about that as well. But yeah, it hurts, and I guarantee you that most women and girls hate it just as much as you do. We're riding the red tide of anger and pain together."

Alex giggles and eats more of her pancakes.

I switch on her stereo and let her listen to music while I start cleaning up the house. I'm sure Cash added something to the Excel spreadsheet, and I have, like, thirty minutes until my meeting with Lone Star, so I rush to grab my phone.

I'm just about to check the sheet when my phone rings.

An unknown number.

It can't be Braydon, right? Surely, he's gotten the damn picture by now.

I answer the phone, ready to tell him where to shove his opinions about me and his phone for that matter. "Hello?"

Silence.

"Hello?" I repeat.

"June? Is that you?" The voice is soft, feminine, familiar.

"Uh, yeah. Who is this and how may I help?" Maybe it's someone from Lone Star calling to reschedule? Or, oh God, what if they decided to start the interview early? Did they email me, and I didn't see it?

"June, it's Olivia."

The world slows around me. My gaze moves around the interior of the room, the same room where I spent the night with Cash, and I let out a breath.

I move to the bed and sit down, the phone to my ear, speechless.

"June? Helloooo, are you there?" Olivia's tone is singsong. A forced happiness.

"Olivia," I say, scarcely comprehending that I'm saying her name. Olivia who abandoned her child. Who lied to Cash about my feelings, who went behind my back and literally impacted the course of my future by doing so.

"It's been so long," Olivia says. "I just wanted to call and check in on you."

She wants to check in now?

"June?"

"Yeah, sorry," I say, "but I'm a little shocked by the call. I haven't heard from you in years. How did you even get my number?" Olivia never wanted to write to me, and she didn't try to keep in contact by phone, email, social media, or anything else. She never replied. It was like the minute I left Heatstroke, I ceased to exist, even though she spent most of her high school years living with Mom and me.

The pain of losing a person I thought was my friend mingles in with all the other emotions, and I have to take a breath.

"Do you need something?"

"Like I said," she says, in that happy-go-lucky tone, "I just wanted to talk."

"About?"

"Well, you know, I didn't want to lose touch with you all those years ago," she says, "but it is what it is. I guess we just went our separate ways. Happens, right?" Olivia laughs but doesn't give me a chance to correct her. "You know, I always thought you were jealous of my relationship with Cash, so it would be better to keep my distance, but it's been over for years now."

"So, you thought you'd call me out of the blue?" I ask, unable to tamp down on my hostility.

"Well, yeah, why not? It's never too late to rekindle an old friendship, right?" Olivia laughs again, a hollow sound. "Anyway, I thought you should know that Cash and I are over, and that he cheated on me, so I guess you weren't missing out on anything with him after all."

The revelation is tossed out there with such carelessness. He cheated on her?

"You know how it is," Olivia continues, "men like that always cheat. I kind of don't blame him. Cash was never the faithful type, and he was a celebrity for shit's sake. Like, it makes sense that he would—"

"So, let me get this straight, you called me for the first time in fifteen years to tell me that you and Cash broke up years ago, that he cheated on you, and that you want to be friends?"

"Yeah," she chuckles, "I guess."

"Olivia." Do it. "Olivia, I don't want to be friends with you. And I don't believe a word you're saying. You abandoned your child. You lied to Cash about me. Fuck you." And then I hang up, my heart beating a mile a minute.

I don't care that she signed away her rights legally. All I care about is the look Alex gets when she's upset over something, and she feels as if she has no one to turn to. The fact is, Olivia could have been a co-parent. Cash has the money to look after Alex, and all Olivia had to do was try to be present. As a girl whose father walked out, it eats me up that she would choose not to be part of her child's life. And if that makes me a bad, judgmental person then so be it. It's the hill I'm going to die on.

You don't abandon your child, not when you have the means to be in their life, and Olivia had the means and the support system, and Cash would've made sure of that, cheating or not.

Olivia doesn't try to call back, and I'm relieved.

I don't believe her about Cash, and I don't trust her anymore.

I check the time on my phone, my hands shaking. Twenty minutes until my meeting with Lone Star. I have to get it together.

Thirty-Six

CASH

I'M TAKING my lunch break, seated on a stool near the in-progress bar when the door to Chuckles opens and Dad stumbles in. He's drunk. The sight is painfully familiar, and I'm up and moving toward him before he's a foot inside the bar.

"Dad," I say, and catch him underneath one arm.

His blue eyes, once so sharp and focused, full of mirth, are hazy and unfocused. He hiccups and sighs. "Wanted to grab somethin' to eat but they kicked me out of the damn Heartstopper!" The last word comes out as a shout. "That damn Marci Walsh thinks she owns the place."

"She does." I direct him to a chair at one of the nearby booths. We haven't finished reupholstering them yet. "Dad, Marci's owned the place ever since Nic died."

"Yeah, yeah, well, she coulda given me a damn burger. Something to line the stomach. Is it my fault that I'm drunk?"

I grit my teeth as I study him. It was foolish to think his behavior would change, and the most frustrating part of it all is he won't listen. He won't get help, and there is nothing we can do but watch it all fall the fuck apart.

"Dad, I need you clear-headed if we're going to fix this place up."

"Don't see that we should."

"What?"

He hiccups and meets me stare for stare, a little of his old self shining through. "I said that I don't see we should fix it up."

"What?" I bite the word out.

My father grumbles under his breath. "I'm gonna sell it."

If I say anything now, I'm going to lose my shit.

"I think I might sell it," Dad corrects himself. "I'm not sure yet."

"You can't sell it, Dad. This was your place with Mom. This is our place. Our family's place."

"Think I don't know that?" Dad asks. "I built this place with my own two fucking hands when you were still in your diapers." He tries to stand but flops back down. "But it's too much, Cash." His tone softens. "It's too much after everything that happened."

"You can't do this."

"I can do whatever I want. It's my business," he says.

"Mom would not want you to sell it."

"Your mother is dead."

The words ring in the silence, in the sawdust and the smell of sweat, and I stare at him with a hatred that reminds me of being a teenager again. It's an irrational anger, and I struggle to keep the beast under control.

"I don't know if I want this bar anymore," Dad says.

"How can you know what you want when you can't even walk straight?"

"Don't you talk to me like that, boy," he replies. "I am your father."

"Then fucking act like it," I roar.

My father doesn't flinch but considers me through those weary eyes. Weary, unfocused. Arguing with him like this is pointless. The best I can do is give him a fucking ride home and leave him at Ganny's to sober up. Not that it will make a damn difference.

We've tried getting rid of all the booze in the house, even tried talking to the owners of the local bars, but he always finds a way, and I am sick of it.

It's a disease, but I am at the end of my rope.

"If I wanna sell it, I'll sell it. And there ain't a damn thing you or any of your siblings can do about it," Dad says. "It's my business." He glares up at me for a moment, and then the fire seeps from his eyes. He lets out a sigh and rests his head on his forearms on the table.

He looks old and worn, but I'm still furious.

I take him by the arm and help him up. "Come on, Dad."

"Where?"

"I'm taking you back to Ganny's. You can't work."

"Take me to Longhorn's."

"Longhorn's is closed," I say.

My father grumbles under his breath but doesn't fight me as I guide him out of Chuckles and to my pickup. I feed him into the passenger seat and clip him into his seat-belt. This is bullshit. This whole thing is bullshit. I stayed. I tried. Why can't he?

I couldn't do this to my child. So how can he do this to us?

We drive to Ganny's in silence, mostly because Dad has fallen asleep, snoring with his head resting against the window. I carry him inside and sit him down in the living room, then fix him a cup of coffee.

Dad doesn't acknowledge it.

"I'm going back to Chuckles," I say. "To work. Join me when you've sobered up."

"Told you not to bother. Might sell it."

I freeze in the doorway, balling my hands into fists. "No," I say, "you won't because it's the last thing this family has left. Leo's gone. Hannah's leaving. Jesse's got his own life, and we hardly ever see Lily. It's just us, Dad."

He doesn't answer.

I leave before I say something I'll regret. The only thing that's keeping me in line is the thought of Alex and June waiting for me at home.

"YOU OKAY IN HERE?" I ask Alex, popping my head into the living room.

"I'm good. Thanks, June." Alex lies on the sofa, a heating pad on her stomach, flipping through the channels. She hasn't had much screentime today, and her pain seems to have subsided at least. She was pretty cheerful over dinner—steak and greens—whereas Cash was silent and brooding.

I head upstairs, my thoughts on the outcome of my meeting with the college counselor today.

The fact is it went great. Sasha, my counselor, told me there's plenty of space for students wanting a bachelor's degree in teaching. That's the first step. After studying that, I'll need to complete an Educator's Preparation program, take certification exams, and submit a state application. It sounds like a lot but taking that first step is exciting. And there are several colleges with rolling admissions.

The only hurdle left is tuition, but even that might be

doable. There's financial aid and scholarships, and a straight up loan. I'm part excited, part terrified.

I don't want to leave.

I hear strumming. Cash is playing guitar in the library again.

I follow the sound into the room—it's my favorite in the house—and watch him.

He's on the floor, wearing jeans and a cotton T-shirt that bites at his muscular arms, the guitar in his arms. He picks and strums, then pauses and writes something down on a sheet of music in front of him.

"What are you doing?" I ask.

Cash looks up at me, smiling. It sends more of those butterflies fluttering in my stomach. "Sit."

I sit across from him, my legs tucked to one side, my ankles crossed.

He strums a few chords, his blue eyes full of unspoken emotion as he stares at me, and I shiver. The melody is beautiful, almost haunting, and I'm lost in the moment. Him playing. Me listening. Afterward, he makes changes to his sheet music again, then absently reaches over and strokes my ankles and feet.

I suck in a breath.

Cash tucks the pencil behind his ear and gives me a look that could melt the clothing off my body. He moves his calloused fingers up my legs, my thighs, toward the hem of my shorts.

"Cash, we—"

"Hmm." He sets the guitar aside, then grabs the sides of my shorts and scoots my butt along the floor, dragging me toward him. Cash leans in, pressing his mouth to my ear. "Do you know why I started writing music?"

"Because you loved country music?" The warmth of his breath against my neck and ear gives me shivers.

"Because of you."

I stiffen, turning toward him, so that our noses almost touch. "What?"

"I started learning guitar because of you," he murmurs. "Started the band because of you."

I'm stunned.

He presses a gentle kiss to my lips. "Remember that summer we went to the music festival in Austin? We were thirteen."

"Your mother took us."

"That's right. And you were infatuated with that one asshole who played the guitar? He sang some croony bullshit country song that made you all weak at the knees?"

"I remember."

"Well, I figured if you liked him so much, then maybe if I started playing country, you'd like me too." He presses his forehead against mine. "Anything for you, June."

I've never heard Cash talk like this. "Anything you want." His lips dip toward mine, and I'm already burning for him.

The doorbell trills downstairs, shattering the moment, and I shake my head and move away from him. "I'll get it," I say, and jump up before we can go any further.

We shouldn't be getting this close with Alex downstairs anyway. I walk past the living room where Alex is still watching TV and answer the door.

And it's like the world has inverted, or rather, like I've stepped back in time.

Olivia is on the doorstep.

She arches an eyebrow. "Hi."

She looks worn. Like she's lived a hard life, and she looks older than thirty-three, her platinum blonde hair pulled back into a tight ponytail. She's wearing a tie-dyed dress that wraps around her body.

"I'm disappointed, June. I thought we were friends."

"What are you doing here?" I ask.

"Don't just stand there staring," Olivia says. "Get Cash."

Footsteps on the stairs bring my attention back to the house. Alex! And I turn in time to see Cash approaching, and Alex stepping out of the living room with an inquisitive look on her face.

"Who's that?" she asks.

Olivia smiles and waves at her, but Cash steps in front of Alex before she can say anything to her.

"Get off my porch," Cash says, his voice cold.

"Aw, come on, Cashy," Olivia says. "Is that how you talk to old friends? Seems to me like you treat them real nice." She sweeps a hand toward me.

"June, could you take Alex upstairs, please?" Cash asks.

"No problem. Come on, honey." I guide her up the stairs and away from Olivia and Cash. Right now, all that matters is making sure Alex is fine.

"June," Alex says, as we reach her room, "who was that lady?"

"That's something you and your father will need to discuss," I say.

"But why can't we discuss it?"

"Because it's not my place, honey. That's a conversation you need to have with your dad," I reply, with a smile that hurts me.

Because it's true. It isn't my place, and I'm so confused about everything I couldn't have this conversation if I tried.

Olivia is back. And I have no idea how Cash is going to handle this situation.

Thirty-Eight

CASH

THE UNIVERSE ISN'T DONE BEING a cocksucker today.

I shut the door behind me with a snap, then walk into the front yard and out onto the sidewalk. Olivia hesitates, standing on the porch with one hip popped, her hand on in. "Are you serious right now, Cashy?"

"Stop calling me that."

She rolls her eyes then comes down to meet me. "We're just going to stand here on the sidewalk and hash it out? You can't even invite the mother of your own child into the house to have a grown-up conversation?"

"You are not Alex's mother," I say. "You signed those rights away to me. And you agreed you would not come looking for her by court order." I'm trying to remain calm if only for Alex and June's sakes. "You will not drift in and out of Alex's life. You will leave because you have no legal ground to be here."

"Cash, come on." She stamps her foot like she always

did when she didn't get her way. The same way she did on the day we broke up after I found her in bed with Kev. "You can't just kick me out. You have no idea how hard this has been for me too. You of all people should know that after what I went through when we were kids. My parents abandoned me. And when I fell pregnant, I didn't know how to handle it. So, I fucked up. Everybody fucks up."

I take a breath. I'm not into this manipulative bullshit. She pulled the same thing with me whenever she messed up. It was always an excuse. Deep down, Olivia is desperate for love that she'll never get because she doesn't allow it to happen. It's a self-fulfilling prophecy. "When Alex needed a mother the most, you weren't there. And it will stay that way. Now, get lost before I call the cops."

"The cops," she says.

"That's right. Court. Order."

Still, Olivia hesitates. She folds her arms, trying to press her breasts upward. "You know I wouldn't come here unless it was absolutely necessary. I'm not even going to mention how weird it is that you and June are living under the same roof, but—"

"Don't talk about June."

"Whatever," she trills. "Look, the truth is, I need your help. I need money, and—"

"Enough. I offered you everything you needed. I begged you to stay in Alex's life, but that time is done. Leave now or I'll call the cops."

Olivia's angry, but she knows she's beat. She can't be here without getting in trouble with the law.

"Fine," she says, "fine." She lifts her hands in supplication. Finally, she saunters off down the street. There's no car in sight, which is worrying. Where the fuck did she come from?

I exhale into the night sky, tucking my hands into my pockets, the reality of what just happened hitting home. Alex and June are upstairs waiting for me, and I turn toward the house and start walking.

Olivia made her choices, and they included drugs, alcohol, and my bandmate. Her needing money isn't my problem anymore. But it enrages me that she would endanger Alex by coming here.

Upstairs, I find June brushing Alex's hair.

The two of them look up at me expectantly. One pair of green eyes, clouded with worry, the other pair blue and curious.

"Who was that, Dad?" Alex asks.

"I'll leave you two alone," June says, scooting off the bed and setting Alex's hairbrush on the bedside table.

I almost want to stop her, but this is a conversation I should have with my daughter in private.

June sweeps past me, carrying her intoxicating citrus scent, and I breathe her in. She's the opposite of Olivia in so many ways. Her attitude, personality, her strength, and loyalty. I made the wrong woman a mother and it's bullshit, but I can't go back in time and change it now.

I sit on the edge of my daughter's bed and take her hand, noting how much bigger it is than it used to be. I remember the first time she held my finger, her tiny chubby hand wrapped around it, her eyes closed in her bassinet. I knew then that I would do anything for Alexandra, and that feeling hasn't abated or changed. No matter the years of sacrifice or the hard times or the attitude.

"Was that my mom?" Alex asks shrewdly. "That blonde lady?"

"That was her," I say. "Your biological mother."

"Why was she here?" Alex asks. "I don't get it. It's not like she ever wanted to see me before, so why now?"

I don't want to lie to my daughter, but I don't want to hurt her feelings either. "I'm not sure what her real intentions are, but she's not allowed to be here. You remember what I told you, right?" I've been an open book with Alex about this. "She's not allowed to come here because she chose that, but it's not a reflection on you."

"I remember, Dad," Alex says. "And I know it's not about me, it's about her."

I'm struck by the wisdom of my eleven-year-old.

"I have you, and I have June," Alex says slowly. "And Daisy and her moms too. If she'll ever talk to me again."

"She will." I stroke her hair back from her face. "If you ever want to talk about any of this—"

"I know, Dad," Alex says.

I draw her into a hug and squeeze my daughter to my chest. I'll do anything to protect her. I can't deny the effect June's had on our family, on the house, on Alex. My daughter is more confident, she's happier, and she's resilient.

And June.

I thought I was a strong man before her, now I'm realizing how much stronger I can be for her and Alex. She's teaching me that strength doesn't have to mean being alone.

It means accepting that she might leave and being willing to take the pain.

I kiss my daughter on the head and tell her to get ready

for bed then leave her room, determined. I'll do whatever
it takes.

Thirty-Nine

JUNE

SEEING Olivia after all these years is a shock to my system. I stand in the guest room in Cash's house, staring down at the side of my mother's place, and the part of the street that I can just make out. Warm night air drifts through the open window, accompanied by the chirp of crickets, and it feels like I'm here and in the past at the same time.

I don't know what I was thinking, but I feel guilty for having been with Cash, even though I know that Olivia isn't right for him. That she isn't right at all for the things she's done. But at the same time, I feel like a shitty, judgmental person for even thinking that.

I have college applications to prep, and standing around thinking about what could have been or what I should have done is not getting me anywhere.

I open the door of the guestroom and stop dead.

Cash stands on the threshold, one hand up as if he's about to knock. "I was going to write you a letter," he says, "but I figured we've never been that good at telling the truth on paper."

My body flushes hot at the proximity. No matter how much I plan on moving past him, on working on my personal goals, I'm stymied by his presence.

"June," he says, sweeping his hand down my arm. "You all right?"

I suck in a breath. "Well, you could say I've been better. Is Alex all right?"

"She's fine," he says. "Sleeping. We talked about what happened, and she's, yeah, she's going to be fine."

"You made the hard choice by telling her everything," I say, a little of my admiration for him coming out in my tone. "Hard and honest."

His fingers work up my arm to my throat, and it's becoming increasingly difficult to concentrate.

Cash rests his hand against my skin, grasping my chin gently, and tilting my head so he can take me in. I've never enjoyed a man's touch this much. Maybe I've been reading too many romance novels, but the way he touches me and moves me, makes my knees weak. He's in full control, as he walks me backward into the room and taps the door shut with his foot.

"June. I'm going to do unspeakable things to you." Cash moves another hand upward and he cups my cheeks in both hands, as if he's holding water and he's afraid it will seep through the cracks between his fingers. "You," he says, "June. You've always been the reason. You've always been the one I want. I was fucked when Olivia told me that you weren't interested in me. I was done. And I was a dumb kid for believing it," he says. "But I'm an adult now and I'm not going to let anything stand in the way of what I want again, not when it comes to you."

I swallow, my mind racing alongside my heart. These are words I wanted to hear when I was young. When things were simpler.

"Every part of me wants you to stay. Every single part of me wants to keep you here so that I can have you as mine," Cash says, and my skin prickles with goosebumps at the emotion in his voice, "but I know that you've been through enough. The summer's coming to an end and you're going to leave to be who you were meant to be. I have always believed in you, just like you believed in me."

"Cash." My bottom lip trembles. No one has ever spoken to me like this before. Not my mother, not Braydon, no one.

"You deserve the world on your own terms. And I want you to know that whatever you want to do, I will support you. I will pay your tuition. I will buy you a car if you need it. I will buy you a fucking house, June. I will do whatever you want and need."

"You can't do that," I say,

"You're everything I've ever wanted from a friend, a woman, a lover. And whatever comes, if you want me by your side, June, I will be there to support you every fucking step of the way."

I'm trembling all over. He leans in and kisses my tears away, murmuring under his breath, the warm words lost on me but penetrating my soul. This man is something special.

There isn't a chance in hell I could doubt him. I've known him since we were kids, loved him since I was old enough to start thinking about him as more than a boy, and dreamed of being with him. Cash is a rock. A grumpy, solid, sweet rock. He might not show the world how he feels, but he's shown me, and that's enough.

I won't let what Olivia or anyone else says get in my head. I want Cash. I want him so bad it hurts, even with my doubts and fears about the future. Even with the complications.

Could this really work between us? Could we move on from what happened when this town is full of hurtful memories?

"You don't have to make any decisions now," Cash says, his hands moving to my waist. He pulls me close, murmuring the words into my ear. "But June, I can't keep my hands off you. I swore I wouldn't let another woman into my life, but you wear me down."

I shiver and run a hand through his hair, tugging gently.

He grunts and nips my throat then kisses me, his fingers biting into my waist and pulling me toward him.

I kiss Cash with the heat that's been building inside me.

Cash lifts me off the floor effortlessly. I wrap my legs around him, and he walks us backward to the bed. We tumble onto it together, breathing hard.

I'm lost in him, at ease with him but so wet I'm struggling not to lose control.

"Breathe," he says, muttering it in my ear. "You have to breathe."

I'm trying but it's difficult when my senses are overwhelmed by him. Cash slows down the pace, stripping me and leaving trails of wet kisses along my skin. He reaches the white cotton panties I chose this morning and tears them off me.

"Fuck," he says. "You are so perfect, June. I want you to sit on my face."

I whimper, pressing my fist to my mouth. "You—"

"Do you want that?"

I nod.

"I want to wear you like a fucking crown. Come here." He strips his shirt off one-handed then lays down on the bed.

Cash positions me over his lips, grabbing handfuls of my ass cheeks, and parts me. He guides me downward, and I grab the back of the headboard to keep myself steady. His blue eyes blaze up at me, full of desire and promise.

"Rock back and forth," he says. "Do what feels good." And then he closes his lips over my pussy, and I'm lost.

I circle my hips at first, eyes closed, the moist sounds of him eating me filling the room. I bite down on my bottom lip just as he slaps my ass. My pace is erratic as I slide over him, his tongue hot and hungry for me.

Cash takes control, holding my weight, moving me back and forth, sucking my clit into his mouth then reaching around and inserting two fingers into my pussy. I'm laid bare for him, everything on display, and again, he's got me in the palms of his hands, taking me where I need to go.

He grunts against my pussy, sucking the delicate flesh, thrusting his fingers inside me, and the pleasure is exquisite.

"Cash," I moan. "Oh God, Cash." I clap my hand over my mouth to shut myself up, and ride him, my thighs quivering. I can't hold on any longer, and I grasp the head-board with both hands arching onto him and rocking through my orgasm.

Afterward, Cash helps me down and gives me a dirty grin. "Let's see how many more times we can make you come like that." And then he flips me onto my back and pins both of my legs up.

"Hold on," he says, his hands fixed on the insides of my thighs. He sucks my tender clit into his mouth and sets to work again.

I block my screams again, trying to be as silent as possible, especially now that he's got all the control. I'm breaking apart for him again before I even know what's happened, my body utterly sated by his adoration.

But Cash keeps me there, feasting on me like he can't get enough, lavishing me with attention I've never had before. "Again," he says. "I'm going to show you what you deserve, June."

I quiver underneath him, breathless, dripping with sweat, and watching as he dips his tongue inside me. He pumps it in and out a few times before returning that focused attention to my clit, and my third orgasm sends me into spasms. My eyes roll back in my head.

"Yes," Cash says. "Yes, that's so fucking hot. You're delicious when you come." He slaps my pussy gently, blows on my clit then pulls my legs down.

He rises on his knees in front of me and unzips his jeans, pulling out his thick cock. His rock-hard cock, throbbing, already dripping pre-cum, but he waits a second, allowing the tension to build between us.

Cash gets up and drags me to the edge of the bed. He folds my thighs back again, then holds his dick and runs it through my lips. "So wet for me," he says. "So wet and swollen."

"Please," I say, rising onto my elbows and staring down at us. "Please, Cash. I want it."

"Hmm."

"Please."

Cash inserts the tip, parting me, and my head slams back on the bed. I kick my legs like I want to escape the pleasure, even though that's the furthest thing from my mind. It's just too good.

He holds me down, pressing deeper and deeper.

I pant.

"Almost there," he says. "You're going to take all of it tonight. Every night from now on."

And then he sheathes himself fully. Cash's pace is fast at first, but he lowers himself over me, cupping a breast in one hand and kissing me. It turns sensual and hot, a slow burn that leaves me breathless and whimpering.

Cash turns me onto my stomach, angling my ass into the air and reaching around to access my clit.

"Bite down on the pillow."

I have a second to do as he says before he unleashes himself on me, pressing against my G-spot, playing with my clit, slapping my ass so hard the pain turns to pleasure. I whine and moan his name, catching glimpses of him over my shoulder, his muscles glistening with sweat, his gaze fixed on my ass and pussy.

He takes me mercilessly, not allowing me a second of reprieve, until finally, I shatter for a fourth time. Cash fills me up again, holding back a moan of his own, his fingers punishing my flesh, marking me as his.

"I don't want to pull out," he says, scooping me up and

keeping his dick inside me. He lays us down, on our sides and cuddles me close.

"You're amazing," I whisper.

He laughs, a low sexy noise that thrums through my back. "You're mine."

Forty

CASH

I SPENT most of the night inside June, or with our arms and legs intertwined. Either I'd wake her up or she'd wake me for more. I want more of her, even as I write her a letter early the next morning.

See you tonight. I'll show you how much you mean to me.

I want every cell in her body to hold a memory of me. I want to possess her entirely and keep it that way.

I leave the letter on her bedside table then sneak out of the room and into mine. A quick shower later, I peek my head into Alex's room and find her sleeping, then stop by the library to grab my laptop. I wanted to check in on a few emails with suppliers today, but the lid of my laptop is open.

June's been working on it, using it to make college applications.

She deserves her own space. Her own method of inter-acting with the world, and I'm pretty sure she has none of that because of her piece of shit ex. I leave the laptop where it is so she can use it, then resolve to buy her one later today.

Summer is almost over, and I can't fucking stand it. If I could force it to continue forever, I would, as selfish as that is.

But today, there's work to be done, and I need to check whether my father has decided to come into work or if I'm going to have to fetch him from Ganny's and babysit him. Letting him do whatever the fuck he wants clearly isn't an option anymore.

I take the drive toward Chuckles at a crawl. The sun has only just come up, but the heat's already building, and I'm not looking forward to work.

My phone rings, and I frown. It's Jesse. "What now?"

My brother only ever calls me when we need to talk about problems. We see each other so often, whether it's at Ganny's house or around town, that calling each other to chat isn't a thing.

I pull over and answer. "What?"

"There he is," Jesse says. "You know, I've been trying to call you for a half an hour, you asshole."

"I was busy."

"Busy with June, the hot nanny?"

"Hey," I grunt. "Keep a respectful tongue in your mouth when you're talking about her."

"Huh. That what you're doing, brother? Keeping your respectful tongue in your mouth?"

"I swear to God, Jesse."

He chuckles, and I wish he was here so I could sock

him in the stomach. "Relax, old man," he says. "I get it. She's your lady now."

"I wish," I grumble, before I can stop myself. I don't open up to people, least of all my brother. As much as I love him.

"She will be," Jesse says. Clearly, my brother can tell mocking me about this would be inadvisable. I'm sure he'd jump on the opportunity otherwise. "The woman's in love with you, Cash. I thought she was going to let you carry her home from the quarry the other day."

"Hmm."

"Can I ask you something?"

"What?"

"Does it make it hotter? The sex? You know, since you're her boss and she's the nanny? It's like something out of a porno," Jesse says, adding in a feminine voice, "Oh please, mister country music star, please. Take me now."

"Shut the fuck up." This is the dichotomy of Jesse. One second he's a caring guy giving great advice, the next he's a degenerate. I'm just glad I got to June first.

Jesse chuckles. "Yeah, yeah," he says. "You know I'm just fucking with you. If it's meant to be, make it so. That's the Taylor way."

He's not wrong. Taylor men don't stop until we get what we want. Hell, even the Taylor women are like that. Look at Lily, with her big fancy job out in the city, and Hannah with her determination to live her life exactly as she wants it, her nose buried in a book behind the counter in the library. She wouldn't let a man tell her what to do, her brothers included.

"Jesse, I got to get to work. Talk."

"I heard a rumor," Jesse says, "you know how us men love to gossip."

"What the fuck are you talking about?"

"Olivia's back in town."

I grunt.

"I take it that's a yes? Your caveman grunts are difficult to, uh, decipher over the phone."

"She was in town. I told her to get lost."

"Is Alex okay?"

I grunt in the affirmative.

"Right," Jesse says. "Look, you need me to handle it, I'll handle it. I've got you."

"Thanks, but she's gone." She'd better fucking be. There's a reason I got a court order to stop her from seeing Alex. She came back once after signing away her parental rights. She threatened to take me to court if I didn't give her money. Olivia was drugged up, and I, like a fucking idiot, tried to help her. But things only got worse, and I was forced to get the court order to keep her away from our child.

"Probably better you stay home with June and Alex today anyway."

"Huh?"

"Just saying," Jesse clears his throat, "that it might be a good idea for you to head on home and be with them today."

"I have work. At Chuckles."

"Right, right, but maybe not, you know?"

"Huh?"

"Maybe you don't go to work and you stay home."

"Are you having a stroke? Smelling burnt toast?" I ask.

Jesse clicks his tongue. "For once, take my advice and

just go home. Don't go to work today. Let's meet up at the Heartstopper right now. Grab some breakfast. I want to talk to you about something, Cash, it's serious."

"God forbid."

"Brother, I need to talk to you."

"Not now, Jesse. Catch up with me this evening. I'm driving, I'll call you back."

"Cash—"

I hang up.

What the hell was that about? Not go into work? Why? June and Alex are fine at home, and as much as I'd love to spend the day with them, I've made a commitment to my father. That's another thing Taylor men don't do. Go back on their word.

The way Jesse talked about the bar has me suspicious.

I start the pickup. As I pass cars, their drivers raise a hand over the steering wheel in greeting, and pedestrians or folks opening up stores on Main Street wave at me from the sidewalk.

Heatstroke is our town, and as much as coming back here felt like a death sentence, I can't picture leaving now.

Not even for music?

I grit my teeth and park outside the bar.

The doors are shut, the inside is dark, and there's a For Sale sign in the window.

I involuntarily grasp the steering wheel so hard it creaks. "Fuck," I say.

All the hard work for nothing. Trying to piece together the family, trying to make it so that the Taylors mean something in this town. Gone. Gone because he can't lay off the fucking sauce and deal with his problems.

And you're so fucking great at that, aren't you?

I start the engine again. I tear through town, not bothering to greet anyone, ignoring the view of the bay, the sand, the happy people starting their day. It all blurs into one mocking tableau.

Ten minutes later, I'm parked outside Ganny's house. The car ticks and cools as I sit there, staring up at her grand house that's been in our family for generations. I open my door and charge up to the porch, balling and releasing my fists.

Ganny's in the living room crocheting, and she smiles up at me as I walk in. "Cash, honey pie, what are you doing here?"

"Where's Dad?"

"Not here. He went out to some business meeting earlier." Ganny pats her fluffy white hair, and I'm struck by how much older she looks. She's still spry, even though she's well into her eighties, but I worry about her more and more. Part of the reason Dad moved in with her was to make sure she was all right, and now he's the one who needs the fucking babysitting.

"Ganny, he's selling the bar."

My grandmother sighs and sets aside her piece. "Oh, honey," she says, "I'm sorry."

I don't reply. Sorry won't cut it.

"Your daddy's always had a mind of his own when it comes to the business," Ganny says. "I talked to him about it. I told him how much this means to you, but his mind is made up."

"We can't let—"

A car door slams outside, and my father emerges from a sleek black sedan.

"Now, Cash, honey, don't do anything you'll regret."

"Stay here," I tell Ganny.

"It takes me five minutes to get out of this chair," she says, lifting her the piece she's crocheting into her lap. "You really think I was gonna jump up and follow you?"

"I'm getting you a caregiver," I say.

"I've got—"

"Ganny, you don't have my father. He doesn't even have himself." I'm not having this argument with her again. The caregiver is happening.

I go out onto the porch.

"Dad," I say, I vaulting over the picket gate. "Dad, what were you thinking?"

For once, my father doesn't smell of alcohol, and he considers me with a sharp-eyed gaze. "Cash, what in the hell are you doing here? And what do you think you're doing, talking to me like that? Boy, I ought to tan your hide."

"Tan my hide? You haven't been in your own fucking hide for the past month."

Another car door opens, and Seth Deveraux emerges. He's dressed in a suit in this summer heat, wearing tattoos across the backs of his knuckles, and a grin I want to wipe off his blocky head.

"What have you done?" I ask my father. "What are you doing?"

"Your father sold me the bar," Seth says, before my dad can respond.

"Now, Cash, calm your—"

I circle around to Seth's side of the car. "You fuck," I say. "I told you to back the fuck up." I point a finger in his face.

"Your father wanted to sell his business," Seth says, "I

gave him a good price for it. Not my fault you didn't get the memo, buddy."

"Buddy?"

I'm on him in a second, fisting the front of his fancy suit and pulling him close. Adrenaline pulses through me and my vision tunnels. "Who's your fucking buddy? I'll break you like a twig."

Seth laughs. "Do it then, tough guy."

"Cash!"

Seth grips the front of my shirt, and I press my forehead against his, butting him backward. I'm going to teach this interfering piece of shit a lesson.

"Cash." A hand grasps me and tugs me to one side. "Let it go, man. Let it go." My brother's face appears, but I look past him toward Seth.

Seth's laughing. "You're gonna let your brother stop you?"

"I'll kill you," I say, trying to leap past Jesse, but my brother holds me back.

"It's not worth it," Jesse says. "It is not worth it. Calm down."

"He bought the bar, Jesse." My mouth is dry, and I'm barely managing to keep myself under control.

"I know, but it's not worth it—"

"Guess you won't need that nanny for the rest of the summer, huh?" Seth calls, his eyes flashing. "Maybe I'll hire her. Always wanted a personal assistant."

I roar and push past Jesse, charging toward Deveraux like a raging bull.

Forty~One

JUNE

"YOU GUYS SOUND GREAT!" I say, clapping my hands. "You're really getting it. I'm so impressed."

Both Daisy, hair in cornrows and wearing a gap-toothed grin, and Alex, with ribbons in her hair, clap and give each other high fives.

"There's a part near the chorus that's a little pitchy from you, Alex, but we can work on that," I say. "I think you guys are almost ready for the talent show. I'm so proud of you both."

Alex is feeling way better today, and, of course, Daisy was only concerned about her wellbeing and not upset about her running out on the slumber party. The girls have been practicing hard for the end of summer talent show, and they've gone from out of tune to rocking it in a few weeks.

"We couldn't have done it without your help," Daisy announces. "I think this calls for a round of cookies."

"Yeah!" Alex grins. "That's fine, right? I'm allowed sugar today?"

"There's nothing indicating otherwise on the sheet. So, yeah, I'd say so. But we've got to head home afterward, okay?"

"Got it!"

Daisy and Alex run through the comfy living room in Daisy's moms' house and into the kitchen. I sit on the leather sofa, grateful for the AC. It's hot as hell out there, and thinking is out of the question in this weather.

That's probably for the best, though, since thinking means worrying about my applications and Cash, and all the complicated feelings that are bubbling beneath the surface.

"Heading out?" Sara smiles at me from the doorway. She's tall and elegant, and it makes me wonder if she was a ballet dancer at some point in her life.

"Yeah, Sara, thanks," I say. "I think we're done for the day."

"I don't know if anyone's told you this," Sara says, "but you should be a music teacher."

"What?"

"I've watched you with the girls, and you're amazing at it."

"You're too kind," I say. "You really think so? A music teacher?" I hadn't considered it. I'm not sure what qualifications are necessary for that, but it's an interesting idea.

"You did mention you wanted to get a teaching degree, right?"

"Correct."

Sara opens her arms as if to suggest that it's decided. I'm a music teacher now. I laugh at her enthusiasm.

"Here's the thing," Sara says, "you've helped Alex and Daisy so much over the past few weeks. I'm actually looking for a nanny, and with your skillset and the way you've been with the kids? I don't want to poach you from Cash, or whatever, but let me know if you're ever available."

"For real?" I ask, my heart skipping a beat.

"You've got my number," Sara says. "And feel free to tell Cash that I asked. I don't want him to think I'm being shady."

"Thanks, Sara. I appreciate the offer. I'll think about it." I don't want to be a full-time nanny, but it's good to have options like this. And I like Daisy. She's a good kid.

Alex darts back into the living room to grab her backpack, cookie crumbs clinging to the corners of her mouth. "I'll call you tonight, Daze."

"Talk later, Lexi!"

I grin at the stage names they've picked then say goodbye to Sara, and we head out. Alex and I stop for ice cream on the way back to the house, and the summer vibes are immaculate. She eats her ice cream on the hood of the car, getting smears of it on her face and hands, and I help her clean up as she regales me with tales of the last show she watched. The folks who pass by grin and wave.

This is the perfect summer, and just that thought gives me butterflies in my stomach. It's going to end soon.

We get back into Ol' Rutsty, and Alex turns to me. "You're the best nanny ever, June. I wish you would never leave."

"Thanks, honey." I give her a side-hug. "Seatbelts on. Let's hit the road."

Alex lets out a whoop, and we drive back toward the house.

I'm just telling Alex to make sure she cleans up when

the screen door at my mother's house bangs. Mom marches down the porch steps, glaring at me, her fists on her hips.

"Uh-oh," Alex mutters. "Your mom looks angry."

"Head on inside," I say. "I'll be in in just a second."

Alex hurries inside with a concerned backward glance. My mother has the good grace to wait until she's gone before circling around to Cash's picket gate and opening it. She hesitates, checking that his car isn't parked in the garage or driveway, then steps onto the property.

"June," she says.

"Mom?"

"You've got some real nerve, you know that? You come back to town, tell me you need my help, and then disappear." She taps her foot on the front path. "You know, I expected more of you. I graciously offered you a room in the house, and all I asked for was a little financial help. Instead, you're out here—"

"Mom, I told you that I wanted to get back on my feet and save up to study. And I'm not staying under your roof, eating your food, or using your electricity. I don't owe you money." It feels so good to say that. Those are the words I've been afraid of saying for years.

When I was with Braydon, I had an "allowance" and I'd send as much of it back to my mom as possible.

"You said you would pay," Mom says, pointing a finger at my chest.

The last time she was here asking for money, Cash told her to get lost. Now, it's my turn. "I'm not giving you money."

"How dare you! How dare you talk to your own mother like that? After the trouble you caused me? I wouldn't need any of this help if you'd just kept my secrets."

"Those should never have been my secrets to keep," I said, shaking my head. "You ruined your relationship with dad. You were the reason he left. And how dare you think you have the right to step onto this property and cause a scene when there is a child inside who needs my care? How dare you interfere in my life? My private affairs? How dare you!"

A weight lifts off my shoulders.

My mother takes a step back.

"You haven't supported my decisions unless they directly benefit you," I say, and it hurts because it's true. I'm not sure my mother loves me.

The screen door at her house slams a second time, and Olivia emerges, adding another layer of awful to this encounter. I can't have her over here. Not with Alex to care for. I spin around, scanning the front of Cash's house, my heart pounding against my throat, but Alex doesn't appear to be watching.

Olivia comes to a halt next to my mother. "I know I didn't hear you raising your voice at Patricia."

I blink.

Olivia's always been "out there," willing to make people uncomfortable, and I think that's what my mother likes about her.

"You can't be here," I say stiffly.

"What are you going to do about it?" Olivia asks.

"Call the cops."

"You can do that," she says, pressing her fingers to her chin, beneath her lips and itching furiously, "but it's a waste of time. I'll just say that I was never here, and that I live next door. What am I supposed to do about that?"

"Move," I say. "You're not allowed here."

Olivia narrows her eyes. "You really think you're hot shit, don't you?"

I take a breath. "You have thirty seconds to leave this property. If you're not gone by the time I reach the front door, I'm going to call the cops." Heck, either way, I'm going to call them and Cash. Olivia's presence is a serious problem.

"Thirty seconds." Olivia laughs. "Just remember, I had him first. He'll always be my man. And she'll always be my child."

"Wrong on both accounts," I say, and then I turn and walk away before I explode and make the situation worse than it already is.

Olivia wants me to descend to her level and make a scene, and she wants that so she can color me with the same brush as her. I'm not sad that I don't have her as a friend anymore.

The girl who used to stay up late with me, painting our nails and gossiping or reading, is gone. Or rather, I've changed. I can see her for who she really is.

I open the door and my cell phone rings in my purse before I can pull it out to call Cash.

Forty-Two

JUNE

I RIP my phone out of my purse, hoping that it's Cash calling, but it's another unknown number. I peek into the living room and find Alex lying on the sofa, watching TV. She grins at me, and I smile back before heading through to the kitchen—it has the best view of the front yard.

Olivia and my mother have gone inside, but I'm going to call Cash and Jesse regardless.

I have to put my desire to avoid confrontation second, and Alex's safety first.

For the first time in my life, it feels easy to do that.

My phone quits ringing, and I lift it to start dialing Cash's number, but the screen lights up again. Another caller.

"Hello?" I answer irritably.

"Juney baby." Braydon's voice is like oil. "Don't hang up, please! I'm sorry about the other night. I shouldn't have talked to you like that. You're not boring in bed. And you're not a fat slut. It was wrong, but Juney, I—"

I don't remember him calling me "a fat slut" but that

just adds to my anger. Not just slut-shaming but fat-shaming too. What a gem of a guy. I can't believe I fell for his narcissistic bullshit facade.

"Don't call this number again," I say, and then I stab my finger down on the screen to end the call.

But Braydon calls back again.

And again.

He's relentless. He won't take "no" for an answer, and I'm betting that's because he grew up with a silver spoon shoved so far up his ass, he tastes metal when he coughs.

"Leave me alone," I answer. "Braydon, stop calling me. It's over. You cheated. I've moved on."

"Juney, you can't just throw away what we have because of one misunderstanding."

"Misunderstanding? You, and I quote, 'squirted every-where.' That doesn't sound like a misunderstanding, Bray-don," I hiss, keeping my voice down and checking Alex wasn't on her way out of the living room.

"That was a one-time thing. Please, Juney, I need you in my life. You've always put me first, and I miss that. I miss your support. I know you're angry about what happened, both with that girl who meant nothing to me. Nothing. And because I got drunk and said a few insensitive—"

"Insensitive? The girl who meant nothing? She meant everything, Braydon, because she cost you our relation-ship," I say. "But that doesn't matter now. Don't you get it? We were over years ago."

"Juney, come on." His voice takes on a whiney quality that irritates me. It reminds me of my birthday party, moments before the sound from his phone cut. "I'm going on the campaign trail this year and I need a woman by my side who shows what type of man I am. That I care about the little people—"

"I couldn't give a shit." Apparently, it's the day for saying how I feel. And man, is it liberating. "I'm done caring about what you want, Braydon. For once, I'm looking out for myself."

"That's the thing! That's the thing, Juney! I can help you. I know how you've always wanted to go to college and be, uh, yeah. I have connections at so many Ivy League schools, and universities across the country, honey. I can get you in anywhere you want to go. I'll pay for your full tuition. Please, Juney baby, I'll do anything to—"

"What do I want to study? What do I want to major in?" I ask because this is base level knowledge that he should have. "Go on. Tell me."

"Well, you've always wanted to do science. Right? I remember you talked a lot about girls in STEM and—"

"Goodbye, Braydon. Do not call this number again. We are over. We are done. I don't want to hear your voice or see your face ever again."

"What, are you going to get that big goon to threaten me again?" Braydon asks.

I head upstairs as he talks, ensuring that Alex can't hear this conversation. I walk to the window in the guest room and watch my mother's house for any sign of movement. "Goon? He's my boyfriend," I say, even though it's not true. It's exactly what Cash said, and I know he'd want me to say it now. "He's my boyfriend, and he's fantastic in bed. Like, I can't even describe how hard he makes me come." If this guy is determined to make me uncomfortable with phone calls, then I'm going to do the same right back. "He's got a massive cock. And he—"

"June!"

"He knows how to use it. Unlike you, Braydon. Remember that time I fell asleep while you were on top? Yeah, that wasn't because I had a long day, it was because I could barely feel anything," I say, and then I hang up.

This time, he doesn't call back.

I'm assuming that's because he's reeling from the revelation that he isn't a God in the bedroom. I dial Cash's number, tapping my nails on the windowsill nervously.

"Pick up, Cash. Come on."

Next door, Olivia emerges onto the porch and lights up a cigarette. She's way out of line, and it makes me sick to my stomach. She doesn't glance over at Cash's house, but she takes her time with the cigarette.

Finally, she strolls off the porch and down the street, disappearing from sight.

I let out a breath.

I wish I had the power to solve this problem on my own, but Cash is the one with the court order, he's the one with the lawyer, and Alex is his kid.

Even though I wish she was mine too.

Alex deserves a mother who loves her. Every child does.

Cash doesn't answer the first or second call I make, so I switch to calling his brother. But Jesse isn't picking up either.

"What the hell is going on?"

I'm not sure what the court order says. Is Olivia allowed to be next door? How close can she come to Alex? Calling 911 seems like a bad idea. This is not technically an emergency.

Marci's number pops up on the screen before I can put in a call to the Heatstroke police station.

"Marce? Are you—?"

"Cash is in a fight," Marci says, breathless.

"What?"

"I just heard from Tilly. She saw him grabbing Seth Deveraux by the collar outside Ganny's house. He's in a fight. Jesse's there."

My body goes cold. The last time we ran into Seth Deveraux, Cash acted like he wanted to tear into him. There's tension there because of the bar and his family.

"Shit." I swallow. "Do you know why?"

"No, but I know that two squad cars just drove past the diner heading in that direction."

This is bad. This is really bad. "I need to call the cops."

This is so messed up.

"What? Why?" Marci asks. "Oh, my God, is it Olivia?"

"Yeah, but I can't talk now." I hang up and make the call, hoping that reporting this will at least help provide the evidence for Cash to use against Olivia in court.

This is messy. Every part of this is messy, and I'm not sure how we can fix it.

Forty-Three

CASH

JESSE CATCHES me before I can turn Deveraux's face into a pulp. He struggles to hold me back, and this time my father steps in front of me to stop the fight. Not that it will be much of a fight. I'm going to pulverize Deveraux for ever stepping between me and my family.

"That's enough, son," Dad says. "That is enough."

Two police vehicles scream around the corner and skid to a halt outside Ganny's house, their sirens wailing and lights flashing. Two officers approach, frowning at the commotion we've caused, and good sense finally wins out.

I step back, shake off my brother's hands, and clear my throat.

Seth's watching me with a glint in his eyes, and I meet his stare head on. One day, someone's going to teach this motherfucker a lesson, and I hope I'll be there to see it or at least to help.

"There a problem over here?" Officer Bronson asks, shifting his belt. He's been an officer in this town since I was in my teens, and he eyes me. "Causing trouble, Mr. Taylor?"

"That won't look good in them fancy tabloids," the second officer says. He must be new to Heatstroke because I don't recognize him.

"All under control," Jesse says.

"That so?" Officer Bronson looks up and down the street, smacking his lips. "Cuz we got a call about a domestic disturbance from a couple of your neighbors. Apparently, there's been some kinda fight out in the street."

"Some lady called to tell us that Mr. Cash Taylor, the famous musician, was about to beat up a guy in a suit." The second officer, who's fast making my shit list, nods to Seth.

Deveraux lifts both his palms. "I'm the only guy in a suit around here," he says, "and I can tell you that nobody was going to beat anybody else up."

At least he's not a snitch.

"That true?" Officer Bronson spears me with a glare.

Deveraux has the power to fuck with me, right now, and I know it. I nod, trying to keep the sneer from my lips.

"Everything's fine here." Jesse's a deputy, not an officer, but he works closely with the local station since they service the two main towns in our county. "All under control. You boys can head back to the station."

Officer Bronson hesitates. "I'm going to have to ask y'all to clear out of the street anyways."

I nod again.

"I was just on my way back to the office. Mr. Taylor," Deveraux says, directing that at my father, "I'll be in touch.

You made a smart choice today, and I look forward to turning your bar into what it was always meant to be."

"Thanks, son."

Son.

Jesse squeezes my shoulder painfully to distract me.

Seth gets into his car and drives off. I move off the sidewalk and up to Ganny's house, closely followed by Jesse and Dad.

The cops leave after a little more blustering and checking that everyone's where they should be, and my grandmother appears in the doorway. "Y'all done acting the fool out there?" she asks.

"Ganny." Jesse gives her a hug. "You got any of those chocolate chip cookies? My favorite ones?"

Ganny gives him a radiant smile that wipes the years from her face. "Anything for you, Jesse-Poo." She pinches his cheek, and then shuffles back inside.

Jesse eyes me. "Don't do anything dumb."

I point at my chest. "Me? Me?"

"Don't," he whispers, and then follows Ganny inside.

My father sits down on the porch swing, rocking himself by the heels. He watches me. I'm equal parts tired and pissed.

"You shouldn't have done that," I say. "Sold to Deveraux. He's a shark."

"I know it."

"Then why—?"

"You know, Cash, for a smart boy, you can be blind dumb sometimes," Dad says.

I take the insult like a lashing, my jaw clenched, focused on a point over his shoulder. "I've done everything in my power," I say, "to keep this family together and functioning. All I want is for Alex to have what I had growing up, but you are refusing to—"

"See, that's your mistake," Dad says. "You've given her more than we ever gave you, your mother and me. Just because she doesn't have a mother, doesn't mean she doesn't have family. She's got us."

"The bar was part of us. Part of the family. I worked my ass off trying to help you fix it up, and—"

"You wanted Alex to have a whole family," Dad says. "And I know I haven't been much of a father to you, or a grandfather to her over the past year. Since your mother died. Fact is, I've been a piss-poor excuse for a father."

That shuts me up.

"There are things I've done that I'm not proud of," Dad continues, "and trying to redo that bar was me trying to fix things. But I couldn't do it. Like I was wandering around in a dark room, bumping into things when I'm the one trying to fix the lights."

"That's why I was helping you."

"Cash, that bar was never going to be yours. It was never your destiny to run it. You weren't made for that," Dad says. "You were meant for bigger things than looking after someone else's old dream. And sometimes, when you love something, you've got to let it go. I'm letting the bar go."

I leaned against the balustrade.

"And I'm leaving for a while," he says. "So that I can get help. There's a place in El Paso, one of those rehab centers, and I'm going to go."

Relief washes over me. "That's great news, Dad."

"Yeah, I heard what you kids were saying. Got a call from Lily the other day, and she chewed me out too. I know I've been letting you down, letting the family down, but I'm not going to do that anymore, even if it means giving up the bar."

"Probably not the best business to be in, in that case."

"That's what I'm thinking," Dad says. "Funny thing is, alcohol wasn't a problem for me before. It just sort of crept up on me after your mother died. And then it kept creeping every day until I couldn't remember what time it was or what day it was or where I was meant to be."

A silence drifts between us, and I run a hand over my face, releasing the tension that's been seated in my chest.

"This is what's best for the family and for me. I'm sorry, son. I'm sorry for disappointing you, but I want you to learn from my mistakes. We Taylor men, we're stubborn as hell. We'll stick with something right to the bitter end. Don't stick with what doesn't serve you. Don't shut yourself off from the people you love because you're afraid of getting hurt."

I nod, and I can't talk. I clear my throat and sit down next to my father. He places a hand on my shoulder and squeezes then pulls me into a one-armed hug. It reminds me of when I was a boy, and it leaves me choked up.

"You in love with this woman?" he asks.

"June?"

"Yeah, her. You two were inseparable when you were kids. I figured you'd wind up together one day." He laughs, soft and slow, like he's got all the time in the world. "You want my advice?"

"Sure."

"If she makes you smile every day, if you feel lighter around her, if you'd do anything to keep her happy, keep her in your life," he says. "Because when the bad times come, there's nothing you need more than a good friend by your side. Take it from a man who's loved and lost."

I rise from the swing seat, feeling light, and head down to the pickup. I've got things to do, and all of it involves proving to June how much I love and need her in my life, and how I will work to make sure she knows it. Even if I don't need a nanny anymore, I will support her and protect her.

I get into the car and check my phone, and my entire body tenses. I have several missed calls from June, followed by a series of text notifications.

> **JUNE**
> Cash, are you all right?
>
> I heard you were in a fight.
>
> Olivia and my mother are living together next door. They came by today and were on your front lawn, so I called the cops to report it, just so there's evidence of Olivia overstepping.
>
> Let me know when you get this message.

I send a text in response then start the car and tear off down the street.

CASH

I ARRIVE HOME with the setting sun with two bouquets of flowers. I walk into the house and find June in the kitchen, finishing up dinner. It's pasta tonight and it smells amazing. I set one of the bouquets on the table.

June turns around, clutching a slotted spoon. She scans me, as if she's afraid that I'm hurt, then sighs. She looks genuinely happy to see me, but her gorgeous smile falters at the sight of the flowers in my hand.

"Alex is upstairs," she says.

"These are for you." I hold them out to her.

"Me." She takes them from me, and before she can move her hand away, I catch her wrist and bring her into my arms.

"You deserve every flower in the world."

"That would be terrible for the environment. And the bees. You know, the entire ecosystem would collapse."

I kiss her lips gently.

June pushes away from me, her gaze teasing, and nods toward the kitchen doorway. "Don't be naughty, Cash."

"That's all I want to do with you," I say.

She smells the flowers and peeks at me over the petals.

This woman will be the death of me.

"So," she says, pointing the flowers at me. "Judging by the lack of bruising and the fact that I didn't have to bail you out with my nanny salary, you didn't get into a fight with someone?"

"Technically, no." I did text her, but I like that she's worried about me. "Thanks for texting me about Olivia. I've spoken with my lawyer, and Olivia won't be giving us trouble any more. She's not allowed to live next door, and the police will take care of it."

June nods. "That's good. That's good for Alex. I didn't want her to see anything that would upset her."

"You're a fucking angel, you know that?"

"Then what are you?" she asks.

"An idiot who gets in fights and never talks about how he feels until it's almost too late."

She frowns. "What do you—?"

"My dad sold the bar to Deveraux," I say. "Which means I don't have to fix it up anymore."

June's head dips downward, and her shoulders sag. "You don't need a nanny."

I hate how sad she sounds. I hate it, but that small, evil fucking part of me craves it because it means that she wants to stay, even if it's not my place to tell her to.

"I don't" I say. "But June, I want you."

She looks up at me. "Cash, this is—"

"I want you," I repeat. "I don't care if we have to do long distance while you study. I don't care what it takes. I'll provide for you. I'll pay for your college tuition. I will make sure that you have everything you need."

She's already shaking her head. "I can't let you do any of that. I have to do this on my own. I spent years with a guy who paid for everything and treated me like something to be wheeled out for guests or parties. I don't want that life. I want to be who I was meant to be." Tears shine in her eyes and start spilling down her cheeks. "I want you too, but I have to be—"

"Stop." I can't stand to see her cry. "Stop. You don't have to take my money then. I'll help you find a job or something. Anything. Anything for you."

"I think I've already found one," June says. "Daisy's mom, Sara, asked if I could nanny for them. So, I can do that temporarily until I find out where I've gotten in. If I've gotten in anywhere. That's still up for debate."

"You'll get in somewhere," I say with confidence. "Any college would be insane to turn you down. You're a hard worker, you're intelligent, you're beautiful—"

"I don't think colleges care how beautiful you are," she says, laughing, swiping tears from underneath her eyes.

"Fair," I say, "but you will get in. I believe in you."

A grin spreads across her face. It's like she's a sunflower turning toward the light. "Thank you."

"I know that your life is heading in that direction," I say. "You're going to be who you were destined to be, June, I have no doubt about that, all I'm asking is that you let us be a part of your journey." I step toward her, sweep her hair back from her face, and kiss her.

The kiss is soft and salted with her tears.

"These are big steps, I know," I say, "but we can take it as slow as you want. But I need you to know that I'm all in, June."

"All in?"

"Yes."

"At the beginning of the summer, you told me you didn't want anything to do with love or romance or commitment. What changed?"

"Me. I changed. I realized I was being stubborn. And that if you want the good, you've got to take the bad with it. The pain of love."

Footsteps clatter down the stairs, and she backs away from me hastily. We haven't even gotten the chance to discuss how we're going to break it to Alex. The fact that we're dating or the fact that she's not going to be the nanny anymore.

"Dad!" Alex runs into the kitchen and I grab the second bouquet off the table.

"For you." My toxic trait is ensuring that any man who dates my daughter one day will have to endure her criminally high standards. "You look pretty today, sweetheart."

"Thanks, Dad." She sniffs the flowers. "Why did you bring me flowers?"

"Because you're special, and you deserve them."

Alex beams at me. "June, can you help me put these in water?"

"Sure can," June says, and guides my daughter over to the sink.

"Dad got you flowers too?"

"Yeah, he did," June replies. "He's a real gentleman, your dad. He got them as a farewell gift."

Alex frowns. "But there are still two weeks left of summer. You're not leaving yet, are you?"

"I'm afraid so," I say. "June's time with us is up because I'm going to be home from now on, honey." It's better to get this part out of the way. And it will give us an idea of how she might react to our relationship.

Alex's bottom lip trembles. "But—"

"It's okay," June says, and draws her into a hug. "We can still be friends. We—"

Alex breaks out of her grip and runs up the stairs without another word, the flowers left forgotten on the counter.

June clasps the edge of the sink. "I think we could maybe have handled that better. My fault."

"Mine too," I say, and take a step toward the door. I frown at myself. "Do you want to talk to her?" Because it's their relationship, and while it's my decision who's the nanny, I know that Alex just wants June in her life.

"Yeah," June says. "I do. I don't want her to be upset." And there's guilt written all over her face. I don't want June to feel bad for following her dreams, and I hate it that Alex is hurting. It's a strange feeling.

June moves past me, and I catch her hand, sweeping my thumb across the back of it. I love her, but now isn't the time to say it. When I tell her how I feel, June is going to be so overwhelmed, she won't know how to respond. I'm going to show her how a real man treats his wife, because that's what I want for us.

She blushes at the intensity of my stare.

I kiss her once on the lips. "Tomorrow night, you and I are going out. Alone."

Forty~Five

JUNE

I **FEEL** like I might be crazy for having this much faith in a man, but my heart is open to Cash.

You're a fool. My mother's voice sounds in my head as I take the stairs.

Alex has closed her bedroom door, so I knock on it. "Alex? It's June. Can I come in?"

"Yeah." The squeaky reply sounds heartbroken.

Guilt wracks me, but ultimately, this isn't my decision. I'm not needed here anymore, and it would be seriously inappropriate to stay on and pretend to be the nanny just so I can have a relationship with Cash. And staying next door to my mother while that's all going on, with the potential for Olivia to be around at any time, just complicates things.

I step into the room and shut the door behind me.

Alex sits in the middle of her bed, her covers draped around her and over her head. She looks like a budget Star Wars character, and it's adorable.

"Hey," I say. "Are you good?"

"No."

"I'm sorry. Is there anything I can do to help?"

"You can stay," she replies. "You can stay and never leave. You can be my nanny forever."

I walk over to the bed and sit down beside her, releasing a breath. Alex is mature for her age, but it's moments like these, when she's at her most vulnerable, that show how young she still is. I remember what it was like to be eleven and worried about things I shouldn't have been. Or coping with school and bullies. Or just wanting my mother to be nice.

I take her hand and squeeze her fingers. "I've had the best time being your nanny," I say. "I've loved every second of it."

"Me too."

"And you know, just because I'm not going to be your nanny any more doesn't mean I'm not going to be your friend. I'm only a phone call away."

"I don't have a phone."

"You have a phone in the kitchen. You can call me any time," I say. "Any time. And with your dad's permission, we can go out to the beach or we can go shopping together again. Besides, I'm still going to help you and Daisy prepare for the concert at the end of the summer."

"You are? For the talent show?"

"Of course," I say. "You didn't think I'd just let you fend for yourself, did you?"

Alex shrugs and looks down, her bottom lip quivering. I stroke her hand and choke back tears of my own. I have to go slow with Cash, if we're going to do this, if this is really going to be a thing, because I cannot afford to hurt this little girl. She's already been through enough with Olivia.

"I would never leave you guys to figure stuff out if you weren't ready," I say. "But I have to admit that you two are rock stars. You're going to kick butt at the talent show."

A smile appears. "And you'll be there."

"Of course, I'll be there. You'd have to tie me down to stop me from being there. I'm going to be the one cheering the loudest. I'm going to cheer so loud you're going to be a little freaked out by it."

Alex laughs, and then she squeezes my hand back, which I take as the first sign of forgiveness for my betrayal.

"So, remember how I said I want to study to be a teacher after the summer?" I ask.

"Yeah."

"Well, turns out, you need a lot of money for that. Or a scholarship. Or both, sometimes," I say. "Your dad doesn't need me as a nanny anymore, but Daisy's mom asked me if I could help her out. I don't want that to be weird for you."

"You'll be Daisy's nanny?" Alex asks.

"Maybe. Not sure yet. But maybe," I say. "Depends on how things work out with all my college applications."

"That's fine," Alex says, lifting her chin. I can tell it bugs her, but she's being strong about it. "That just means I get to see you when I visit Daisy and when we do practice for the talent show." She squishes out from underneath the blanket and gives me a hug.

I hug her back, relishing this moment. I've always wanted to work with kids, just because of how joyful they are, how free, and how amazing it would be to help shape them into the best versions of themselves they can be. But this is difficult. I didn't think I would get this attached to Alex.

I choke back tears as she squeezes me even tighter and mumbles something under her breath.

"What's that, honey?"

"It's dumb."

"No way."

Alex hesitates. "I said I wish you were my real mom."

Oh my God. "Oh, honey." I wish I was too. But it wouldn't be helpful or responsible to say that to her right now when she's feeling this way. Instead, I hug her and don't let go until she wants to.

She wipes her tears away and grins at me. "You promise I can call you any time?"

"Unless it's past your bedtime. Because then we'll both get in trouble with your dad."

"Hey," Cash says, knocking on the door. "I heard someone blaspheming me in here."

Alex and I laugh as he opens the door. I lose my breath at the sight of him but cover my tracks. Even if Alex feels like she wants me around permanently, it's still not the right time to tell her. Not until we're sure. Not until I know what's happening with college.

Cash comes over and grabs Alex. He hugs her and she giggles hysterically as he tickle-fights with her. The sounds of joy fill the room, and I can't help but laugh along.

I wish every day could be like this.

Forty-Six

CASH

I'VE ALREADY DROPPED Alex off for the evening at Ganny's place. She spent her last day with June as her nanny, shopping, going to the beach, visiting with her friend Daisy, and making fried pickles, which I ate under June's watchful stare.

I stand at the base of the stairs waiting for June to appear. She went up to get dressed for our night out a half an hour ago, and I'm anxious to see her. To touch her and hold her and show her the fuck off in front of everyone in town.

I do not give a damn what anyone has to say about it. Don't care if it winds up in the news. But I need to make sure June is prepared for that on the off chance it does happen. I'm not a "star" anymore so there are fewer articles about me online these days, but one pops up every now and again, and Jesse loves to annoy me with them.

"You going to be ready this century?" I call up the stairs. "I'm growing a beard down here."

"You already have a beard," she says, out of sight at the top of the stairs. "Almost done."

I can't fucking wait to take her out tonight. I can't wait to have her to myself, then bring her home and make her scream my name. I want everyone to fucking know she's mine.

Heels click on the landing, and I look up.

I'm stunned.

She's a vision in red, descending the stairs with her hand on the balustrade. The dress she's chosen tonight clings to her body, accentuating every curve, and my mouth waters for her. Her hair falls around her shoulders in golden waves, and she's done her makeup so that her green eyes look even bigger than usual.

"Christ on a fucking cracker," I murmur.

"What?" She laughs.

"You are...fuck."

"I am fuck?" She pouts her lips. "Well, you, sir, are looking mighty fuck yourself."

She's halfway down the stairs, but I rush up to meet her and lift her into my arms. June gasps as I squeeze her to my chest and lower her onto the stairs, pressing her against them and showering her neck with kisses. "Keep talking like that and we won't leave."

"Don't make promises you don't intend on keeping," she murmurs back, and I catch her bottom lip between my teeth. "Lipstick," she yelps.

"Could not care less." I kiss her hard, and she moans into my mouth. By the time we break for air, her lipstick is smudged, and I don't doubt it's all over my lips.

June laughs at the sight of me, and I rise from the stairs,

lifting her with me. I walk her down them, and we head into the downstairs bathroom. I watch June reapply her red lipstick, picturing it all over my cock.

"I'm going to punish you for wearing that dress later," I say.

She grins, showing a confidence that makes me want her and love her even more. I place my hand on the small of her back and guide her out of the house and toward my pickup.

"Wait," she says, "let's take Ol' Rusty."

"Why?"

June shrugs. "It's silly, but it reminds me of when we were young."

"We're in our thirties," I say. "We're still young."

She touches her fingers to my beard. "I swear there are grays in there."

I catch her arm and kiss her hand. "Watch it. You're playing with fire. Keys."

"Huh?"

"Give me the keys."

There's a flash of defiance in her eyes, but June hands the keys over to her car. Once we're inside, she giggles. "You look huge in the driver's seat."

I fully plan on christening this car with her at some point. Maybe on the hood, given that I'm too big to fit in the damn thing without hunching over. I start the engine and we drive off. June hums under her breath, and I love the sound of her voice, and how happy she looks.

We park along the boardwalk, and I clear my throat. "Baby," I say, "you realize that I'm not going to stop touching you once we're inside."

"Oh?"

"I'm not going to be able to keep my hands off you," I say. "And if you don't want people knowing about us, then we should head home now. Tell me what you want."

June reaches out for my hand, and I squeeze hers. "I want to be seen with you," she says.

That's a good answer. I get out of the car, circle around to her side, and open the door for her. I take her hand and help her out, then press her against the side of Ol' Rusty and run kisses along her neck again. Her skin is already red from being grazed by my beard, and I love that. I want to mark her.

We head inside together, and I love the fact that her nipples are plucking at the fabric of her dress. The music in Longhorn's is loud, and every head turns as we enter. People stare, and I loop my arm around her waist, drawing her closer to my side, my hand moving over her ass.

June is pleasantly pink, and she smiles up at me as we move out onto the sand. She kicks off her shoes, and we sit down on the bench outside.

"I'm overdressed," she says.

"You're perfect. But if you want to get rid of the dress, I'm more than happy to help."

June bites down on her bottom lip, but the server arrives before she can tempt me any more than she already has. We give her our orders, and I take June's hand as it rests across the table, the gentle wash of waves hitting the shore are the perfect backdrop to our evening.

"I'm so happy to be here with you," I say. "I'm the luckiest man alive."

June's leg rests against mine, and I clench my jaw at the contact. I have to focus on her face rather than the things I want to do to her.

"I never thought this would happen," she says.

"Me neither." And that's the God's honest truth. "I've wanted you for so fucking long, I never thought this would happen." She's broken me down in the best ways. She's made me whole again. "What do you want out of life?"

June presses her lips together, considering. "Peace. I want peace. And I want the freedom to be myself. I want to feel like what I want matters, and that what I do with my life brings meaning."

"Hence the teaching."

"What about you?" she asks. "You don't have your daddy's bar to work on anymore, and I know Alex is everything to you, but what about you, Cash?"

I still get royalties from my music, but I know what she means. She means what am I passionate about. What do I see myself doing. "I've been treading water for so long, I don't know what that looks like," I say. "I wanted to give Alex the best life. That's been my purpose. Then it was to make sure Dad didn't collapse in on himself after Mom died, and now…"

"Now?"

I wet my lips. "It was always music."

"But it's not anymore?"

"It might be," I say. "Funny thing is, I feel a lot more like singing now that you're around."

June rubs a hand over her chest, blushing again. "Then you have to do it. You have to go for what you want."

"Hmm."

"Seriously, Cash. You've been so encouraging to me, it's my turn to be the same to you. You can't let your dream die because of an asshole."

It catches me off guard, and I chuckle. "Yeah, both of 'em were assholes, and you're right. But I can't see myself leaving Heatstroke. Alex has her whole life here."

"There must be a way."

The server returns with our drinks and a bread basket, and June tucks her feet underneath herself. She eats two slices of bread, which I butter for her, liberally, and I love the way she eats. Like she can't get enough.

I excuse myself, walk to the restroom, splash water on my face, and put in a quick call to Ganny to check on Alex. She's having a blast watching Frozen and is attempting a rock rendition of all the songs. I say goodnight to her then head back to the table.

I'm halfway across the dance floor when I see June, standing on the beach with another man.

He's blond, shorter than me, wearing an arrogant expression with a weak chin. He's got one hand on her forearm.

June's eyes are wide, and she tugs away from him, but he grabs her again.

Red heat washes over me, and I charge across the sand toward them.

"Let go of me, Braydon!"

Braydon. This was the asshole who cheated on her. This was the dumb motherfucker who spoke to her with disrespect.

"You think—"

"Hey!" I bark it out, and Braydon turns toward me.

He squares up like he stands a fucking chance.

I whip my fist back and right hook him square on the jaw. He hits the sand like the sack of shit he is. "I warned you," I say, standing over him. "I warned you not to contact her again."

Braydon cowers in front of me, choking on sand, his hand on his jaw. He's wearing one of those rich boy suits, and I reach down and grab him, lifting him up by the front of his shirt and holding him there.

"I warned you," I growl.

"Please," Braydon whimpers. "Just—"

"Cash, stop," June says. "Just stop. He's not worth this." Her hand comes to my arm. "I don't need you to do this."

I hear what she's saying, but it's difficult to think of anything other than ruining this idiot.

"What did I tell you I would do?" I shake him.

Braydon is a mute. Lost all that hot air he was releasing not a couple of minutes ago.

"Let me remind you." I crack my head against the bridge of his nose and then throw him onto the sand.

"Stop!" June shrieks. "That's enough. That is enough."

Braydon rolls around in the sand.

The music in the bar has cut off, and everyone is staring. The bartender is already on the phone to the cops, and I swear under my breath.

"You shouldn't have done that," June says. "I had it under control."

I turn to her, but the asshole ex speaks first. "I'll sue you for this! I'll—"

The whoop of sirens cut across his words, and I know

that I am in the deepest shit possible. Jesse marches into the bar.

"June," I start.

But June is pale, trembling, her gaze staring through me rather than at me, like she's seeing me for the first time. The real me.

I can't lose her now that we've finally found each other.

Forty-Seven

JUNE

I THINK there's something wrong with me, because while I'm pissed at Cash for breaking Braydon's nose, a small, sick part of me was turned on by that.

It's been a couple of days since Cash was nearly arrested at Longhorn's. Braydon decided not to press charges because I told the cops that Cash was acting in my defense. I still have the bruise on my arm to prove it.

The look on Braydon's face as he left Longhorn's will forever be ingrained in my brain. Fear.

He won't be coming back.

But that's not the problem here. Cash wants to protect me, but I need him to realize that I have to fight my own battles, pave my own way, otherwise this isn't going to work.

I spent too long with a man who wanted to keep me like a trinket, rather than love me like a woman. And if I'm going to be with Cash, in whatever capacity, I need him to realize that.

I sit in Marci's living room on the sofa, blanket bundled around my waist, and my phone in hand. I have two missed calls from Cash, and I stare at them, my heart pounding.

He's sent me a text message as well.

> **CASH**
> When you're ready to talk, I'm here.

I don't feel pressured to answer him, and I'm not sure what I want to say yet. I miss him so much, it hurts, even though it's only been a couple of days. And I've got other things to deal with. I need to check my college applications. I need to find a job—I'm still waiting to hear back from Sara about being a nanny for Daisy. Just because I've basically fallen head over heels for Cash again doesn't make any of those problems go away.

Marci taps on the living room wall. "You okay in here, bestie?"

I smile. "Yeah. Thanks again for letting me stay here."

"Eh! Don't even mention it," she says. "I'm all for letting a man sweat it out. And for helping a friend in need, of course."

I laugh. "I'm not letting him sweat it out."

"Girl, please. He knocked out your ex and head-butted him in Longhorn's."

I gnaw on my bottom lip. "Is it wrong that I find that kind of hot?"

"No." Marci says and steps into the room. She sits down on the sofa at my feet and pulls them onto her lap. "That's not wrong. It's wrong that he interfered, but at the same time, the dude was just sticking up for you in the most badass way possible."

"But it could have ruined everything, Marce." And I didn't want Cash going to jail on my account. "And I hate feeling like I need to be saved."

"I'm with you. But at the same time, sometimes it's nice to be saved." Marci pointed at me. "But for God's sake, don't tell him that."

I snort.

"Especially not after what he did this morning."

Ice travels through my veins, and I stare at my bestie.

She gives me a mischievous grin and ties her shock of red hair back into a high ponytail. "He stopped by this morning early and left something for you in the diner downstairs."

"You gave me a heart attack!" I slap at her.

Marci continues grinning. "Oh, come on, what did you think he did? Hunted down Braydon and made good on his promise?" She gives me a look and starts snarling. "If you come near her again, I'll rip off your dick and feed it to you. Grar."

"Did you just grar?"

"I said what I said." Marci jumps up and puts out her hands. "Wait here. You're going to love this." She rushes out of the room and returns a second later with something behind her back. She produces a gorgeous, smooth white box and hands it over.

It's got an image of a laptop on the front.

I stare at it, confused, then look up at her. "What?"

"He left this for you. Stopped by while the sun was barely up and knocked on the diner door. He said he didn't want to wake you, but he bought it for you and after what happened that night, he didn't get around to giving it to you."

"Are you serious?"

"I mean, he must be if he bought you a laptop," Marci says. "Swoon. If only they made more men like Cash Taylor.Who am I kidding? I don't have time for hunky guys who like to buy things for their women."

"Not even Jesse?"

She narrows her eyes. "You know I hate that guy."

I burst out laughing, partly because I'm in shock. Braydon bought me stuff when we were together, but it was never thoughtful. It was always upon request. And the gifts never felt like gifts. It felt like an obligation on his part.

This is so different.

Cash noticed what I needed and got it for me without me asking. My throat closes with emotion, and it takes me a second to get it together.

"I'll leave you two alone," Marci says, waggling her eyebrows. The door that separates the downstairs from the upstairs shuts a moment later. The diner will get busy soon, and I don't feel like staying holed up all day. I'll take my new gift to the library. And after that, I'm helping Daisy and Alex with their song for the end of summer talent show.

I unbox the laptop reverentially.

It's sleek and silver with great specs—a sixteen-inch screen, loads of hard drive space, and a powerful CPU.

It's already been set up for me, and "Welcome, June" flashes on the screen. I press my lips together to keep from crying. It's almost too much.

I pick up my phone and snap a picture of me with the laptop, and text him.

> Thank you. Thank you so much. But also, I don't know what to say about the other night, yet.

> > We don't have to talk about it right away. I'll wait until you're ready.

I smile at the text then push myself up from the sofa and start preparing for the day. A half an hour later, I make my way out of the door with my brand-new laptop bag strung over my shoulder and accept the grilled cheese sandwich Marci holds out for me.

"Love you, byeee," she calls. "Go kick some ass!"

Barb, one of the regulars at the diner blows me a kiss as I sail past. The place is already starting to fill up.

The town is alive with tourists, even at this hour. Tourists who are heading to the beach or enjoying Heatstroke's eclectic collection of boutique stores, antique shops, restaurants, and the Heatstroke Museum—one of my favorite parts of the town because it's basically a collection of melted objects, dated with the year that Heatstroke's vicious summers destroyed them.

A low whistle stops me as I walk down the sidewalk.

Olivia waves at me from across the street where she leans against an old Buick, as if I'll go over to her. I ignore her, tension already banding in my chest at the thought of interacting with her again.

But, of course, she's relentless. She intercepts me outside the bookstore. Inside, Mrs. Langemeyer sits behind the little counter with her nose in a book, and I wish I could trade places with her.

"Hold up," Olivia says.

"I have nothing to say to you." I sidestep her, but she matches me.

"Just wait a second, June, we've got to talk," she says.

"No, Olivia. We don't have to say anything to each other. You've made where you stand pretty clear."

"You didn't even give me a chance to explain about what happened," Olivia says. "I know you think I'm a shitty person for what I did to you."

"For what you did to me? What about Alex? What about Cash?"

"Well, shit, I couldn't take care of Alex, and Cash is like, a whole different thing. It's complicated."

"You told Cash that I wasn't into him," I say. "And then you dated him and broke his heart. You slept with his friend and abandoned Cash and his baby."

"He didn't want me involved."

I shake my hair back from my shoulders. "Cash told me he offered you support, a place in Alex's life, and you refused. You threw it away before you knew what you had to lose."

Olivia's mouth opens and shuts. She brushes her fingers over her lips, and I'm struck by how tired she looks. There are dark circles under her eyes, her cheeks are sunken, and she's trembling when she moves.

"He offered you help even though you slept with the drummer in his own fucking band," I snap. "And now you roll back into town expecting handouts and to ruin relationships? You don't care about anyone but yourself."

"You haven't walked a mile in my shoes," she says. "You don't know."

"Everything that's happened has been a choice. You chose this." I don't care how harsh I sound.

"June, you're not perfect. I know you like to think you are, but you aren't. Did you ever think about how difficult it was to be me? I was always the third wheel. Everybody loved you. You made friends wherever you went. Hell, you didn't even need me as a best friend. You could've picked any other girl because everybody loved you. I just wanted something for myself. I wanted to feel special."

Olivia's eyes fill with tears, but she blinks them away, and then it's almost as if her face sharpens. Like all the dark, gritty edges of her come out in the light of day. "You've finally learned how to stand up for yourself, but it doesn't change anything. You're still just June. June the weak little victim who needs everybody's help."

The words feel like physical slaps, but I refuse to react to them.

"You might have the people in this town wrapped around your little finger, but you're not me. You'll never be Cash's first love. You'll never be Alex's mother."

I let the words roll off me. This is her last attempt to mess things up, and I won't allow it. Compared to living with Mom, this is nothing.

"You mistake me for giving a shit about your opinion," I say.

She sucks in a breath, hating that I haven't broken down. "I just came to tell you I'm leaving," she says. "And I was going to tell you to enjoy your time with my ex-fiancé, but it looks like you two are over before you began."

"Huh?"

"I saw a nice big for sale sign outside Cash's house," Olivia says. "Looks like he's leaving town, just like me."

I take a breath. "Goodbye, Olivia. I hope you find what you're looking for." And then I walk past her and down the street, my insides twisting and turning. Cash is selling the house? Why?

Forty-Eight

JUNE

DEAR MISS JACKSON,

Our Committee of Admissions has considered your application with great care, but we regret to inform you that we will not be offering—

I stop reading the email and move to the next one. And the next.

I've been rejected by all four of the colleges I applied to. All four.

I squeeze my eyes shut. In the Heatstroke Public Library the occasional cough or turning of a page, the soft sounds of footsteps on carpeting, the creak of a wooden chair, the tap of keys is my only company.

It's going to be okay. It has to be okay.

Rejected.

I can't give up on this. The colleges I applied to all had rolling admissions, but there have to be more options. I need to call my advisor and see what she has to say about this.

I step out of the library, phone in hand, and dial Sasha's number.

"Good morning, June," she sings. "How are you?"

"I got rejected. Everywhere."

Sasha pauses. "All right, that's not the best news," she says, "but there's no reason to panic yet. You still have options."

"Options?"

"Just because you didn't get into a physical college at this time, doesn't mean that you can't apply again," Sasha says. "You can reapply at a future date, try different colleges, or you can try applying for online courses right now."

"Online?" My heart skips a beat.

"That's right. There are plenty of great colleges offering accreditations online," Sasha says. "Let me email you about this, June."

"I would really appreciate that."

"Of course. Just don't lose hope or give up."

"Thanks, Sasha." I hang up. I have options. And wouldn't online courses be cheaper too?

It's almost time for me to go over to Daisy's place and help the girls with their routine, so I pack up my laptop, wave goodbye to the librarian, and head out into the sunlight. Today has been a rollercoaster. First the laptop, then Olivia, then the rejections, then Cash putting his house up for sale and now fresh hope.

I arrive at Sara's house to find Daisy and Alex on the porch together, about to go inside, and Cash on the front path.

Seeing him stops me in my tracks. It's the first time we've come face-to-face since what happened at Longhorn's, and I'm breathless at the prospect.

Cash is wearing a T-shirt that fits him perfectly and stretches over his muscular biceps. His hair is mussed and slightly damp as if he's just come out of the shower, and his beard is trimmed. He turns his head and locks eyes with me, and I'm done. Melting inside.

Cash gives Alex a hug goodbye. The girls rush inside together, chatting excitedly about their plans for the talent show.

I adjust the strap of the laptop bag on my shoulder and smile.

He stops a foot away. "I prepared a bunch of shit I wanted to say to you, but now that you're standing in front of me, it's gone. I can't remember a goddamn word. Feels like we haven't talked in years, not days."

"We have some practice with that."

"Don't remind me," he replies.

I take a step toward him without thinking, and his gaze grows hungry.

"I figured that I wouldn't have the words," Cash says, and reaches into the back pocket of his jeans. He extracts a letter and gives it to me. "This is for you."

I take it from him and our fingers touch. It's electric.

I glance past him at the house, checking that the kids aren't watching from the front window. We haven't told Alex anything.

"June," he murmurs, "I'm sorry for what I did the other night." He hesitates, running a hand through his hair and laughing under his breath. "I'm not sorry that I hit that dumb motherfucker. Anyone who lays a hand on the person I love will get what's coming to them, but I am—"

"The person you love?"

He smiles at me, a softness taking over harsh features usually drawn into a scowl. "I'm sorry that I interfered. I'm sorry that I made it seem like I don't trust that you can look after yourself."

My insides twist.

"I know you can look after yourself. I believe in you, June, I always have. I just struggle to contain myself around you. Sometimes, I wonder how far I would go to protect you, protect Alex. To the ends of the earth. To dark places if need be."

"I don't want that," I say immediately, still shaken by his earlier comment. "I want you to be safe. That would make me happy."

"I know you don't like conflict," Cash says, "and I should have just pulled him off you and called the cops. Should've done the rational thing. For that, I'm sorry."

"Thank you," I say.

I'm at a loss for words. I've never seen Cash lose control like that. Not once in our time as friends, maybe because nothing that he really cared about was ever threatened.

"If me backing off will make you happy, I'll do that. I'll do whatever you need me to do. I can't imagine my life without you, June, but if you're going to leave, I'll respect it." He leans in and brushes a kiss across my cheek. He walks past me.

It takes all my energy not to go knock-kneed like a fool. Because whether I like to admit it or not, I am a fool for Cash.

His pickup starts, and he drives off, waving as he takes to the street.

The letter is still in my hand, and I open it greedily.

Dear June,

I'm sorry for acting like an asshole. I want to make it up to you.

Please meet me tonight at eight at Old Miller Road, near the entry to the trail that leads up to Diver's Point.

Cash.

I frown. His solution is to ask me to meet him at the quarry that nearly killed me twice? I'm too intrigued not to go, but it's a strange request.

Regardless, I trust Cash, and I want to go. I want to find out why he's put his dad's place up for sale.

"June, are you coming?" Alex appears on the front porch.

"Coming, honey," I call out, and then I walk over to join her. She hugs me and grins up at me.

"I missed you," she says.

"I missed you too. Ready to rock out?"

"Heck yeah!"

Forty-Nine

CASH

MY PALMS ARE SWEATING. I check my watch for the fifty-millionth time since I arrived outside the entrance to Diver's Point. It's one minute until eight, and she's not here yet. She might not have forgiven me.

I hear the crunch and putter of Ol' Rusty's approach, and a sense of certainty slides into place.

She's here.

This is my shot.

June parks the car, and I open the door for her and offer her a hand, and she takes it.

She looks classically beautiful as always, blonde hair tied back, wearing a blouse covered in hot peppers, and a pair of cutoff jeans. She's tied another ribbon in her hair, and her lips are bright red tonight.

"June, you look stunning."

"I wasn't sure what to wear," she says, pointing at her sneakers. "You said the quarry. Which, uh, have to admit I was confused by."

I laugh. "You think I'm going to make you hike up to it in the dark?"

"Maybe? I don't know what to expect in Heatstroke. This place turns people crazy."

"The only thing I'm crazy for is you," I say.

She takes a breath, looking up at me through those long lashes.

"I wanted to show you something," I say, and then I take her hand and walk her through the entrance to the trail. "It's not Diver's Point."

"That's a relief." She laughs.

"But I thought it was important we meet here instead of at the main gate."

"Main gate?"

I nod, guiding her along a side trail that runs along the border fence. "You know that the quarry is privately owned property."

"Sure. Mr. Carter's place," she says.

"He owns the land, the ranch house, the quarry itself. He's getting on in years. Has been struggling to maintain the quarry and Diver's Point, even to run his ranch. He's sold all his cattle."

"Oh." She sounds mildly confused.

I lead her around the corner, and June gasps.

With the porch lights on, the ranch house, a sprawling, three-story wood cabin, looks cozy as heck. The pathway toward it is lined with lanterns, and the trees that border the house itself have been decorated with fairy lights that twinkle in the darkness.

"It's beautiful," June says.

"It's yours."

"W-what?"

"Or ours," I say. "I bought it. I bought it and the quarry."

She's speechless, staring at me on the path, shaking her head in disbelief.

"I bought it because I can't see a future where we live together with your mother next door, always putting pressure on you," I say. "Clinging to my childhood home is pointless. And we can make new memories here together. We already have one at the quarry. It's not the best one, but we can change that. We can make this place our own. We can make it a safe place for our family."

June's bottom lip trembles.

"I know that this is a lot," I say, "but June, I want the world for you. I don't care if you have to leave to study, as long as you know you'll always have a home to come back to here. A home where we'll be waiting for you. I acted like a dick the other night. I know that was the wrong thing to do, and I'm going to back off so that you can be who you want to be, June. I don't want you to be just mine. I want you to have the space to you as well. Your own person. I think that's something you never really had, not with your mom, not with your ex."

Tears wet her cheeks, and I catch them with my thumbs, because I can't help myself. I can't stand to see her upset.

"But what about Alex?" she asks. "What if she doesn't want this?"

"Ultimately, Alex is my daughter and I choose what's best for her until she's of an age to do so for herself. I choose you. And Alex has too. She adores you. She wants you in her life. And so do I."

June's tears keep coming. "Why?"

"Because you're loyal, you're kind, you've changed my life. You've brought a smile to my daughter's face. You've taught me that I don't have to be a rock, that it's okay to be happy. That I'm allowed to sing."

"Cash."

"You don't have to move in right away," I say. "When you're ready, we'll be here. We'll be waiting. You can live with Marci or in your apartment. All I'm asking for is a chance to make it work, June. Please."

She loops arms around my neck, and I kiss her. A kiss that I've been waiting for my entire life.

She's not holding back. She's giving me everything. Her hope, her loyalty, and her trust, and I can feel it.

There's no weight to those feelings. There's only a desire to reciprocate. I will never let June down.

I hold her against my chest as she trembles, her heart beating like crazy against mine.

"I can't believe this," she says. "Are you serious, Cash? Are you serious?"

"Yes," I say. "Anything for you. Anything."

She's quiet for a while, and I live in the moment with her, enjoying the sounds of nature, the sensation of her body pressed against mine. I run my hand over her bare skin, and she shivers against me.

"Are you ready to talk to Alex?" I ask.

Her chin lifts, and she frowns at me. "Now? Are you sure?"

"She's here," I say, nodding toward the house.

"That fast? You moved that fast?"

"I wanted to make things happen, and I'm privileged enough to have the funds to do so," I say. "So yeah, she's here. She's helping unpack the kitchen, and I told her you might come by tonight. But no pressure if you're not ready."

June takes a breath. "I'm not ready to move in with you, Cash. I do need to find my own way because I've never had my own life. But I want to make this work with you. I want to be with you. I'm ready to try."

"Me too." I take her hand.

We walk toward the house together, and I hold the door open for her. Inside, Alex lets out a squeal.

"June! You came. Yay! What do you think? Isn't it cool? We have the biggest house ever. I chose a room on the top floor. I can see the whole quarry from up there. And I have a walk-in closet and everything."

"That's amazing. I can't wait to see it."

"Hold up," I say, shutting the front door and gesturing for Alex to sit down on the sofa. "We've got to talk to you first before you start giving house tours."

Alex sits down and the leather squeaks underneath her. "What did I do?"

June laughs at that, but I can hear the nerves in her voice.

"We need to talk to you about something important," I say. "Very important."

"Okay." Alex tucks her hands underneath her legs, tilting her head to one side.

"I really like June," I say. "A lot."

"Me too! June's awesome."

"Yeah. I agree. But I like her as more than just your nanny or as a friend," I say. "I like June as a girlfriend."

Alex falls silent. A tiny frown creases her brow. She looks from me to June. "Do you like him as a boyfriend?"

June blinks repeatedly. "Yeah," she says. "I really do. I

know that might be confusing for you because I was your nanny, but I do like him. A lot."

One second, Alex is on the sofa, the next she's up and running toward June. She collides with her in a hug, crying hard.

"Alex?" June says.

But Alex is hiccuping and crying so loud, I'm not sure she can hear.

"Easy, honey," I say, taking my daughter by the shoulder. "Easy."

But Alex won't let go of June.

"Alex, talk to us, honey," I say. "Come on."

"What are you feeling?" June asks.

"H-h-happy," she says.

The relief is so strong it nearly knocks me on my ass.

"Happy?" I repeat.

"Yeah," Alex says. "I was s-scared June was going to leave forever, and now she can't. She can't leave, and she has to stay with us. She has to stay and be my friend."

I have a feeling she wanted to say something else, and it's a bitter-sweet feeling. Alex just wants a mom, and June has been more of a mom to her than Olivia could ever be.

"Alex, I'm not going to move in right away," June says, "but I'm going to be a part of your life forever."

"You're one of my best friends, June. I'm happy. Especially because Dad will be happy too."

June sinks down and hugs her, and I join the group hug, drawing them both into the protective circle of my arms.

Fifty

JUNE

THE NIGHT AIR in the Heatstroke town square buzzes. It's like the air has turned electric. I stand beside Cash, standing on tiptoe every now and then to check if I can see Alex waiting near the side of the stage.

Cash holds my hand, stroking his thumb over the back of it. "They're going to do great," he says. "Don't worry."

"You think? Because they worked so hard on it. I just want them to have fun."

Cash lifts my hand and kisses it. "They'll be great. Alex has got Taylor blood. She's going to kick ass."

People mill around, waiting for the show to start, buying food and drinks from the food trucks that have been set up nearby. Even Mrs. Crouchbottom is in attendance, accompanied by one of her daughters, who's pushing her around in a wheelchair to be safe. She waves at us, and I smile back at her.

I crane my neck. "I want to get closer to the front. I can't see her from here." We're underneath a massive oak tree, and I'm already getting annoyed with our position.

"All right," Cash says, and then he starts walking without hesitation. He parts the crowds with his presence and gets us all the way to the front. Anyone who has anything to say about it shuts up the minute they see the look on his face.

"I didn't mean we had to cut to the front."

Cash gives me a look that makes my insides gooey. "You want to be at the front, we'll be at the front."

Bridget, who's a member of the town council, comes onto the stage to warm up the crowd. Everyone cheers through her speech, and I can tell there are a lot of tense parents waiting to see their kids. I'm right there with them.

"So, first to the stage, welcome your very own Daze and Lexi, the Kicks."

I scream so loud my throat hurts and jump up and down as Daisy and Alex walk onto the stage. They're wearing black and purple and glitter, and Daisy's moms had taken her hair out of braids and done it in a kick-ass mohawk.

Alex spots us and grins broadly. She doesn't seem to have a hint of nerves, and I'm so impressed by her. I could never do this.

I give her a double thumbs up, and Cash claps and shouts her name beside me.

I spot Leah, the girl who excluded Alex, standing near the side of the stage, her arms folded and lips pursed, but the friends surrounding her—all wearing eighties getups —are shouting and cheering for Alex and Daisy as well.

The music starts, and Alex grabs the mic. Daisy is on the drums and hammering away at them as the backtrack plays. And then Alex starts off the song with a rocker shriek that sends excitement tingling to my toes.

The girls have chosen "I Love Rock and Roll", the version Joan Jett sang—a few of the lyrics changed here or there so they can be sung by the kids—and they are killing it. Alex is singing, and I'm so proud I could cry. She sounds amazing. She hits the notes perfectly, beating out the rhythm and marching up and down the stage like she was born to be on it.

I look up at Cash, and he's staring at her, his eyes moist.

Alex lets out a triumphant rock star shriek at the end of their performance and the crowd goes berserk. I'm right there with them, cheering and hollering and losing my mind. The girls come off the stage, but it takes a good couple of minutes for the place to settle down.

I spot Daisy and Alex celebrating next to the stage. "We've got to get the ice cream," I shout, turning toward Cash, but he's gone.

What the—?

I can't find him in the crowd either, which is weird, but maybe he's rushed off to buy them something to eat?

I hurry over to join the girls but slow my approach at the sight of Leah chatting to them. She's got her attitude out on full display. She can't seriously be—

"—okay, I guess," Leah says. "If you like that kind of thing."

One of Leah's friends laughs. "It was amazing! It was so cool, you guys. I wish I could sing like that."

"Or play the drums," another girl says, beating away in the air. "Like, how? How?"

Daisy and Alex link arms. "Thanks!" Alex says. "It was fun."

"But it was an easy song," Leah replies.

"Oh," Alex says, meeting her gaze. "Well, then you should try it." And she doesn't say it with malice. She meets the other girl's gaze with zero fear. "I'm sure you'll be great, Leah."

Leah's cheeks turn pink, and she looks away.

The other girls keep tittering and chatting, and I'm so happy to see Alex getting on with them. Not so much Leah, but I don't really want her getting involved in Alex's life. It seems like Leah has some stuff she needs to work through.

The microphone distorts and a couple of people cry out.

We all turn toward the stage for the announcement of the next act, and I sidestep over to join the girls and quietly congratulate them and give them high fives.

"You were amazing," I whisper. "You rocked it!"

"We have a special treat for you all tonight." Bridget is at the microphone again, and she's squirming like she wants to jump out of her skin. "It's with great excitement that we welcome to the stage, for the first time in over a decade, a real celebrity, Cash Taylor." Bridget cheers and claps.

My jaw drops. Alex and Daisy clutch each other, then they start laughing and clapping, joining in with the crowd.

"Are you happy, June?" Alex asks.

"You knew?"

She nods excitedly.

I walk back to our spot in a daze, watching as Cash comes onto the stage. He's wearing worn blue jeans and a plaid shirt, rolled up to show his tanned forearms. He's holding his guitar, the strap against his chest. He sits down on a stool that's been placed in the center of stage and adjusts the microphone in front of him.

And then he searches the crowd until his gaze lands on me.

"June," he says, "this is for you."

CASH

I SWORE that I would never do this again.

That I would never hum again. But I did when she came back into my life.

That I would never play the guitar again. I did that for her too.

And now this.

I strum my fingers over the strings, keeping my gaze fixed on her as I pick out the tune that's been trapped in my head for months. If I'm honest, it's been in there for years. Ever since we were kids.

Snatches of a song that I could never quite find until now.

I lean into the music, gazing out at the starlit sky and then back to June's face. She's crying, smiling, as I croon words I've written for her. She's the only person who exists to me.

I want her to feel what I've been feeling inside. I want her to know how much she means to me, because I wouldn't do this for anyone but her.

I reach the chorus, holding the guitar steady, my voice breaking with emotion.

> Before you, I was dark and cold
> Spent my life chasing a dream that ain't mine
> But you came in, baby, and showed me right
>   from wrong
> Cos, honey, you're not my sunshine
> You're my sun
> Baby, you're not the reason
> You're my only one.

I finish the song, and the crowd roars. Jesse and Hannah appear next to June, cheering like crazy, but I only have eyes for her. I set my guitar down, balancing it against my stool, and then I walk toward the edge of the stage.

I bend down and grab June underneath her arms and lift her up to meet me.

The crowd goes wild.

I hold her to my chest. "I love you, June," I say, making sure she sees it on my face, feels it in the way I hold her.

Her feet aren't touching the ground, and she leans into me, her arms looped around my neck. "I love you too, Cash."

I kiss her in front of everyone, tenderly, then with more pressure, more need. She responds in kind, grasping the back of my neck.

"I love you," I murmur against her lips. "I love you. I love you. I can't live without you."

She squeezes me tight, and I take a step back and

promptly trip over a cord on the stage. We collapse onto the wooden boards, and the crowd gasps and cries out.

I raise a hand. "We're okay."

The cheering resumes, louder than before.

June lies on top of my chest, blinking away tears and laughing, and I can't help but laugh too. Because this is the first day of our forever. There's not a damn thing that will stand in our way.

———

ALEX IS STAYING at Daisy's house tonight, and I'm so fucking grateful Daisy's moms are fine with dealing with two incredibly excited, sugared up pre-teens.

I have June all to myself.

I park the pickup outside the house then get out of the car and circle around to her side. I open the door and bring June out. "Hold onto me," I say, "put your legs around my waist."

June's chest is already heaving, and her pupils are dilated. Seeing her want me this bad makes me want to fulfill every promise, every wish and dream she's ever had.

I lift her into my arms under the light of the full moon and press her against the side of the truck. My lips find hers, and I press my tongue into her mouth, claiming her again. Claiming her in the open, for the world to see.

"I can't wait," June whispers. "Please, I can't wait, Cash. I need you."

I put her down gently and take a blanket out of the back of the pickup and lay it out on the grass, right there in the moonlight. "Lie down."

June follows my command, and I join her, bringing my lips to hers again. We neck like we're teenagers again, and I consider it making up for lost time.

"I love you," she whispers.

"I love you more," I reply, and then I rip her top and free her breasts. I suck one nipple into my mouth and then the other, moving against her, pressing my fingers between her legs, dragging her panties aside underneath her denim fuck-me skirt.

I swear, she's been challenging me not to fuck her all night, and she's about to pay for it.

She's wet for me, and I slip my finger over her clit, moving in all the ways that bring noises from her throat.

"That's right, June," I say. "You can make us much noise as you want now. You're mine."

"Cash," she whines. "Cash, I'm going to come."

"Already? Good."

And then she breaks underneath me, her body arching and moving underneath the moonlight, and I swear she's the most beautiful creature I've ever seen. It's like she was made for me.

"I need you inside me," June says, grabbing the front of my shirt. "Please, Cash. I need you now. I don't want to wait."

"Nobody said you had to." I free my cock from my jeans, grab her thighs and drag her toward me, kneeling on the blanket. I bury myself inside her, groaning at the warmth, the sweet pleasure that is uniquely her.

She cries out as I make love to her, leisurely at first and then harder, more urgent, I reach between us and work her clit. The view is immaculate, my shaft wet with our combined juices, her pussy spreading for me, her thighs tensing with every thrust.

"Cash. Cash. Cash!"

"That's it. Howl for me." I want her to let it all out.

And she does, crying and clawing, and coming so hard she draws my orgasm out. I pin her down and fill her, thrusting deep and hard.

"I love you," I say, kissing her lips, her nose, her forehead. "And I'm going to spend the rest of our lives making sure you know it."

Epilogue

JUNE

Two years later…

"YOU'RE NOT SCARED, ARE YOU?" Alex teases, stretching out her arms as she waits for me at the start of the trail that leads up to Diver's Point. "Is it too far to hike? I know you're all old and stuff."

"When was it you started developing this attitude?" I ask. "I swear, you were hugging me and sweet as sugar a couple of weeks ago."

Alex gives me her best shit-eating grin. "I still hug you. I just tease you too."

She's as full of it as her dad, but I'm willing to let her get away with a bit of sass today. She's reached the age where she wants to spend more of her time with her friends rather than with me or with her dad, and it's nice that she specifically invited me out here today. I should be studying, but I can take a break to spend the day with her.

"So, have we got everything?" I ask.

Alex swings her backpack down off her shoulder.

"We've got snacks, dried and fresh fruit, two bottles of water, extra pairs of socks, and a sleeping bag, just in case." She pats the roll on top of the hiking get up.

"Who taught you how to pack, your Aunt Hannah?"

"Yeah, why?"

I laugh. "No reason."

"Let's gooooo." Alex starts off up the trail, and I fall into line with her. It's a warm summer's morning—so not the best time for a hike—but the plan is to head up to Diver's Point, then hike back down and have a picnic at the water's edge.

I haven't told Alex about my incidents at the quarry, but I don't need to. I've been living with Cash and Alex for a year now, and things have been perfect. Better than I expected.

"Come on, Mom, hurry up," Alex says.

"What's the rush?" It still brings me so much joy whenever she calls me that.

"No rush," Alex says, coolly. "The longer we're down here, the more we have to walk."

"That's interesting logic."

Alex grins at me, and we head up the hill, taking breaks to hydrate along the way. I'm already getting tired, but I can't let Alex down, so we forge on.

"First one to the top is a caramel egg."

Alex races off, leaving me in her dust with a bottle of water and zero will to continue up the hill. I sigh and forge on anyway, because there's no reason to give the teenager more ammunition to use against me.

I finally reach the top, but Alex is nowhere in sight.

For one horrible moment, I'm certain that she's fallen off Diver's Point and into the water below.

No, there was no splash, and Cash made sure to build a sturdy guard rail for visitors. He's revamped and made the entire area safe since he bought the land.

"Alex?" I call. "Come on, Alex, where are you? This isn't funny."

Leave rustle behind me, and I spin around.

Cash and Alex emerge from the underbrush.

Alex is pink-cheeked and grinning. "Ah. You finally made it."

"You little…" I point a finger at her and waggle it, but I'm distracted by the fact that Cash is home.

He's been spending most of his time teaching kids music either at the local middle school or in private lessons requested by parents. He shouldn't be home today, but he's here.

"Cash?"

"June," he says, blue eyes holding me in place. "Sorry we had to get you up here with subterfuge, but we figured it's the only way you'd visit the quarry again. You've been avoiding this place." He comes closer and takes my hands. "And I told you, we're going to make this place our own."

Alex hangs out on a bench next to a picnic table at the lookout point, watching us halfway between joy and cringe.

"June," Cash says, "you've made our family complete. You're the only mother Alex has ever known. Ganny loves you. So do Dad, Lily, Jesse, Leo, and Hannah. You're part of our family now, and the only thing missing is the Taylor family name. I love you. I love you with everything I have."

My heart pounds in my chest.

He reaches into his back pocket and pulls out a ring

box. He drops to his knees in front of me. Not just one knee, but both.

"June Jackson," he says, opening the ring box, "will you do me the honor of being my wife?"

"Cash. Oh, Cash." I drop down with him and throw my arms around his neck. "I love you. I love you so much."

He squeezes me to his chest, and I hold onto him for dear life, like he's my raft in a sea of chaos, because that's what he's become. That's what our life has become.

"Is that a yes?" Alex calls out, and she's got her phone out recording the moment.

"That's a hell yes!" I laugh, tears on my cheeks.

Cash wipes them away as he always does, and then he removes an elegant ring from the box and slips it onto my finger. The diamond is surrounded by two smaller stones.

"Three," Cash says. "One for each of us." He wraps me in his arms and holds me close.

After a couple of minutes, Alex comes over and joins the hug, and even her eyes are moist. "I love you guys," she whispers. "Seriously. I love you guys, a lot, but can we have a picnic now?"

Cash's laughter rumbles out over the water. "Yeah. Let's eat." He heads back through the trees and returns with a picnic basket that's superior to the trail mix we were going to have. And we spend the afternoon drinking fizzy soda to toast our engagement, eating M&M's and grilled cheese sandwiches.

It occurs to me, while I'm lying against Cash's chest, listening to Alex regale us with tales from her summer, that this is it. This is everything I've ever wanted.

A cozy home to call my own, a man to love, a child

who loves me, and a future full of love and hope and sunshine.

———

*Join Bailey's mailing list at www.baileyhartromance.com and read more of Cash and June (and Alex) in a **bonus epilogue!** **Scan the QR CODE below to get it.***

Pssst! Can you guess whose book is next?

Marci and Jesse in a... cottage with one bed. She's facing the wall cos they're fake wed. ;)

About the Author

Bailey Hart writes small town swoonworthy romance that leaves readers with all the tingly feels. She loves wearing her nails long, eating Mexican food, and dancing like nobody's watching. When she's not writing, she's at dance class, spending time with her son and husband, or daydreaming about her next story idea—spicy scenes included. She lives in Cape Town, South Africa, and desperately wants a cat in the near future.

Come visit her at www.baileyhartromance.com

Bailey's Babes

Come join Bailey in the Facebook Group and hang out with other romance babes just like you! You'll get sneak peeks from new books, access to giveaways, and bookish conversations that will make your reader heart sing.

Acknowledgments

This book has been a beacon in the dark for me, and I'm so grateful that I had the opportunity to write it. There's nothing quite like waking up every morning excited for the day ahead!

I'm going to miss writing about Cash, June, and Alex, but I'm pretty darn sure they're going to be in the next book in their own special way.

There are so many people who have inspired this book, and I'm going to do my best to thank them all.

My ass-kicking husband who supports me every single day and is always willing to listen to me ramble on about books and character arcs and spice levels.

My intelligent, wonderful son who helps me with my "boomerisms". Pretty sure that was one of them.

Claire, my assistant, who has amazing insights and keeps things running when I feel like they're running away from me.

To Echo, your kindness and patience, and, frankly, downright spunkiness kept a smile on my face throughout the cover design process. You really *care* and it shows. You're awesome!

To the ladies in our little mastermind group, Andi, Leilani, Lynn, Scarlett, and Wendy. You've lifted me up when I'm down more times than I can count, through kind words, laughter, and encouragement.

To my new ARC readers! Thank you for reading June and Cash's story. ARC readers are the backbone of an author's career and the real rockstars. <3

And, of course, to any reader who picks up this book and falls in love with the characters. You're the reason I started writing in the first place.

That and Cash was super hot and I needed to get him out of my head and onto the page. ;)

Made in the USA
Middletown, DE
21 January 2024

48277109R00191